TERMINATION ZONE

A LANDON JEFFERS THRILLER: BOOK 2

ADAM BLUMER

Meaningful
Suspense
Press

Kill Order by Adam Blumer

Published by Meaningful Suspense Press

ISBN: 978-1-7337134-1-2

Copyright © 2020 Adam Blumer

Cover design by Elaina Lee

Editing by Lesley Ann McDaniel

For more information about this book or the author, visit AdamBlumerBooks.com.

Library of Congress Cataloging-in-Publication Data

Blumer, Adam

Termination Zone / Adam Blumer 1st ed.

Printed in the United States of America

To my daughters, Laura and Julia,
God's amazing gifts.
I love you and will always cherish you.
May God go before you and be
the Light you seek in dark places.

You can go to the hospital in the morning and leave by the afternoon. And [getting the brain implant] can be done without general anesthesia.

—Elon Musk, Neuralink Event, August 29, 2020

I see another law in my members, warring against the law of my mind, and bringing me into captivity to the law of sin which is in my members. O wretched man that I am! Who will deliver me from this body of death? I thank God—through Jesus Christ our Lord!

—Romans 7:23–25

PART 1

A SINGLE NAME WHISPERED

1

Thursday, March 24
Trader's Hill Campground
Folkston, Georgia

The *zip* of someone opening the large tent's door jerked me out of the bliss of sleep in the dead of night. My eyelids snapped open.

Who else could it be but Gordon Hamilton? Maybe he regretted downing that supersize soda hours earlier and had hustled to the outhouse just in time.

But when I glanced to my left, Gordon lay in his sleeping bag a few feet away, though there was room for up to six people in here. His bearish snore serenaded the Georgia crickets.

"Jade?" I whispered toward the door, rising on my elbows.

No answer from my ex-girlfriend. And yet a shape hulked in the ambient haze just inside the opening. Too big to be her.

Few options remained. One I hated to accept.

The drones, the brain-implant controlled assassins, had come for me.

Tingles dancing up the back of my neck, I glanced at my wireless-signal-jamming watch, Jade's gift, but the dial emitted no glow.

Dead?

How could my protection over the last four months have suddenly abandoned me? Jade had earlier asked for my watch, offering to replace the batteries. She'd given it back without following through?

My Beretta 9mm handgun must lie there somewhere in the dark, but my fingertips brushed emptiness.

Gone too?

No time to search for it now.

Whoever lingered in the dark pounced on me, his fist plowed into my gut; the sleeping bag muted the impact but not by much. Longing to shout Gordon's name, I could barely breathe past the agony.

While the masked man straddled me, something glinted in his hand. A hypodermic syringe glistened in the meager moonlight seeping through the tent's windows.

The assassin hadn't come to kill me but to immobilize me so the puppet master, the person or persons driven to control my life through my brain implant, might claim me. This wonderful reunion with Jade, Henry, and Gordon yesterday had been nothing but a setup. I needed to—

The syringe swung toward my neck, but my mind screamed "no." Even while I grappled with the man's powerful arm, the needle inched closer.

"Gordon!" I cried.

The Vietnam vet sprang to his feet and kicked my attacker's wrist. The syringe cartwheeled into the shadows. Gordon grabbed the intruder and put him in a headlock.

We had agreed that I should run if trouble came. Grabbing my backpack, I hurried toward the door, nearly colliding with another faceless shape. The second drone brandished a knife, glittery in the half-light.

I pulled back, but he must have been programmed not to hurt me, because he stepped toward Gordon and swung the blade at him. My friend sprang to the side at the right moment, maintaining the head-

4

lock on the first drone and using him as a human shield. Intruder nearly impaled intruder.

"Run, Landon!" Gordon yelled. "Get out of here."

Indecision stalled me. How could my friend expect me to abandon him with two against one?

Gordon's fist collapsed the syringe-wielding drone, but the knife brandisher, fleeter of foot, sidestepped him just in time.

"Landon, what are you waiting for?" Gordon shouted. "Go!"

They'd claim me once Gordon no longer stood in their way. His selfless act gave me the opportunity to flee.

Exiting the tent, I made a beeline across the moonlit campsite toward Gordon's unlocked truck. I found the second wireless-jamming watch in the glove compartment, where I'd stowed it earlier for safe-keeping. But the screen failed to glow in response.

Both wireless jammers sabotaged on the same night?

They'd been fine yesterday before Jade and Henry had shown up at my campsite and surprised me after several months of hiding away. Too much of a coincidence?

Abandoning the lifeless gadget, I sought my fail-safe backup. Months ago I'd found an old football helmet at a flea market and wrapped it in steel plating. That way if the jammers ever failed me, I had one last resort to block any controlling or tracking signals to my brain.

Fleeing the drones would be pointless until I blocked their means of hunting me down.

I dashed to the truck bed, barely visible in the moonlight. But that image became the last to grace my eyeballs, because just then I became a blind man.

No.

The puppet master had found me. Without functional jammers, he'd claimed control through the implant. Next, he'd terminate every sensory gateway, making escape futile.

Gasping in a panic, I searched the truck bed like a blind man with outstretched arms. Hands seeking but not finding.

C'mon, c'mon. Where is it?

Night sounds ceased. My hearing had been unplugged too. Ice water coursed through my veins.

Hurry!

Using something like an app on his smartphone, my enemy could now still my racing heart. The nightmare would be over for all of us, but then the puppet master would win.

Unacceptable!

Fingertips grazed a familiar cardboard box. Fumbling around inside, I grabbed the helmet. Slapped it on.

Sight and sound returned, and in that instant, the implant nestled in my cerebral cortex ceased broadcasting my GPS coordinates to my enemies.

Renewed, I spun away from the truck, debating next steps. Other drones—maybe even the puppet master himself—must be on their way here to ensure this endgame concluded successfully.

By no means could I return to Gordon for the keys. Which meant I couldn't take the truck. What better place to hide than in the woods?

Lingering in the cool spring air, wearing nothing but shorts and a T-shirt minus shoes, I scanned the campsite's perimeter for signs of other drones coming my way.

No one.

All those months of hiding in the woods, using a fake identity, and resisting the temptation to contact Jade and my mom—in spite of all those precautions, how had they found me?

Grunts coming from Gordon's fight with his attackers in the tent snapped me back.

Run, Landon. Get out of here. They're coming.

I'd been so happy to see my friends after my months of isolation, but I'd become nothing less than a trouble magnet. Logging as many miles between me and this place as possible would make everyone safer.

Offered no other alternative, I ran.

2

Inside the tent, illumined by a kerosene lantern, Jade Hamilton held her dad's arm above his heart. He moaned. She applied more pressure to the arm wound, ears straining for the first clues of an approaching ambulance.

Nothing.

"Just hold on, Dad. You'll be fine."

He grimaced. "But those guys are still out here, looking for Landon. He needs my help."

Gordon tried to sit up, but Jade forced him back down on the bloody sleeping bag. "There's no way you can help him with a wound like this, so just lie still. I'm sure Landon can take care of himself."

She bit her lip. The tourniquet should have worked by now, but it hadn't. The last time she'd checked, fresh blood spurted from the wound. Had the knife nicked a major artery?

Some nurse I am if I can't even help my own father.

Blowing blonde bangs out of her face, she applied more pressure with a fresh wad of paper towels. "You're not going to be able to help anybody if you don't rest. Besides, I still need to stop the bleeding."

"It's that bad, huh?" He panted, still trying to catch his breath after wrestling with the two intruders.

A rustle outside snapped her gaze to the unzipped door flap, and her heart revved. Minutes ago the strangers had fled into the night before she, awakened in the second tent by Gordon's shouts, had been able to get a good look at them.

New fears sank their talons into her mind. Could the strangers come back? Doubtful, if they were after Landon.

But still she glanced around, planning how to defend herself if necessary. After all, they'd just been attacked, and Landon had gone … where? According to Dad, he should be deep in the wilderness by now.

On the other side of the tent, something glinted in the half-light. Sure enough, Landon had left his Beretta behind. If pursued, the odds didn't weigh in his favor. He'd be okay in the woods as long as the drones didn't catch up to him. She prayed he'd found another means of blocking the puppet master's tracking signals.

What was I thinking when I disarmed his wireless jammers? Landon's never gonna forgive me for this. That is, if he's able to survive the night. It's all my fault.

Biting a fingernail, she peered through the screen window at the truck where Henry waited inside, his worried eyes peeking at her through the driver's side window. Awakened by her dad's cries for help, she'd hustled her son in there and told him to lock the doors behind him. Thankfully, being locked in there also spared him from seeing all this blood.

Her arm ached from keeping her dad's arm elevated. Gordon's eyelids fluttered, his tongue dragging across his lips. "Landon was right. The lie was assuming we were safe to come looking for him. We never should have come."

She hadn't confessed her mistake to him yet. He'd learn the truth at some point and think less of her. Let him live in ignorance for now. "Shh. Save your strength, Dad. It's gonna be okay."

He panted. "Does anything about this situation look okay to you?"

"I just mean—"

"Did you see where Landon went?"

"No. He was gone by the time I found you lying here."

"Probably never expected he'd be on the run again. Poor guy."

Just like her dad to be thinking about others when he might soon face a serious situation of his own. She'd given the emergency dispatcher her dad's blood type over the phone. Surely, they'd bring plenty of blood with them. What could be taking them so long since her 9-1-1 call from the ranger's station?

Swirling red and blue lights washed the forest in a kaleidoscope of changing colors.

Thank God.

The sucking sensation in Jade's chest, which had prevented her from drawing a deep breath, eased. "Now just hold on, Dad. Help's on the way. Keep applying pressure. I'll be right back."

Hustling from the tent and toward the gravel road, she waved her arms. The ambulance lights swung toward her in concert with squeaky brakes. Two uniformed men hopped out and followed her.

The EMTs busied themselves with checking Gordon's vitals and working their magic. Soon they carried him on a gurney toward the ambulance.

"He's lost a lot of blood," said the EMT with the spiky, bleached hair, "but he should be okay. We'll give him a transfusion on the way."

Relief kneaded her tight neck. She thanked him and whispered gratitude to the Almighty.

The figure of a woman registered in Jade's peripheral vision. Jade turned, and the stocky brunette in jeans and a green sweatshirt approached her and flashed her eyebrow-raising credentials. "Hi, I'm Special Agent Maggie Songbird with the Federal Bureau of Investigation. I understand there's been a stabbing here."

An FBI agent here? In response to a stabbing?

"Yeah, that's right. Two men attacked my dad before they ran off, chasing a friend of mine."

Compassion softened the woman's dark-brown eyes. A shock of gray streaked through the middle front lock of her hair. "I'm so sorry. Is your father going to be okay?" she said with a slight southern twang.

"I hope so."

"What about your friend? Do you know where he went?"

She shot a worried glance at the trees, bathed in blue and red. "No, I don't. I hope he's all right."

"Well, the local police should be on their way. I'm sure they'll see if they can find him. Actually, I'm here on probably an unrelated matter, but I'm wondering if you could help me, especially if you've been staying at this campground."

Jade shoved strands of errant bangs out of her eyes. "Well, I haven't been here long, but I can try."

"I'm looking for *this* guy. Have you seen him? Somebody reported seeing him here at the campground, and he's of interest to the FBI."

The agent gave Jade a back-and-white photo of Landon Jeffers, a glamour shot for one of his piano CDs. In the picture, he made footprints on a beach, handsome in blue jeans and a white T-shirt, face lifted toward the sun.

Guilt chafed Jade, shoving tears into her stinging eyeballs. Her hand flew to her mouth.

"Ah, so you *have* seen him," Maggie said. "Do you know where he is?"

Wow. Is there any possible way I could have messed things up worse than I did?

Taking two weeks of vacation, she'd been so excited about the reunion with Landon. But she'd been so gullible to believe the man on the phone, the one who claimed to be from the FBI and said it was safe for Landon to come out of hiding. His words had prompted her trip to Georgia with her dad and her son to find her friend, but the man's words must have been a trap to flush Landon out.

Clearly the FBI hadn't called her; otherwise, an FBI agent wouldn't be here now, looking for Landon. And because she'd been too trusting, she'd removed the batteries from Landon's wireless jammers to prove he no longer needed to live in fear. Only to have fear come calling with a vengeance in the dead of night.

Maggie gave Jade's shoulder a comforting squeeze. "I'm sorry, honey. Are you okay?"

Jade smeared her tears away. "How do I know you're really from the FBI? No offense, but others in the past have said the same thing. They weren't legit either, and Landon almost got killed as a result."

"So you know Landon Jeffers?"

"Of course, I know him. But I'm not saying another word until you give me some proof beyond a fancy badge that you're really who you say you are."

The EMT with the thick, gray beard jogged up. "Ma'am, if you want to follow us, we gotta go now."

"Hold on a sec." Jade ignored Maggie and checked her smartphone. No reception, so forget checking the agent's creds here. But the hospital would offer Wi-Fi.

"Can I ride along with you in the ambulance?" Jade asked the EMT. "I'll need to bring my son, too."

"Sure. No problem," he said and jogged away.

"I'll follow behind," Maggie said.

The agent's tenacity impressed Jade. "What on earth for? If you're looking for Landon, he ran off into the woods about a half hour ago." If Maggie worked for the puppet master, she should have already known this. Evidence she was who she said she was.

"Don't tell me," Maggie said. "Those two men—"

"They came for Landon all right, and my dad's in a world of hurt because he defended him. That means if you're really who you say you are, you just missed your best chance to help Landon Jeffers."

Maggie's shoulders sagged. "I'm coming anyhow. If Landon finds a way, I bet he'll get in touch with you."

Jade stalked toward the truck to get Henry, Maggie hot on her tail. "And why would you say that?"

"Your reaction when I showed you his picture. You're not his sister, are you?"

Jade stopped and faced her. "He doesn't have a sister."

Maggie flashed a second photo, this one of Jade and Landon hanging out together years ago. How had the agent gotten her hands on that?

"Let me guess," Maggie said with a faint smile. "You're Jade, his high school sweetheart. Something tells me he hasn't forgotten you. You can bet he'll try to get in touch. And when he does, I'll be there."

3

Running has never been a regular part of my routine, but it's amazing what I can do when somebody wants to kidnap or kill me. I paused to catch my breath, lungs aching, legs trembling from exertion.

Thirty yards away, a stick crunched underfoot.

Darting behind some brush and holding my breath, I prayed the man who'd been tailing me would walk on by. At least a half hour after venturing into the dark woods on foot, I'd wrongly assumed I'd gone far enough for him to have lost my scent.

Another drone? Must be. Who else would be shadowing me in the woods at this hour?

My muscles tensed, the tree hiding my bulk when he drew near. A human form in dark clothes, face hidden in shadow. He paused and took stock of his surroundings, not moving, just waiting and listening.

A thick stick lay mere inches from my fingers. I grabbed it and hurled it far to my left.

The commotion in the distant brush jerked the man's head toward the sound. He darted away in pursuit.

I forced myself to wait two full seconds before adrenaline sent me sprinting in the opposite direction.

How long and far I ran, I don't know. But soon my legs resembled Jell-O more than muscle, bones, and sinew. My sweaty head itched beneath the helmet, but I dared not take it off.

T-shirt sticking to my chest, I panted hard and forced my achy legs to keep going. By now I'd put at least a few miles between me and the drone, but no longer could I assume I'd gone far enough to ensure safety.

Slowing to a fast walk, I planted my hands on my sore hips and peered ahead through the moonlit darkness, seeking any breaks in the thicket or unseen fallen logs that might block my path or trip me. The flashlight in my backpack might have helped, but turning it on now would have been like waving a T-bone under the nose of a rottweiler.

The forest held its breath. My ears tuned in to the chorus of frogs, the whooshing of leaves in the trees, and the shuttling of air through my lungs. A gentle breeze caressed my face, cooling my sweaty skin and calming my racing heart. The aroma of pine needles filled my nostrils.

Stopping, I listened and scanned my surroundings. No sign of the drone anywhere.

I wiped my parched mouth on my arm and tried to ignore my severe thirst. Checking the backpack earlier had revealed beef jerky and other snacks but no water beyond a half-filled canteen, which I'd drained a half hour ago. If I found a stream, I might chance a drink despite potential bacteria. A TV survivalist had strained river water through a sweaty sock.

Was I that desperate? Not yet.

Listening for any unusual sound, I chose not to let the deceptive sense of calm fool me. Again the reality of my situation hit home, reminding me of how ill-prepared I'd been to head out on my own, unarmed.

You can't run all night, Landon. Plus you need water. And without a map, you have no clue where you're going.

Until the drone interrupted me, I'd been heading in a general southerly direction, but only God knew how true my course had been.

Finding a place to hunker down, maybe near a drinkable creek, and grabbing some much-desired rest ranked high on my priority list. Then, in a clearer state of mind, I could decide what to do next.

But what were the odds of finding shelter in the middle of nowhere? In a place safe from drones?

My mind rewound to my flight from the campground. Maybe Gordon had overpowered both drones. Had Jade and Henry stayed safe through the attack? If only I could contact them and let them know I was okay and check on them. But getting in touch might be a colossal mistake.

Why couldn't they have left me hiding in the wilderness on my own? Everyone would have been safer that way.

Recent memory skipped back to the moment I'd spied Jade and Henry breaking through the trees for our unexpected reunion. What incredible joy to see them again, but look at what had happened since.

I forced myself into a jog and persevered until I discovered a dirt road, a sign of civilization. Interest piqued, I managed a fast stroll and followed it ... until I almost collided with a medium-sized structure. An impenetrable wall of blackness rose vertically from the forest floor.

Could it be?

Yes, some sort of hunting cabin rose before me, with sturdy log-style walls. Drones would look here first, but part of me no longer cared. Maybe they'd already been here and wouldn't return to a place they'd already checked.

The doorknob yielded, and the door failed to squeak. I eased into blackness.

No discernible mustiness. Could the place be uninhabited? If so, maybe I'd crash right here on the floor.

Dare I call out? A sixth sense told me not to.

Meager moonlight seeping through the nearest window revealed little of the interior.

I barked my shin against something solid, one of two chairs stationed around what must be a small wooden table. And yes, a lantern occupied the middle. I picked it up, and liquid inside sloshed. The pungent aroma of kerosene permeated the air.

Matches. There must be some here somewhere.

Wait.

Across the room, the red lights of an electric heater glowed.

Alone? No.

The click of a rifle being cocked. I froze.

"Stay right there. Drop the backpack and put your hands up," said a man's voice in a thick southern accent from the room's blackest corner.

4

Reflexes shoved me a step away from the voice, my back meeting the door. "Oh, sorry. I didn't know anybody was in here. I'll go."

"No, I don't think so." The stranger struck a match and lit the lantern, the flame revealing a bushy, brown unibrow and a round, chubby face peppered with a few days' reddish stubble. The husky man wore blue jeans and a red plaid shirt.

Sitting on the edge of a cot, where he'd apparently been sleeping, he pointed a hunting rifle toward my chest. "I said, put up your hands."

I complied. "Look, I don't know what this is all about. I got lost in the woods and was just trying to find shelter."

Eyebrows lifted. "You were wandering around in your bare feet?"

"It's a long story."

"Well, I've got time. Take a seat." The man shoved a chair toward me with his foot, and I obliged. Maybe I could talk my way out of this situation and sleep on the nearby sofa.

The cabin was larger than I suspected. Beside the brown faux leather couch against the far wall stood a tiny TV perched on a side table. Next to the heater sat a blue cooler to the man's left, along with a twelve-pack of bottled water. Hunting supplies, mainly turkey decoys and fish tackle, lay scattered around with little rhyme or reason.

The stranger rose and stepped toward the table, still pointing the rifle at me. With his other hand, he snatched a piece of paper from the tabletop and studied my face in the half-light as if comparing my likeness to something on the page. A wanted poster?

"What's with that weird helmet?" he said. "Take it off."

"Sorry, but I can't."

"Can't or won't?"

How much could I tell this guy? "Look, you don't understand. I take this thing off, and some nasty people will show up. Believe me, you don't want that."

He studied me, eyes shining. "You wouldn't happen to be Landon Jeffers, would you?" He handed the paper to me. There I was, in a photo taken for some magazine interview a few years back.

"A man came by a few hours ago," he said. "Told me to keep an eye out for you. Said you're dangerous and that I should call him if you drop by."

A drone? "Did he leave his name and phone number?"

His suspicious expression softened. "Don't matter. You don't look so dangerous to me, just exhausted. And you probably could use some antiseptic for those cut-up feet. You're probably pretty thirsty too. I see you eyeing those water bottles."

"I'm that obvious, huh?"

The rifle lowered. "If you're on the run, you must have your reasons. That's none of my business. What *is* my business is when I take a few days off from work to go turkey hunting, and some bully shows up, points his gun in my face, and starts ordering me around. I don't care for people like that. No sirree."

He huffed and shook his head, his stern look melting into a small smile. "My name's Sam, by the way."

We shook hands. "Nice to meet you, Sam. You already know my name."

"I think I've heard of you. Don't you play the piano or something?"

"Something like that."

"Well, you're welcome to stay here the rest of the night if you want."

"I hoped you'd say that. The couch would work."

"Be my guest. And tomorrow, if you want, I could give you a ride to town. Could even cover you with a tarp or something in the back of my truck in case what's-his-name comes calling."

"Thanks for the offer."

"No problem."

"Have you seen anybody else around other than that guy you mentioned?"

"Nope. So how long you been out in them woods?"

"An hour or so."

"What on earth are you doing out there in the dark at this time of night? You running from somebody?" When I hesitated, he said, "Sorry. That's none of my business. You hungry?"

"More thirsty than hungry."

"Then help yourself to that water. Drink as many as you want."

Within seconds, I'd drained my first bottle and started on my second.

"I've got some stronger stuff stashed away," he said, "if you're interested."

The grimace came without conscious thought. "No, that's okay."

"I've got some beef jerky somewhere, too. Or maybe you'd prefer some canned pork and beans."

"No, it's okay. I'm really not that hungry." I drained the second bottle and decided to let it settle before I opened a third.

Leaving the rifle on his cot, Sam bent over the cooler and rummaged around inside, his back to me. "Well, you gotta eat something. Otherwise I wouldn't be a very hospitable—"

Sam never saw the bullet that hit him. It shattered the window, spraying glass, and sent him sprawling facedown over the cooler with a grunt.

I tumbled off the chair and flattened myself on the wooden floor. Another volley of gunfire shattered the table lantern, extinguishing it at the same time. Darkness fell on me like a heavy blanket. My heart pounded through my rib cage.

5

Charlton Memorial Hospital
Folkston, Georgia

Jade accepted the steaming cup of coffee from Maggie Songbird and murmured a thank-you. She did her best not to disturb Henry, who'd curled up on his waiting room chair, his head cradled on her lap.

Not usually a coffee drinker, she sometimes made concessions, and right now she needed to stay awake. The strong brew, consumed black, nearly burned her lip.

The FBI agent's eyes were glued to her phone. Probably checking messages. Maggie set her phone and coffee down on the side table and tore open a packet of stevia.

Great. A health nut.

Maggie's dark features made Jade wonder about her heritage. Mexico? Or somewhere farther south?

Jade rechecked her watch. When would somebody come with news about her dad? At just past two in the morning, they could all use some shut-eye. The ER met expectations; everything took longer than

ADAM BLUMER

it should, and she wouldn't get a wink until she received word about her dad's status.

So much blood … The sight in the tent had unnerved her. He'd be okay, wouldn't he? And what about Landon? Had he escaped those drones on his scent?

Studying Maggie over the top of her coffee cup, Jade mulled over the FBI agent's mysterious appearance. Shortly after their arrival at the hospital, Jade had looked Maggie up online, confirming she was the real deal. Now questions swirled around in her head, questions that needed answers.

Jade kept her voice low, not wanting to disturb Henry. "You were gone a while. I hope it didn't take that long just to get coffee."

Maggie poured in some creamer from another packet and began stirring it in. "I needed to call my partner and fill him in on what's going on with Landon."

"Sorry you had to get him out of bed."

"No, he was still up. A real night owl."

Jade blew on her joe. "So you know all about why Landon's been on the run since Thanksgiving?"

"Yeah, I was thoroughly briefed about his situation a few days ago."

"So how did you know to look for him at the campground?"

The FBI agent stared at her for a second, as if stunned, before tearing her gaze away. She must have detected the ping-pong game going on with Jade's pupils; the side effect of her lifelong journey with nystagmus went hand in hand with her ocular albinism, a condition that limited her ability to see objects far away and explained her blonde hair and faint blue eyes. But Maggie was classy enough not to say anything about it.

"There'd been a reported Landon sighting at the campground," Maggie said, "and I came to check it out. I knew if he was on the grid again, he would be in danger. Unfortunately, as you know, I just missed him."

Time to be frank.

"Look, I don't mean to be rude, but if you're really here to help

20

Landon, I need to know more about what you know to feel confident you're up to the task."

"So you doubt my abilities."

"No, not your abilities. Your understanding of the situation."

"I see. Well, how about I tell you how much I know, and you can let me know if I'm missing anything important. Sound good?"

Jade nodded.

Maggie tasted her joe. "I've read the dossier on Landon's case. Quite the story since his diagnosis of brain cancer last fall. Mind control through a brain implant?" A low whistle blew through her lips. "If there wasn't such a trail of violence and death, I'd be tempted to wonder if the story came from some upcoming sci-fi thriller rather than from real life."

"It's all a little hard to swallow, isn't it?"

Maggie nodded. "After everything Landon's been through, I can understand his lack of trust in the FBI, or really anyone else for that matter."

"Then you understand why he chose to run and hide?"

"To a point. We offered him the witness protection program last November. If he'd accepted it, he'd be a lot safer right now."

Jade raised an eyebrow. "But that meant he'd have to trust the FBI. He didn't know if he could do that. Remember, a brain doctor who said he'd come on the FBI's behalf nearly got Landon killed last fall."

Maggie shook her head, her face a mask of disgust. "Yes, I know all about Brady O'Brien, the imposter."

"But see, Landon didn't *know* he was an imposter. He thought he could trust this guy."

"I'm sorry, but we can't help that somebody showed up, pretending to work with us. We're the real deal. If you can't trust the FBI, then who can you trust?"

Jade couldn't withhold the chuckle. "Is that supposed to be a rhetorical question? I might as well be transparent about my reservations. I'm not blaming you personally—you weren't even in the picture at the time —but the FBI didn't exactly shine last fall. So maybe you can understand why Landon and I still have some trust issues when it comes to the FBI."

Maggie set the coffee cup down and folded her arms. "I don't think I read this part in the dossier. You'd better fill me in."

"Sure you want to hear it?"

"If we can improve our game, I'm all ears."

"There are still two unresolved issues that maybe you can help me with."

"Only two?" The whiff of an adversarial spirit permeated the air.

"Possibly more, but let's start with those first. I'd like to know why the FBI dragged its feet when Landon asked for help through my uncle. Your colleagues showed up all right but when it was almost too late to do any good. I mean, Landon died in my arms."

"I'm well aware of that."

"Then you also know that by some sort of miracle, we brought him back to life. All I'm saying is, if the FBI had treated the issue more urgently and gotten on location sooner—"

"Things might have turned out better for everyone?"

"Exactly."

Maggie paused and moistened her lips. "I'm sorry you feel like we blew it. At the same time, all of you were told to wait a few days for us to get some agents on-site and set things up for reverse tracking from Landon's implant. It isn't our fault Landon grew impatient and decided to go rogue."

"But Ray Galotta, the crooked cop, was searching the town for him and us. We didn't have time to wait."

Maggie shrugged. "It was the best we could do under the circumstances. I'm sorry we didn't meet your expectations."

"You're forgiven. But I just can't help feeling that if the FBI had taken our concerns more seriously from the get-go, some people who are dead wouldn't be. In fact, we may not even be sitting in this waiting room right now, and Landon wouldn't be who knows where."

"I'm not trying to make excuses, but do you have any idea how many crackpot calls the FBI gets every day? We needed more information about Landon's situation before we could send a bunch of staff to the north woods."

"I still think you folks dragged your feet."

A brief pause. "Clearly we aren't going to see eye to eye on this issue. You're looking at Landon's situation from the viewpoint of somebody who was here at the time. We saw his situation from afar and didn't initially have all the data you did. At the time it seemed neither prudent nor wise to send in the cavalry. We came cautiously after we had all the facts."

Jade bit her lip and looked away.

"I can see you're upset."

"Wouldn't *you* be? Do you have any idea how this brain implant has messed up Landon's life? And his mom's life, too? I'm glad the FBI is here, finally. I just wish the help had come a lot sooner."

Maggie leaned forward, elbows on her knees, eyes brimming with sincerity. "I can tell you've been through a lot, and really, that's why I'm here—for you *and* Landon. Thank you for being so frank with me. I can't speak to mistakes made in the past, but what I can say to hopefully rebuild trust here is that I wouldn't even be here if the FBI didn't take Landon's situation very seriously."

She shrugged. "I wish we had taken it more seriously sooner, but like someone has said, hindsight is twenty-twenty. I wasn't on the case then, but I'm here now on his behalf and yours. I'm going to do everything in my power to help him. Any other questions?"

So many spiraled around in Jade's head, almost enough to overwhelm her. "You're aware of the cop, Ray Galotta, who was killed last fall?"

"The one hunting Landon? Of course. Very sad."

"My understanding is that the FBI planned to do a full investigation of his brain implant after his autopsy. Have they been able to track down who's behind the implant?"

Maggie scribbled on a notepad she'd pulled from her purse. "I'm not supposed to discuss pending investigations. I need to talk to my partner, Brad, before I can give you an answer on that. Do you have any other questions?"

Jade shook her head. Sipped her coffee.

"In that case, if you don't mind, I'd like to hear your account of events last fall as you remember them. Hearing your side of the story might help me. I feel like I need to review everything I know so far. Maybe there are details other investigators missed."

So Jade told her everything she could recall. She concluded with confessing to turning off Landon's wireless signal jammers. "Thanks to me, the puppet master knew exactly where to find him."

"The puppet master?"

"That's what we call him or them—whoever is pulling the strings." Jade lifted a hand in bewilderment. "I know, I know. Why on earth did I do it? Landon was showing symptoms of classic paranoia. I thought I was doing him a favor by turning the jammers off. I thought maybe he just needed to realize he was safe without them."

"And now you're afraid you made things worse?"

Jade sighed. "No, I *know* I did. And to make a bad situation more difficult, now he's on foot and probably lost somewhere. And those guys who hurt my dad—now they're after him, too. I feel just terrible."

She leaned forward and ducked her head, so not wanting to cry in front of this stranger. "Here he'd been safe hiding in the woods all those months, and I had to show up and ruin everything. It's all my fault. He wouldn't be in this mess if I hadn't interfered. And if he wasn't paranoid before, now he'll really be."

Maggie reached toward Jade and patted her knee. "Hey, sounds to me like you're being a little hard on yourself. Remember, he didn't stab your dad—one of those evil men did, though someone else was probably controlling their actions. He had to know danger would come calling at some point and was probably prepared for it."

Jade straightened. "Wait. The helmet. I don't think I saw it in the back of the truck."

"The helmet?"

She explained, a slow smile spreading across her face. "He's in the woods, all right, but those guys won't have a clue where to find him. He might be okay after all."

"How are his survival skills?"

"Until recently, I would have said nonexistent, but he's been camping out for a while. He may have learned some things just in case something like this happened." She shook her head. "But he's going to be so mad when he finds out what I did. I wouldn't blame him if he never forgave me."

"He's pretty special to you, isn't he?"

"Of course. We've been friends since like, forever."

"No, I mean something more than that. But really, it's none of my business."

Maggie's phone rang, and she rose to answer it. She strode a few feet away and spoke in soft tones. Moments later, she returned, eyes sparkling with renewed energy despite the late hour. "That was the sheriff. I called him on the way here. One of the assailants left a syringe behind in your dad's tent. They're going to check it for prints."

"That's great."

"If they are successful and we get a hit in the database of known offenders, that might take us straight to one of the guys responsible."

6

My gaze scoured the darkness of the cabin, searching for a way out. Gasps bursting out of me, I waited for the inevitable. Who else could be out here on my tail except for more drones?

But why shoot Sam? Had they somehow confused him for me? We didn't look at all alike.

Sam didn't budge. Had the bullet killed him? From my angle, any wound lay hidden in shadow.

Breathing hard, I stayed flattened on the floor and waited. Weighed my options.

Moonlight filtered through the shattered window and illumined Sam's rifle on the cot. If I grabbed the rifle, at least I'd have a weapon. But I'd also place myself in the line of fire.

The cabin door crashed open. I tensed.

A dark figure entered and slammed the door shut behind him.

The person I assumed must be a man swept past the other side of the table and crossed to Sam's body, bending over him. The intruder in black clutched something at his side. A rifle.

My gaze swiveled to the door. Perhaps while the stranger focused on Sam, I could hightail it out of here.

The man whirled toward me, face shrouded in shadow. "I know you're here, Landon Jeffers. It's okay. I'm a friend. You don't have to hide from me."

Yeah, right. You just shot Sam in cold blood.

"I know things look bad"—the intruder crossed to the broken window and peered out—"but you gotta trust me."

"Trust you? I don't even know who you are."

"But I just saved your life. That has to count for something."

Saved my life? What could he mean?

He pulled out a flashlight and turned it on, then upended it. Set it on the table, its illumination spreading across the wooden-beamed ceiling.

Before me stood a man in his sixties with gray, neatly combed hair and a matching goatee; he wore a black jogging suit and athletic shoes. If he was a drone, he couldn't be the run-of-the-mill variety. The thickness of his torso and the absence of any obvious gut suggested a man in decent shape for his age.

"You keep eyeing that door, and that tells me you're about to try something foolish," he said. "I can put a bullet in your back just as easily as I put one in this guy here."

"Why did you kill him?"

"I didn't. He just passed out from a minor shoulder wound."

He held up a syringe, and I cringed. The last time I saw one of those, it had been meant for me.

"I also gave him a shot that'll ensure he stays asleep for a while," the stranger said.

"Who *are* you?"

"It's time we had a chat. Have a seat."

He pushed a chair toward me and chose Sam's cot for himself, resting on it with a sigh, the rifle still in his hands. A spasm rippled across his strong-featured face. Was he in pain? Or wounded?

I rose and took a tentative step toward him, searching him for injuries and finding none. "Are you all right?"

"I'm fine, but don't think you were the only one being hunted tonight. I faced a few of my own obstacles to reach you in time. But those are irrelevant." A shrug. "C'mon, sit. I don't bite."

27

"Why don't you put that gun down first."

His eyes glittered. "Because others like this guy could be nearby. And we don't want their kind showing up unannounced, now do we?"

"What do you mean?"

"You'll understand, Landon, as soon as you give this man here a once-over." When I hesitated, he said, "Don't tell me you're squeamish, not after everything you've seen and done."

Our gazes connected. "You don't know anything about me," I said.

"Actually, I know a great deal."

"Care to enlighten me?"

"You're Landon Jeffers, an award-winning pianist who has several best-selling recordings to his credit. You were diagnosed with terminal brain cancer last fall, but it was all a ruse so a surgeon of nefarious intentions could place an implant in your brain. When you learned others were using the implant to make you do bad things you couldn't remember, you cleverly used wireless signal jammers to go off the grid and try to find help. After you and your friends nearly got killed a few times, you defeated your handler and got help from the FBI."

I waited for more.

"Your trademark is your curly black hair, which you secretly hate and I suspect is hiding under that ugly helmet you're wearing. If you had to choose a snack, you'd rather gorge yourself on salted pistachios, not to mention Jack Daniel's or cigarettes when you can hide them from your religious mother, who wouldn't approve."

He paused. "Need I go on?"

"Can you?"

"You're in love with Jade Hamilton, but you're afraid that being near her will endanger her, so you stay away. Very chivalrous of you, I must say. That's why you decided to play Walden in the woods for a while. In high school you and Jade were sweethearts until Joey Bartholomew attracted Jade's attention. During a fight you pushed Joey, who accidentally tripped on a tree root and fell to his death. Then, at the Christian school you attended, you shot two men in the back after they tried to kidnap Jade and—"

"Who *are* you?"

"Do you trust me now?"

"Why—just because you know a lot about me? Some folks who aren't my friends know a lot about me too. That doesn't tell me who you are or why you're to be trusted."

He got up. "We're wasting time. I want you to take a good look at this man here. I think what you find will end our stalemate."

"His name is Sam. I still don't understand why you shot him."

"So you trust Sam more than you trust me? C'mon, take a look."

I stepped toward Sam, feet crunching on broken glass from the shattered lantern.

Nobody with eyeballs, not even in this meager light, could have missed the scar running across the back of his head. Poor guy. Another drone sent to do somebody else's dirty work. If only I could find more people like Sam, show them the way out. Last fall I'd tried to help the cop, Ray Galotta, but he'd rejected my invitation.

Only to die mere seconds later.

Right before my eyes.

"Sam would have waited until you were asleep," the stranger said. "He probably would have injected you with something, unless he planned to put something in your food. Either way, he would have drugged you or killed you. If so, he found you in the perfect termination zone."

"Termination zone?"

"The place where you're most vulnerable, lacking aid or anyone to help you. But he didn't count on me coming along."

Backing away from Sam, I collapsed on the chair and cradled my helmeted head in my hands, the aroma of spilled kerosene filling my nostrils. "He's another drone."

"A what?"

"That's what I call them, the remote-control killing machines."

"You mean an operative, a servant of the Justice Club."

I stared at him. "Justice Club?"

"Sounds swanky, doesn't it? Like a bunch of fat cats smoking cigars in a country club. Don't let the name fool you."

"I'm not fooled. But their underlings—their operatives—are people just like you and me, who can't help what they do but still pay the consequences."

"I understand your sympathy, but these folks can be deadly, too. That's why I'm here—to help you."

"But wait. I still have this helmet on. How did Sam know it was me?"

"The old-fashioned way." He gestured to the kerosene-splattered wanted poster. "They knew you were somewhere in the vicinity and lacked shelter. Probably sent out a few like Sam just in case you dropped by. Odds were in their favor you'd show up."

He reloaded the rifle with ammo from his pocket. "Now that Sam's unresponsive, others will be coming to see what went wrong. Time for us to move."

"What if I don't want to?"

He raised an eyebrow. "You stay here, and they'll either kill you or take you. There's no choice."

"I need more. How do I know I can trust you?"

"There's no time for that now. You're coming with me because you want to live."

I didn't budge. Just stared him down.

He sighed and reached into his pocket, then pulled out a keychain. But not just any keychain. It bore a round raised piece of metal, shiny white. On it a black train was superimposed over a large red cross.

I inhaled a quick breath. "Where did you get that?"

He smiled. "You've seen this before, haven't you?"

"My dad. He was in a special train club with a few Christian buddies. You know my dad?"

"I more than know him. I was in his club years ago. We met on Tuesday nights."

I stared at him with new eyes. This guy? A friend of his dad's? "That's right. 'Train Tuesdays.'"

He nodded. "Only six keychains like this one on the planet. That makes it special." He paused, sliding the keychain out of sight. "Are you coming with me now?"

Grabbing Sam's rifle from the bed, he thrust it toward me. "Take it. It might come in handy. I'm trusting you not to shoot me in the back. Would you just try to extend the same trust?"

I accepted the rifle and leaned it against my chair. Why trust me if he were my foe? Besides, my father would never have given that keychain to someone who couldn't be trusted.

He said, "Sam's boots appear to be about your size. Grab 'em, too. You'll need 'em."

"But they're not mine."

"Believe me, he won't miss 'em, and you'll need 'em for our journey. Besides, he's a dead man."

"A dead man?"

"No time to explain now. Take the boots." When I hesitated, he said, fire leaping into his voice, "You don't get it, do you? This is war, Landon, and he's the enemy. Deprive the enemy every chance you can get."

I removed Sam's boots, then sat down to pull them on. "Where are we going?"

"Just trust me." Glancing out the window, a tuneless whistle under his breath, he grabbed several water bottles and handed one to me. "We've got a ways to go, and you'll need it."

And here I'd lamely hoped for some much-needed sleep on the couch.

He grabbed the flashlight off the table and flicked it off. Darkness descended. He reached for the doorknob and swung the door open to the night, the whine of mosquitoes greeting us when we ventured into darkness as impenetrable as granite.

"Why did you take the time to explain?" I said. "We could have been miles from here by now."

"Because I didn't want a reluctant partner. You wouldn't have been any help if you didn't trust me. And you do trust me now, right?" A pause. "Your silence is very reassuring."

7

Even on the darkest of nights, hope can promise a glimmer of the dawn.

The stranger maintained a fast, exhausting pace through the ebony woods, pushing through brush like an expert survivalist. He moved doggedly forward like he followed an established trail in the moonlight, but nothing was there. I puzzled over how he could be so certain of his way.

Now the merest hint of the moon glimmered behind a patchy sky.

I struggled to keep up, grateful for the boots on my aching feet. Never had I traveled so far on foot. How much farther before we reached our destination? When I asked him where we were going, he silenced me with, "No time to talk. Time to make tracks."

When the cabin was at least a half hour behind us, he slowed. "Sorry. I keep forgetting you already traveled several miles before we met. Have any questions for me?"

I came alongside him, gripping the rifle. "What's your name? I don't think you told me."

"I'm Montgomery, but my friends call me Monty. Last name isn't important."

Nearby, something unseen growled in the brush. Monty dove into the brush and reappeared moments later, muttering that whatever had lingered in the dark must be long gone. He set a leisurely pace across a meadow, allowing me to keep up more easily. In his hand glowed a battery-powered compass, which he paused and studied.

Ah, so that's how he knows his way.

"How did you know where to find me?" I said.

"A tip came in that some operatives had been sent after you, that you were vulnerable. Finding you was as simple as following them."

"But how did you get the tip?"

"We have a few moles who leak important information to us when we need it."

"Back at the cabin, you said Sam was a dead man. What did you mean?"

"He was commissioned to either kill or kidnap you. Failure to execute his mission on someone of your profile isn't an option in this business. If he failed, he would surrender his life in exchange for yours."

"How do you know?"

"Because I've been watching how the people you call the 'puppet master' work for quite some time, Landon."

"And that's how it always works with these operatives?"

"Always."

We reached woods again. He lifted a branch, and I ducked under it.

"But last fall I was sent to kill a woman," I said, "and I failed."

"She was one of your first assignments, wasn't she?"

"Uh-huh."

"She was only a test. If she had been a high-profile target, you'd be dead right now."

A gnawing truth burned in my mind. Deemed worthwhile as long as they performed, operatives could be just as easily crushed like a paper cup and replaced with the next person in line.

A certain queue of expandability.

He stumbled and winced, grabbing one of his knees. I dashed to his side, but he waved me off, muttering something about rheumatism. Moments later, he straightened and appeared much improved. Or he'd decided to power through.

He shook his head. "I'm getting too old for this."

"So, are you FBI?"

"No."

"CIA?"

"Nope."

"An agent of the government?"

He laughed. "The government doesn't have a clue. I'm more like an independent contractor who is very interested in making sure those in charge of the Justice Club don't succeed. But it doesn't really matter who I am. I'm a nobody, a mere cog in the machine. A friend of the resistance. What's important is who you are."

"Who *I* am."

"Of course. You don't realize how important you are to them, Landon. You're the reason Sam is a dead man."

"But why am I so important? I don't get it."

He stopped and stared me down, face lost in shadow. "You really don't get it? C'mon, Landon. It isn't every day somebody has the gift of hysterical strength."

"Hysterical *what*?"

"You're kidding me, right? In 1985, when your friend Joey Bartholomew was hanging off the edge of a cliff, about to fall to his death, you somehow lifted him, a one-hundred-thirty-pound teenager, with one arm. You did something incredible. Unnatural. Your brain told your adrenaline to kick into overdrive and make you do something you normally wouldn't have had the ability to do."

I waited for more.

"In 2006 Tom Boyle watched as a Camaro hit a cyclist and pinned the boy under the car. Hearing the boy's cries, Boyle ran to the three-thousand-pound car and lifted it for almost a full minute while an onlooker rescued the boy. True story. Boyle had hysterical strength too."

"And now the Justice Club wants to use me for some special purpose. But I don't even know how to use this special strength."

"It isn't something you plan to use, but if they can tap into our brain and cause that same adrenaline rush, just imagine the things they could make you do. Break open a locked door. Lift a heavy vehicle or machine. That's why we need to keep you away from them."

Advice from the past, from my mom's lips, replayed in my thoughts. *You don't have to do what these evil men want. Sin no longer has the power to control you. You can say no.*

Had Mom been in on Jade and Gordon's plan to hunt me down? They hadn't mentioned her, and I couldn't help reflecting on her status, given the latest developments. How much I missed her, even the sermons I didn't appreciate.

Monty moved again, and I followed.

I gave myself a mental shake, still unable to wrap my mind around my situation. Last fall, in a school playground far away from here, an evil man, controlling me through the implant, had ordered me to shoot Jade Hamilton at point-blank range. But I'd surrendered to God's control and in effect severed the puppet master's means of control. Newfound freedom had allowed me to reject the enemy's orders and save lives.

But only hours ago, the puppet master had somehow regained control, yanking away my ability both to see and hear. He'd also tracked my location through the implant so operatives knew where to find me.

But if God had granted me freedom from these sick people, how could the puppet master track and control me now? None of it made any sense.

AHEAD, the tree line yielded to a small meadow; blades of grass and ferns danced, frosted by moonlight. Nearby, a deer lifted its regal head and peered at us, mesmerized, then bounded away with apparent springs in its hooves.

Monty halted and checked his compass and watch. I pulled out my water bottle and took a swig, then wiped my mouth on the back of my hand, my T-shirt clinging to my sweaty torso.

He regarded me with a grim look. "I'm afraid this is where I have to say goodbye."

"What? You're leaving me?"

"I'm sorry. I have my orders."

"You don't get it. I finally found someone who understands my situation and can help me, and now you're going to just leave me here? Do you have any idea how long I've been in the dark about this implant business? Do you have any clue how"—my voice broke —"how lonely I've been?"

"Yes, Landon, I do. Keep your chin up. You'll be okay. Besides, I think you've got somebody else watching your back too, if you know who I mean." He nodded toward the sky.

Whoa. How could he know so much?

"'Greater is He who is in you than he who is in the world,' Landon. When you get discouraged, just repeat those words."

Wow, a fellow believer, too. And now he had to leave me?

He squeezed my shoulder like a father might, and my throat tightened, touched by the flicker of something I'd missed for a long time.

"My mission was to find you when you were in danger and keep you safe for the next step of your journey," Monty said. "I succeeded. But now it's time for you to follow *your* orders."

"Orders from whom? There's still so much I don't understand. I wish we had more time to talk."

"You have enough to get started. I don't want to overwhelm you. Believe me, it's better this way."

"But I want more."

"You mentioned the puppet master and a crime network of what you called 'drones.' There's another network, an alliance of people just like me who are seeking to thwart the Justice Club's plans. Be assured that, like me, they're your friends and are cheering you on. My only regret is that you had to wait so long before our paths crossed. Though we have to part company now, be assured that my friends and I will be keeping an eye on you. Landon, you are never alone."

The sigh of disappointment, impossible to suppress, blew through my lips. "Please don't tell me you're going to desert me here in the middle of nowhere."

His eyes twinkled. "No, I wouldn't do that to you, not after everything you've been through."

"Then why are we here? What am I supposed to do?"

"Your orders are to return to Iron Valley."

"Iron Valley. But that doesn't make any sense. Don't you realize how dangerous it is for me to go back home?"

"I didn't say your next step would be easy or danger free. Yes, you'll be out of hiding, and bad people will be looking for you. Be careful what you tell others, even your friends. Some knowledge can be dangerous."

"What am I supposed to do in Iron Valley?"

"One step at a time." He pointed in the distance. "On the other side of those trees, you'll come to a dirt road. Follow it a quarter mile to the north. I'll leave you this compass and a flashlight to help you find your way. You'll come to a green Jeep parked on the side of the road, facing you. It's fueled up and ready to take you home. Here are the keys."

He pulled them out of his pocket and dropped them in my open palm, cool against my skin. "The Jeep's yours. Consider it a gift from some Landon Jeffers fans."

"Thanks, but I don't even know where I am. How am I supposed to find my way?"

He slid out a second flashlight and flicked it on to be sure it worked. It did. Handing it to me, he said, "Once you start the vehicle, the GPS system is programmed to guide you safely home. For now no one will be looking for your Jeep, but I would advise you to buy different clothes and change your appearance as quickly as possible, though I'd keep the beard. I understand you've done this sort of thing before, so you should know the drill."

I nodded.

"One more thing." He pulled out something resembling a small pistol and, lifting the part of my T-shirt covering my right deltoid, pressed the nose against my skin. When he pulled the trigger, something stung me like a bee. I winced.

"You'll want to put some ice on that later," he said.

"What did you just do?"

"You have the Justice Club's implant in your head, but now you have our implant in your shoulder, effectively canceling any controlling signals from them. You can take that helmet off now. You don't need it anymore."

I removed the helmet, tempted to ditch it, but I kept it handy, the evening breeze refreshing my sweaty head. "But the GPS in the Jeep. Won't this thing in my arm block the connection?"

"Don't ask me why, but it should work just fine. A different frequency or something. You can make cell phone calls too. There's a disposable phone in the glove compartment. Unlimited minutes. Keep in mind that we'll be monitoring any calls you make."

With almost too much to take in, my head swam. "I'm going home. I guess I should be happy."

"But you're scared. You'd be a fool not to be."

"So that's it? That's all you're going to tell me?"

"Patience. There's are two more things. First, your mother needs you. It's important that you go to her." Something hinting of prescience seasoned his tone.

I swallowed. "Is she in danger?"

"One thing at a time, Landon. You don't need to worry about tomorrow or even next week. All you need to think about right now is what you need to do next, and I've told you that."

"Okay, what's the second thing?"

"It's about your father. You need to visit him, too."

"My father. Don't tell me he's somehow involved in all this."

"How well do you know your father? It's important that you go to him. Whisper a single name in his ear."

"But he's mostly unresponsive in a psych ward. I don't understand."

"You don't need to understand. Just trust me."

"Whisper a name in his ear. Why?"

He shook his head. "You're just full of questions, aren't you?"

"What name?"

"Sonora. Do you think you can remember that?"

"Unusual name. Yeah, I think so."

"Word association. Just think of the Disney movie *Wild Hearts Can't Be Broken*. Ever seen it?"

"No."

"The lead character's name is Sonora. She rode diving horses."

"For real?"

"For real."

"Okay, but then what? How will I reach you if something goes wrong? Or if I need advice?"

"You won't reach me. When the time's right, I'll reach you. You're very important, Landon. Remember the moles I mentioned? We could use another one in the advanced program."

"Advanced program?"

"I can't explain now. Just think about it, okay?"

"Okay." But wouldn't that require my being in the clutches of the Justice Club?

"Until you hear from me, enjoy your trip. It'll be a long drive. I think there's even breakfast waiting for you in the glove compartment. Do you like Egg McMuffins?"

"I used to love those things until cancer changed my diet. You guys really need to update your database on me."

He shook his head. "So sue us."

"One more thing. My friends back at the campground—"

"Don't worry about them. They're fine."

"How do you know?"

"I know. That's all you need to know."

"I put them in danger, didn't I?"

"No, because you ran, you took the danger with you. You did the right thing by running when you did."

His watch beeped, and he winced. "Time's up. I gotta go." He shook my hand, pressing the compass into my palm. "Goodbye, Landon Jeffers. I'll be keeping an eye on you. I'm sure we'll meet again." He turned and strolled toward the trees.

"Do you need a ride?" I called.

"If we planned a vehicle for you, do you think I wouldn't have my own set of wheels?" He waved with a grin. "Adios, amigo. Until next time."

Giving me his back, he entered the woods in a direction opposite mine. I watched him go until he vanished from sight. Once again, I found myself alone in the wilderness with nothing but the rustling of leaves in the wind.

But I'd successfully evaded operatives and found an unlikely friend in the resistance, one who possessed answers I lacked.

With a sigh, I slid the compass into my pocket, hoisted the backpack over my shoulder, gripped the rifle and helmet, and tromped across the meadow to what awaited me beyond.

8

"Sorry you had to wait so long," a male voice said. "We've had a busy night in the ER."

Jade's head jerked up from her upraised fist, startling her from sleep. A cocktail of adrenaline snapped her drowsy eyes open. Across from her, Maggie had fallen asleep too, head listing to one side. She stirred.

A young doctor in a white lab coat, bearing blond stubble and bloodshot eyes, patiently waited.

She rubbed her eyes. "My dad—is he going to be okay?"

"He'll be fine. No internal injuries, but the cut was pretty deep. He needed several stitches. He'll have a battle wound to show off for sure. He was also mildly dehydrated, so we've given him an IV."

"Can I see him?"

"Of course, but he's pretty out of it right now. Just follow me."

Jade corralled Maggie and Henry into the room where her father slept after the eventful night. She pulled Henry onto her lap, his head resting against her shoulder, as listless as a wilting plant. Glancing at her watch and seeing it was barely past three a.m., she let Henry sleep.

Jade simultaneously breathed a sigh of relief and aimed a prayer heavenward.

Thank You, God. He's going to be okay.

HER DAD SLEPT on into the morning, and Jade envied his ease at finding rest; she was too keyed up to do much else but doze in fitful spurts. And no word from Landon Jeffers, to Maggie's disappointment.

After lunch in the hospital cafeteria, they had just returned to Gordon's room when Jade's phone rang. "Caller unknown." A sixth sense compelled her to answer it.

"Jade, it's me."

Her pulse sped up. "Landon! You're okay."

"Of course I am."

"It's Landon," Jade mouthed to Maggie, who leaped up from her chair. Jade said into the phone, "Of course? But—but you ran off into the woods. Those drones were after you, and one had a knife. What happened?"

"It's a long story, and I can tell you all about it some other time. Is your dad all right? I hated leaving him behind to fight those guys alone, but he insisted that I go."

She filled him in. "Dad's gonna be fine. Don't worry about him. So how did you get away from those drones?"

"I met a friend along the way who offered protection and gave me a renewed sense of purpose."

"That sounds mysterious. Where are you?"

"I'm not exactly sure. I found a ride to Iron Valley."

Jade's eyes locked onto Maggie's. "Iron Valley. Why are you going there?"

"I can't really explain, except I think I'm supposed to go home."

"*Supposed* to? What do you mean?"

"My new friend, Monty, knows a lot about drones, Jade, and why people in the Justice Club are trying to find me."

"The Justice Club. What's that?"

"That's what he calls the cybercrime network. Either way, I think he can help us."

"Are you sure he can be trusted?"

"Pretty sure. He knew all about me and knows my dad. He even saved my life."

"How did you find a ride home?"

"He gave me a Jeep."

"He *gave* it to you? Landon, you're not making much sense. Who *is* this guy?"

"That's not important. Look, I need your help. People are going to be looking for me, but I don't want anyone to know where I'm going."

Maggie flashed her notepad. Jade grabbed it, forcing it mere inches from her face, due to her ocular albinism. "Landon, can you take a detour? Meet us here at the hospital in Folkston?"

"Sorry, I'm somewhere in Tennessee, I think. I've been driving nonstop since I found my ride."

"Why the urgency? What's wrong?"

"I'm not sure. I just know I need to go home. My mom needs me."

"Is she in danger?"

"I'm not sure, but like I said, my new friend knows things. He said something that gave me the impression I shouldn't delay."

Phone pressed to her ear, Maggie headed toward the door, no doubt calling Brad with the news that Landon Jeffers had been found. She wouldn't betray his destination, would she?

"Landon, are you okay? I mean, after everything that's gone wrong?"

"I am now. I'll tell you all about it the next time we meet."

"There's an FBI agent here, Maggie Songbird, who's been looking for you. Don't worry. I looked her up at the Georgia Bureau of Investigation website. She's legit."

Suspicion flared in his tone. "What does she want?"

"To see you, of course. She wants to help, but she just stepped out. All I know is that she showed up at the campground, looking for you —something about a Landon Jeffers sighting—but you were long gone by then."

"Jade, does this woman know you're talking to me? Does she know where I'm going?"

Jade's throat constricted. "Landon, I—"

"She better be with the FBI this time and not some imposter."

43

The accusation in his voice tightened her fingers around the phone. "Landon, she is. Didn't you just hear what I said? I checked her out. She's the real deal."

He sighed. "Sorry. Lately, I've had a hard time trusting anybody."

Even me. He knows I disarmed his jammers, but he's too much of a gentleman to say so.

She couldn't keep the tremor out of her voice. "Landon, the problem with your wireless jammers, the reason those drones were after you—it's all my fault."

"Neither jammer worked. That was you?"

"That's what I'm trying to tell you."

"But why, Jade? I don't understand."

"You seemed paranoid the last time I saw you, and I was … I was trying to prove to you that you didn't need to be. I thought I could convince you that you were safe by turning off your protection and showing you everything was fine without it. But then, of course, everything went terribly wrong. I really messed things up and almost got you killed. I'm sorry."

"It's okay. I've already forgiven you."

"But you could have been—"

"Seven times seven, Jade. That's how many times we're supposed to forgive each other, right? Believe me, your number doesn't even come close."

She sucked in a breath. "Landon, what's going on?"

"What do you mean?"

"I guess … um … this isn't the Landon Jeffers I remember. What's happened to you?"

"Something wonderful, but I don't have time to go into it right now. Sorry, Jade, but I really need to go. Remember, my mom doesn't believe in using cell phones. I've been trying to reach her at the school where she's been substitute teaching and left a message. She might try to call me back. I'll call again soon. Bye."

9

Chicago, Illinois

Two more people were dead at his hand, but Gavin Dane Morrison slept like a baby.

That afternoon, after several hours of first-person-shooter video games, he went for a five-mile run in the park near the marina. Later, he cooled off by doing some fast walking around the gazebo while checking messages on his phone. His gaze landed on the headline in his news feed, his stomach tightening. UNANSWERED QUESTIONS STILL ABOUND ON ANNIVERSARY OF VAN LANEN MURDER.

The phone slipped out of his sweaty hand. But Nicki, seemingly materializing out of nowhere, caught it before it hit the wooden floor.

"Whoa!" she said. "You don't want to drop that."

"Hey, you're fast. Thanks!" Amazing the way they kept crossing paths lately.

"I wonder what's got you so interested." She eyeballed the news feed for a split second.

"Don't, Nic!" He snatched the phone out of her hand and abruptly closed the news app with his thumb.

"Well, good morning to you too," she said in an annoyed tone, hands on her hips. "I was just curious."

Had she seen the news article? Gavin shrugged, as if making light of the situation. "Sorry. I didn't mean to be so abrupt or secretive there. It was nothing."

"Nothing, huh? You seemed pretty absorbed." She'd apparently been getting some exercise too, based on her shorts, T-shirt, earbuds, and MP3 player.

He'd bumped into her at the library two months ago—a pretty, effervescent brunette reading stories to kids during "story time." From the get-go, her interest in him had been too obvious, too aggressive, and he'd been trying to put the brakes on ever since.

"So why are you being so mysterious?" she said.

"I don't know what you mean." Gavin waved. "Well, hey, another time, Nic. Send me a text. Maybe we can do coffee sometime." He turned and hustled down the sidewalk leading to the Lake Michigan shoreline, hoping she'd get the hint that he wanted to be left alone.

Nope. The Queen of Persistence caught up to him and met his stride. "You don't mind if I join you, do you? You said we could at least be friends, remember?"

He stopped and faced her. "Look, Nic, I'm fine with being casual friends, but I told you from the beginning that I'm not interested in anything more than that. It's just not smart for you to get close to me."

She quirked an eyebrow. "What are you saying? That you don't like getting close to people?"

"No, that's not what I mean."

Her brown eyes flashed, the sun igniting the blonde highlights in her hair. "Then what *do* you mean? Is it me? You just don't like *me*?"

"No, it's not you. You're pretty and nice, but—but you just don't understand." He propped his fists on his hips. "In my line of work, I could vanish in a heartbeat at any time and be headed who knows where. I could be gone for days without any contact. I may not even be able to return calls or texts. To be friends, you have to accept that."

"Okay, so you have a rather hush-hush, bizarre job."

"That pretty much describes it."

"You don't work for the CIA, do you?"

"No."

A small smile. "Oh, I know. You're an assassin like Jason Bourne. Yeah, that must be it."

He shook his head and resumed his walk, rattled that she'd gotten so close. His gaze veered to Lake Michigan on their right, the sun's rays dancing on the surface. Seagulls wheeled overhead, their squawks harmonizing with the rush of the surf.

"Fine," his stubborn shadow said. "We'll never be more than good friends—I can accept that—but surely it can't hurt for me to at least get to know you better."

"I've already told you a lot." He wished they could talk about something else, something not about him. "What else do you want to know?"

"That one time when you let me take you out for pizza, you said you were adopted."

"Yeah. So. A lot of people are."

"But you said there was something not quite right about the adoption. Remember?"

Gavin had said too much, and now, like a bloodhound on the scent, she'd never give him peace until he gave her more red meat. This was why relationships with people like Nicki Sanders were such a mistake for guys like him.

"Yeah, there's more to the story, but I'm not sure I should tell you."

"Oh, c'mon, Gavin. Please."

Those eyes. So captivating.

He sighed. "Just promise me you won't go spreading this around. I'd rather we kept it between us, if that's okay."

"Sure. Whatever. I won't tell anybody."

"My adoptive parents are great people. They loved me as their own, but I always had questions about who my biological parents were. See, the birth certificate from the orphanage said I was born in Hawaii to a Hawaiian father." He paused, gesturing to his face. "Okay, get real. Do I look like I had a Hawaiian father?"

She studied his blond hair and blue eyes. "Not on your life. But you already knew that, didn't you, especially after you did that DNA test you told me about? Don't you have more Scandinavian in your DNA than anything else?"

"See what I mean? No Hawaiian in me whatsoever. Things didn't add up."

He spotted a nearby bench and sank onto it, facing the water. She joined him.

"I had a strong suspicion that there was a bigger mystery to my past than I realized," he said. "I had to find out who my biological parents really were."

She studied his face intently. "So what did you do?"

"That was back when I was in high school. We didn't have the Internet then. Yeah, I know, I'm really dating myself here. I went to my local library and requested printed listings of missing children, especially in Hawaii. I was looking through database pages going back to the 1970s when there was a bombshell. You'll never guess what I found."

"What?"

"A photo of me."

Nicki's jaw dropped. "What? But how could that be?"

"See, there was a baby photo on the page. From it an artist had made a composite of what the missing child would have looked like as an adult of about my age."

So cute when her nose wrinkled that way. "A composite?"

"Yeah, a recreation of the child's face given the passing of time. Here, let me show you." He pulled out his phone and showed her the photo.

She swore. "That really does look like you. Kind of freaky. So what did you do?"

"First, I got in touch with that organization for missing children. All I knew was that I'd been adopted in Hawaii, but I didn't know any other details beyond the birth certificate. Could I really be the same guy in the photo? To find out for sure, the agency asked me to send them a sample of my DNA, which I did. I didn't tell my adoptive parents, because I didn't want to freak them out. Then one day my phone rang with the call that changed everything."

She waited breathlessly.

"The DNA matched. I was that missing child from Hawaii."

"No way!"

"It's true, but I was confused. Had I been kidnapped from my biological parents before I was adopted? Why had I been reported missing? I didn't learn the details until later."

He blew out a breath. "The important thing was that my real mom and dad, as far as I knew, were still looking for me, but I had a tough decision. See, I loved my adoptive parents, but I knew if I didn't at least meet my biological parents, I'd always wonder who they were. So I tracked them down. You've met my dad. Cool dude, huh?"

She nodded. "Yeah, real cool for him to give you the big condo on Lake Michigan. You could have done a lot worse."

Gavin laughed. "No kidding."

"Too bad you never met your biological mom."

He leaned forward, elbows on his knees, gaze fixed on the lake. "Yeah, well, sometimes time buries things, and that's where they need to stay."

After a marital spat, his mom had in fact left his dad, who'd been living in Hawaii at the time, and taken Chris—his real name—with her. That was why his biological dad had reported him missing. She'd changed both of their names and later disappeared, leaving him, an infant, for the state to take care of. Details were sketchy, but the last time anyone had heard of his mom, she'd checked into a homeless shelter, never to be heard from again.

Nicki patted his arm and peered into his eyes. "You know, Gavin, sometimes it's okay to be sad." That was one thing she nagged him about: his inability to show emotion. What she didn't understand was that this stoic facade helped him survive.

He shrugged. "Why should I be sad? It's not like I even knew her."

"But she was your mom."

He looked away, desiring to change the subject.

Why am I telling her all this anyhow? She can't change any of it. It just is.

"So how did your adoptive parents respond?" she said. "I mean, when you decided to find your biological dad, that must have been really hard for them."

"No, they were fine with it."

Because they didn't know anything about him. They thought I was dead. Murdered, in fact.

But she didn't need to know those details.

The moment passed, the morning sun's glow shimmering like jewels on the water. A picture-perfect day.

"That's awesome that you at least found your dad," she said. "You must love him so much."

Gavin remained silent and let her statement hang in the air between them like a wisp of cigarette smoke. Visible but then gone, leaving little more than an odor behind. But a noxious one at that.

He glanced at his watch. 2:07 p.m. Most people were at work right now on a Thursday, but he could linger as long as he wished. And why not? His dad paid the bills, and Gavin had no regular job to go to. This was one of the perks he received for the price he paid.

What else did he have to do but wait for his brain to set his feet on his next mission?

The mission chosen by his father. The head of a massive network that directed people just like him.

Slaves to a system that each day decided who would live. Who would die.

If Nicki knew the whole story, she'd run.

Soon his father would send him to kill again, though Gavin would have no memory of what he did during those dark, lonely hours when most people slept. The only remnant the next morning was an unsettled nagging, a ping from his conscience that he should feel bad about something he had no memory of.

An unsettled existence.

Did he love his father? His frank response would have startled her.

No, he hated him.

Gavin regretted that he'd ever hunted his biological father down and stepped forward as the lost child. If only he'd been content with his average middle-class life with his adoptive parents, where the most exciting thing on the calendar was prom or a Friday night football game.

He would have retained his true identity as Chris Van Lanen.

Instead, he was an amnesiac killer who wanted out. But take one step toward freedom, his biological father had warned him, and his adoptive parents would die.

10

Iron Valley, Michigan

"Are you okay, Jordy? Let me take a look at that, buddy." Sandra Jeffers knelt beside the third-grader, who'd just fallen off a sled and taken a tumble, mostly on his knees. Thankfully, the snow-covered ground had cushioned his fall. Must have hit the sled somehow. "Oh, that's not so bad."

Bloody and oozy? Yes.

Life threatening? Hardly.

Smiling, she gave him an affectionate pat on the shoulder. "You'll be fine. It looks worse than it is."

Pride swelled in his voice. "Am I gonna need stitches, Mrs. Jeffers?"

She pasted on her most serious expression. "No, Jordy, I don't think so, but you've torn your pants and definitely qualify for a big Band-Aid."

"You think so? I mean, do you think my owie is that bad?"

She helped him to his feet and brushed the snow off his coat and jeans. "We'll let Nurse Wendy make the call. Sound good?"

His chocolate-colored eyes sparkled. "Sounds pretty cool to me. Nurse Wendy is a really nice lady."

Ten minutes later, after leaving Jordy in Wendy's capable hands, Sandra checked her watch and winced. *How time was fleeting.* Substitute teaching had filled her days of late and demanded more time than she'd bargained for. Today's after-school errands included grabbing some groceries on the way home; then she had plenty to occupy herself with this evening.

She made a beeline for her car. If she hadn't bypassed dropping by her desk, she would have seen the note that her son had called and wanted her to call him back.

11

———

After getting her dad discharged from the hospital, Jade helped him, with Maggie's assistance, to the truck and dropped by a nearby pharmacy for his meds.

Maggie's phone rang, and she grabbed the call. Minutes later she ended it; disappointment etched her face when she explained that the police had been unable to find any usable fingerprints on the syringe in Gordon Hamilton's tent.

Maggie shrugged. "Maybe some other evidence sill turn up. The police will keep looking."

At a McDonald's, they grabbed a bite to eat and discussed their next decision: find a nearby hotel and take it easy or hit the highway and start the journey home to Michigan. When Jade was filling the tank at a gas station, Maggie's influence helped push the needle.

"Landon's already ahead of us by many hours. We can't afford to delay another minute."

"We?" Jade said. "So you're coming with us?"

The late-afternoon sun blazed just beyond Maggie's left shoulder. "Absolutely. Like I said, you and Landon are my top priority. If he's heading to Iron Valley, then I'm going too. I have permission from the

FBI to follow this lead wherever it takes me, even all the way to Michigan."

Maggie's wedding ring, glinting in the sun, caught Jade's eye. *How odd to be married and follow us all the way to Michigan. Who knows how long she'll be there?*

"If it's that important that you reach him," Jade said, "maybe you should fly. Perhaps you could even beat him home."

"True. But the safety of you and your family are my priority too. Landon isn't the only one."

Alarm spiked in Jade's thoughts. "You think we're in danger, too?"

Maggie's eyes narrowed. "I'm well aware of what happened last fall. You and Landon's mom, Sandra, are very fortunate you weren't seriously hurt or killed. Remember, these people don't hesitate to threaten or kill loved ones to get what they want. You can bet I'm keeping an eye on you and your family."

"But Landon's no longer in hiding. He's in danger too."

"Don't worry about him. He's heading to his mom's house, right?"

"Yeah."

"I'll call ahead and see if I can get some eyes on him. Make sure he's safe there."

Part of Jade regretted sharing Landon's travel plans with the FBI agent. Couldn't Landon enjoy a few minutes of alone time with his mom before FBI agents sprang out of the woodwork?

Maggie arched a brow. "What? Did I say something wrong?"

Jade returned the gas dispenser and screwed on the gas cap, not meeting her gaze. "Look, I know you and your colleagues have the best of intentions, but I hope they're going to be careful not to give Sandra Jeffers a heart attack."

"Of course, Jade. These are professionals from the FBI's Michigan field office who work with local law enforcement all the time. Some cops'll probably just keep an eye on her house. Believe me, their priority is to keep everyone safe."

"Sorry. It's just that the FBI has bungled things in the past. I don't want something else to cause Landon's family embarrassment."

Maggie folded her arms. "I thought you already aired your grievances. So what else is bugging you? If we're going to work together, you need to tell me everything."

Jade sighed. Why not place all her cards on the table? "Okay, what about my uncle, Senator Jedediah Hamilton? Last fall he contacted the FBI on Landon's behalf."

She nodded. "Yes, I remember."

"He told my dad he thought he was being watched and feared for his life. The next day, his car mysteriously drove off a bridge in Washington, DC, and plunged into the Potomac River, killing him. So if he was in danger, why no special protection when he needed it?"

"The consensus of my superiors at the time was that his personal security detail should have been sufficient."

"But obviously it wasn't, and now he's dead. He's my uncle. I can't help feeling like you folks dropped the ball."

"Jade, I'm so sorry for your loss, but we're not the ones who killed your uncle."

"I know that."

"I doubt this helps much, but after several months of investigation, there *is* evidence that someone—we don't know who—forced your uncle's car off that bridge. Like I said before, we didn't know then what we know now and can only act on actionable intelligence in real time. The investigation is still ongoing, and we haven't given up on your uncle. We're still trying to find those responsible."

"Thanks. I know it's not your fault, and I'm sure everyone has the best of intentions."

"But none of that brings your uncle back."

Jade shook her head. "No."

"Anything else we need to talk about?"

Jade leaned against the truck. "A few weeks ago, a man claiming he was an agent with the FBI called me. He said a lot of arrests had been made in connection to Dr. Korovin's clinic in Tucson, where Landon had his procedure, and that it was safe for Landon to come out of hiding."

Already Maggie was shaking her head, but Jade pressed on. "We never would have taken the trip to Georgia to look for Landon if this guy hadn't called me. Now look at the mess Landon's in. Is it possible the guy who called me really was with the Bureau?"

"No. It makes no sense that anyone from the FBI would have called and told you that. Did you get his name?"

"Chad Moyers."

Repeating the name, Maggie pulled out a notepad and jotted it down.

"So what he told me—none of it's true? There haven't been any arrests?"

"I can't give you details about pending investigations. All I can say is that we are still pursuing all leads. If you want more, just google the 'Korovin Cyberhealth Clinic.' My understanding is that Dr. Korovin has vanished, but if there have been any developments in the case, you'll find more information there."

Jade folded her arms. "Okay, so you're one hundred percent certain nobody from the Bureau called me with that information?"

"I'm positive. It looks to me like an impostor was trying to flush Landon out of hiding."

"And he used us to do it. Strange. Chad seemed to know a lot more about the investigation than most folks would. That's why I didn't question his credentials. Who else would call me, knowing so much, except the FBI?"

Maggie brushed a fingernail across her lower lip. "I could get phone records and see if I can track his number down. Would that make you feel better?"

"Absolutely."

"It would help me if I had at least a guesstimate of the date and time."

"I can't recall those details off the top of my head. I'll have to track them down and get back to you."

12

Sandra Jeffers unloaded the heavy sacks in the kitchen, muttering to herself that someone her age shouldn't have to contend with this task on her own. She should have a man around the house to help her with chores like this.

God, please bring my son home.

The silence of the house wrapped its fingers around her, a grip both cloying and unnerving. Knowing she should be used to the reality of living alone by now, she bit her lip. With one of her men half blind and living in a psychiatric ward and the other disappearing to who knew where, worry had lately become a constant battle.

How she missed Landon, her pianist son, who'd driven off on Thanksgiving night last fall and had been missing ever since.

Glancing at the phone, she shook her head. Not a word from Jade or Gordon; of course it didn't help that her voice mail was on the blink. They'd hinted that they were getting closer to tracking down Landon's whereabouts; then they'd disappeared a few days ago without leaving word.

Nothing since then. So typical.

"Heavens, I'm his mother," she said to the empty house. "If they found him, don't you think they'd called me with the good news?"

Then again, as much as she longed to see Landon again, she preferred that he stay away if being found would place him or others in danger.

Glancing at her watch, she sighed. Her after-school chores had taken longer than expected, and now it was after six thirty. Heading to the freezer with some fresh Alaskan salmon, she paused. Why not cook up a fillet for herself? She headed back to the kitchen, the suggestion too tantalizing to pass up.

She placed the fillet in a greased baking dish and sprinkled on some seasoned salt, paper, and paprika before covering it and shoving it into the oven. She booted up her computer for her evening's jaunt through old photos, birth and death records, and several ancestry databases.

She had no time or patience for those pesky telemarketers, who always interrupted her when she was on the hunt. The phone was going off the hook immediately.

Edna Mayhew had mentioned during the last church ladies fellow-ship gathering that one of her forbears came to America on the *Mayflower*, but several of the women had responded with skepticism. Sandra had offered to track down the elusive connections for her and hopefully help her save face.

"But you really need to watch that mouth of yours, Edna," Sandra said to herself with the shake of her head. "It keeps getting you in trouble, and—"

A creak coming from Landon's bedroom jerked her head to the right from her genealogy perch in the living room. The floorboards in the place creaked worse than her achy knees, but Landon hadn't slept in that bedroom for months.

Probably just the wind making the old homestead creak tonight.

She entered "Mayhew" into the database, and—

Another floorboard popped, this time from the kitchen. She spun her office chair around and eyed the dark doorway. "Hello? Is some-body there?"

No answer.

Even from this distance, the refrigerator's hum met her ears. On the wall, the old clock ticked faithfully, though surely lagging behind the pitter-patter of her heart. The phone was in the kitchen. Did she have the courage to find it and dial 9-1-1?

You are such a scaredy-cat.

But if she called 9-1-1, would they believe her? Since Landon's disappearance, she'd developed a track record worse than the boy who cried wolf. Their ordeal last fall had put her perpetually on edge, and too often her imagination got the better of her. Living alone didn't help. Trying to still her shaky fingers, she chided herself for not getting a cell phone after others had been nagging her to do so for years.

She swiveled back to the computer and resumed her time travel along the Mayhew family line, aware of the lights behind her, even the furniture—a tiny image of the room reflected in the shiny corner of her screen.

Clicking a link, she scanned a page of data.

Wowzers.

How many folks had been on the *Mayflower* anyhow?

Something in the room's reflection shifted. What appeared to be a dark shape emerged from the kitchen doorway and crouched low beside the old piano. It almost imperceptibly inched toward her.

She struggled to breathe and resisted the temptation to turn around.

This can't be happening.

But who could be in her house? And why would he be coming after *her*?

The shadow crept closer, low to the floor; the man on his knees must be only twenty feet behind her.

Her neck and shoulders tensed. Maybe she could dash to her bedroom and lock the door behind her. Holding her breath, she swiveled, knowing she'd catch him.

But nobody was there.

She alone occupied the room.

This is what you get for being an old woman with an overactive imag-ination.

Her gaze scoured every centimeter of the room, certain she hadn't been imagining things. Could the man have darted back to the kitchen before she turned around?

"Is somebody there?" Her voice rang across the room, stark and intruding. "I'm going to call the police now. Do you hear me?"

No response.

In the kitchen, silverware clanged.

Now!

In one fluid motion, she unplugged the laptop, snatched it up in her arms, and dashed down the dark hallway toward her bedroom.

Inside, she set the laptop on the dresser, swiveled, closed the door, and locked it. Flicking on the light, she backed away from the door, the tightness in her chest easing by degrees.

No mistake this time. Somebody was in her house.

Breathing hard, hands shaking, she glanced at her computer, wondering whom she could e-mail for help. Or she could climb out the window if she had to.

Hot breath caressed the back of her neck.

13
_____

Snowbanks outlined driveways and blanketed yards, the roads a slushy mess.

Nearly eleven p.m. I circled the block twice, eyeing the familiar house with windows aglow, a burst of sentiment warming my heart. How to enter the house with the least exposure occupied my thoughts. Maybe I could use the back door through the garage to prevent use of the front door; I even had a key.

Thankfully the cover of darkness would work in my favor, but once again, like during my drive north, I wrestled with Monty's advice about returning to Iron Valley.

My presence here still seemed counterintuitive. On Thanksgiving Day, I'd left this place far behind to keep my loved ones safe, because whoever wanted me had a penchant for threatening them. Why would I come back here now? Wasn't Mom safer with me far away?

Unless …

Monty's words came back to haunt me. *Your mother needs you. It's important that you go to her.*

The prospect of Mom being in danger made my stomach knot. Several times during my drive north to Michigan's Upper Peninsula, I'd toyed with the idea of calling and letting her know I was coming.

But what if somebody had tapped her phone? If she didn't know I was coming to Iron Valley, nobody else would either. Best to keep my visit a secret beyond the call to the school in case she was substitute teaching.

I parked the Jeep on the shoulder a block away, then locked it and hoofed my way toward home through thickening shadows on the slushy sidewalk, passing no one on the way. A car turned onto the street, its headlights whitewashing me for a millisecond before it hurtled past without slowing.

March's breeze brushed across my crew cut and beard. Perhaps my new look for Iron Valley would discourage instant recognition should I bump into an old acquaintance.

I crossed the backyard and tested the rear garage door, which Mom rarely locked. As I anticipated, the door swung inward, and I entered, then closed it behind me. Monty's flashlight confirmed my solitary presence.

Mom's minivan occupied the space before me, so she must be home, but the door connecting the garage to the kitchen was locked. Not wanting to scare her, I hesitated, eyes on my house key.

Better to knock.

Wait.

An alarm of some kind blared in the house. Had Mom gotten a security system since I left town? Not that I blamed her. The key worked, and the door swung open.

The alarm's volume swelled. So loud, my ears ached.

I rushed into the dark, smoke-filled kitchen. Smoke and the acrid aroma of burning food wafted from the oven.

Coughing, I flicked on the range light and fan, and grabbed a handful of paper towels, clasping it over my nose. I turned off the oven and chose not to bother checking whatever smoldered inside. Besides, opening the door would only make the smoke worse.

The smoke alarm blared from the wall near the breakfast nook. I grabbed a kitchen chair and disengaged the battery. Silence embraced me, but I descended the chair, sensing something was still amiss.

Mom wouldn't have let her supper burn like that.

"Mom?" I headed into the brightly lit living room to flee the smoke. "Mom, it's me, Landon."

No one. But her van was in the garage; she had to be here. Why else would all these lights be on with food cooking in the oven?

Nothing in the room signaled anything amiss, though her computer had vanished from its genealogy corner. Which suggested she might be working in bed. Yes, that had to be it. But again, why leave all the lights on and food burning in the oven?

She wasn't getting any younger. Perhaps she'd simply forgotten.

I headed down the corridor, floorboards squeaking. "Mom? It's me, Landon." My knuckles rapped the closed bedroom door. "Mom?"

No response.

Anxiety pinging on my concern meter, I turned the knob and opened the door.

Mom lay on her back on the floor, arms spread wide.

"Mom!" I dashed to her side and searched her closed eyes and colorless face.

Had she been shot or stabbed? I couldn't tell which, but there was plenty of blood on her clothes and the carpet. Was she even breathing?

I put my ear to her mouth.

Yes. Thankfully.

My fingers probed her neck and found a slow but steady pulse. The heavy pressure of tension shattered in my chest.

Who could have done this to her?

I pulled out my phone. "Mom, it's okay. It's me, Landon. I'm calling an ambulance. Just hold on."

While I dialed 9-1-1, Monty's words about my mom needing me bannered across my thoughts. Had he known about the attack in advance? If so, why hadn't he told me? Or done something to prevent this from happening?

14

Friday, March 25

"I t's so good to see you again, Son," Mom said from her hospital bed, hazel eyes heavy with fatigue.

"It's good to be seen, Mom." I grabbed her hand and held it, her fingers as cold as icicles. "It looks like I showed up just in time."

If I'd arrived home just a half hour or so later …

"I don't even remember what happened. Am I going to be okay?"

"You're going to be fine. You just focus on resting and getting better."

A small smile lit up her face. "I can't believe you're really here after all this waiting and wondering where you've been."

Four months had passed since the last time I clapped eyes on her. So many warring thoughts and emotions flooded my mind, so much I wanted to tell her.

Smoothing back strands of white-streaked black hair away from her eyes, I said, "I'm sorry if I hurt you by driving away on Thanksgiving night, Mom. I was trying to protect you and Jade and her family. Heading off on my own seemed to be the best way."

"I know. We don't need to talk about all that now. I'm just so happy you're here." Her eyelids closed as if too heavy to keep them open. "I wish I wasn't so tired. I'd love to talk more."

"We'll have plenty of time for that later. Is there anything I can get you?"

No answer. She'd already drifted off.

So much for good intentions to keep her safe. Just look at her.

But I didn't know for sure what had happened. A stabbing? My mother? And no indication of theft?

This was personal. Could the Justice Club be to blame?

Who else would have done such a thing?

Maybe nobody meant to kill her, just to hurt her bad enough so I'd be here.

Right now.

Out of hiding.

In plain sight in a public hospital. Right where the Justice Club could grab me.

Well, it worked.

Except some local cops prowled the hallways, thanks to notification from Maggie at the FBI that I might need protection. They'd agreed to keep my presence here as hush-hush as possible.

Brushing my fingers across my bristly head, I searched the room to ensure nobody hid in the shadows. Left-hand fingers massaged the tender spot on my right shoulder where Monty's wireless jammer lay embedded in my flesh.

Sheesh.

I know what they'll put on my tombstone someday. "He was paranoid all the way until the end."

My phone rang. Jade.

"Hey! I got our voice mail," she said. "I'm shocked to hear about what happened to your mom. Is she okay?"

"She will be now."

Her sigh breathed across the miles. "I'm glad. I was so worried."

"She came through surgery just fine, the doctor said, though things were a little touch and go due to blood loss. They gave her a transfusion and were able to fix her perforated small intestine. With time it should heal nicely."

"Can I talk to her?"

"Afraid not. She's sleeping, and I shouldn't wake her."

"So what happened? Who would want to hurt your mom like that?"

"I don't know, but the doctor said there's evidence she fought back. Maybe this is the work of the Justice Club."

"What makes you say that?"

"I'm not sure how much I can tell you."

"Was it something your friend in Georgia told you?"

"Yeah."

Knowing she'd want to know more, I hesitated. Surely Monty wouldn't have been in favor of my spilling everything, including the information he'd shared with me about the Justice Club and my father. And though I could trust the phone Monty had provided, I couldn't vouch for Jade's.

I nearly jumped when a nurse appeared. "Uh, Jade, I need to go. The nurse says it's time to move Mom to a private room."

"Okay, no problem. We can talk later."

"When will you be back in town? We have a lot to catch up on."

"I'm not sure. Maybe tonight sometime. I'll be in touch. I'll keep praying for your mom."

"Thanks. Talk to you soon." I clicked off.

A glance at my watch made me restless. No way anyone could guarantee when Mom would wake, and I hated to waste even a second. I knew someone trustworthy who could keep an eye on her for a few hours. The cops patrolling the halls would also ensure her safety if I left for a while.

A second mission nagged at me, Monty's instructions about visiting my father.

It's important that you go to him. Whisper a single name in his ear.

15

After another night of violence he had no memory of, Gavin Dane Morrison rolled out of bed at around nine thirty and fixed himself a three-egg omelet with provolone, black olives, and diced tomatoes. On impulse, he tossed in some crumbled bacon for good measure.

Fifteen minutes later, he sat at the breakfast nook and wolfed down his creation, glancing through the blinds at Lake Michigan below. The sky bore a bruised, forlorn look, the water reflecting melancholy shades of deep gray. No promise of sunshine in the schedule.

Should he run today? If he did, he might bump into Nicki again; her probing his life put him on edge and could get her into trouble. Probably better to keep his distance. Part of him regretted telling her so much. What had he been thinking?

You're thinking that you're not getting any younger and that a long-term relationship with her or somebody would be a lot better than the solitary life you're living now.

Except he knew it could never be. Father would never let him.

After washing up and wiping down the countertop, he headed to his closet to get started on laundry. He froze. Backed away from the clothes basket.

In the kitchen he grabbed his smartphone and dialed the super-secret number reserved for emergencies. The robotic male voice told him to activate the cloaking app before resuming to ensure an encrypted call. While pacing the room, he impatiently ran through the gauntlet of mandatory vocal checks so they could be sure he wasn't someone other than who he claimed to be.

Then: "What's up, Gavin?" the female operator said. "Are you okay?"

Tremors in his voice, more from rage than from revulsion. "There's blood all over the sweat suit I must have been wearing last night. Where did the blood come from?"

"Oh, okay. Yes, that's a problem. But I want you to stay calm."

His voice rose. "Did you hear what I just said?"

"Yes, Gavin, I heard you. Everything's going to be fine. Where are you now?"

"In my condo."

Where else would I be? You folks know where I'm dialing from and track every step I take.

"Are you alone?"

"Yes."

"Okay, I want you to take a deep breath and—"

"This isn't *supposed* to happen," he said, his hand strangling the phone. "My father assured me it never would. This connects me directly to DNA evidence. If the cops show up, I'm toast. That wasn't part of the agreement."

The well-controlled voice said, "Gavin, I'm really sorry this happened to you. I agree with you. This should never have occurred. It is completely unacceptable. You have every reason to be upset."

He swore and raked his fingers through his hair.

"But sometimes," she said, "in spite of our best efforts, unexpected things take place."

"Not to me. This has never happened to *me* before."

"I understand, but everything's going to be fine now. Promise. There's no reason to worry, okay? I just scheduled a disposal team to come to your place. ETA is a half hour. Will you be there?"

"Of course."

"Good. Just show them where you, um, made the discovery. There's no reason why you need to see the evidence or anything associated with it ever again. Do you understand?"

He sank into a chair at the kitchen table. "Okay, thanks. What do you think happened?"

"There will be a full investigation, of course. I'm checking the mission stats now to see if there's anything obvious. Let me see ... you were a decoy in Iron Valley, Michigan."

"Did you say, 'Iron Valley'?"

"That's right." She must have slipped. Probably hadn't intended to share that detail.

"You weren't in charge of the assault," she said.

"But how did the bl ... I mean, the evidence ... get on me?"

"There's no way I can say for sure before the investigation, but you might have been paired with a malfunctioner."

"A what?"

"A malfunctioner. He was supposed to clean up, like you always do without remembering, but he didn't. So some of the bl ... I mean, the evidence ... he was supposed to dispose of must have transferred from him to you. With the protocol we have in place, there can be no other explanation for why the evidence would show up on your clothes."

"Okay, that makes sense, but I'd like my father to call me about this."

The voice turned apprehensive, tight. "Really, there's no reason for you to think that—"

"Did you hear what I just said? I want my father to call me."

A submissive, reproved tone. "Of course. Not a problem. I'm putting in the request now. He should be in touch within twenty-four hours. In the meantime, until the team shows up, just stay away from the closet until they come."

Of course. What do you think I'd be doing? Sitting in my closet and staring at the bloody clothes? At the reminder of what I participated in last night?

He preferred to be ignorant of his nocturnal deeds. Then he could always blame others for using him beyond his control and volition. As soon as he had knowledge, culpability entered the picture.

ADAM BLUMER

"Thank you," Gavin said.

"Is there anything else I can help you with?"

"No, I guess that's it."

"Then I hope you have a great rest of your day," she said in a buoyant tone, as if she'd just delivered his order at a fast-food joint.

Gavin put the phone down, processing this news.

Iron Valley. He hadn't been back to his boyhood town in years. Why would the Justice Club have sent him there? Seemed risky.

And why fly him from Chicago to Iron Valley? It didn't make sense if other operatives were closer.

On his phone, he searched Iron Valley news until he found the headline; he didn't pause until he'd read the full story.

Sandra Jeffers, who lived only a few blocks from his boyhood home, had been stabbed in her own house. The police were inviting anyone with information about the attack to contact them.

So that's where I was last night. That's where Father sent me.

In fact, Sandra Jeffers's blood could be on that sweat suit lying in my closet right now.

16

R elieved to be home, Jade unlocked the front door and pushed it open, a slightly musty smell greeting her. She crossed the threshold and set the suitcases down. They'd left town, so hopeful to find Landon. Now they were back, still without Landon, but hopefully they'd be reunited with him soon.

She turned toward her dad, giving him an encouraging grin. "Hey, we made it. You feeling okay?"

He graced her with a weary smile. "I'll feel a lot better once I'm in bed." He headed toward his bedroom.

Meanwhile, Henry, who'd slept a good bit on the way, bounced around the family room, overflowing with pent-up energy. What a contrast.

After unpacking, Jade ran a finger along the hallway table, wishing she had time to give the place a thorough cleaning. She had offered Maggie the guest room, but the FBI agent had insisted on getting a hotel room.

Fine. Whatever made her more comfortable. Still, Maggie would need a place to hang out beyond work and sleep.

Jade glanced at her watch. Soon they'd meet Maggie at the hospital, and she'd see Landon again after his flight into the Georgia woods. As it was, they hadn't enjoyed a private moment since the brief reunion at the campground. Though Thanksgiving was a while back, she still recalled the warmth of his hand in hers when they'd briefly held hands under the dining room table during the holiday feast.

God, would You please break down the walls so we could at least have a friendship now? Or possibly more?

Her phone rang. Maggie.

After exchanging pleasantries, Maggie said, "I forgot to discuss something with you. Now that we know where Landon is, I realized I better prepare you for what happens next."

Jade's hand fluttered to her neck. "Prepare me for what?"

"As I mentioned before, just by being out in the open, Landon has placed himself in danger. When we get to the hospital, some local cops will be waiting for us just outside Sandra's room. They will be posted there for Landon's protection. I just wanted to let you know so you wouldn't be alarmed. Plus, somebody wanted Sandra either badly hurt or dead, so she needs protection, too. But most of this is for Landon's sake."

Jade leaned against the wall. "Of course. Landon doesn't have any jammers. He'll be out in the open."

"So later, after we greet him and visit a bit, I need to escort him out of there and take him to a safe house, where a few of my fellow agents and I will be prepared to debrief him. This is for his own good and yours. Do you understand?"

"Of course."

AFTER CHECKING into her room at the Holiday Inn Express, Maggie grabbed a cup of coffee from the lobby and called Brad McCarthy, her partner. His wife, Cassie, was a secretary in the office pool and one of her best friends.

After greetings, he said, "So what's Iron Valley like?"

"It's small. And there's snow on the ground here."

"Snow on the ground? Mags, it's March."

"Brad, this isn't Georgia. It's Michigan's Upper Peninsula." Maggie sat on the edge of her bed, sipped her hazelnut brew. "I'm in my hotel room, and we're heading to the hospital soon. Landon Jeffers should be there, waiting for us."

"I certainly hope so."

"You don't sound so sure."

"This guy has evaded a number of folks over the last few months. You know what they say. 'Don't count your chickens until they're hatched.'"

"Well, I guess we'll wait and see, but his mom was seriously hurt. You bet he'll show. Otherwise he's a pretty unfeeling son. Thanks for cheering me on to get this assignment, Brad. Beyond my personal request, I assume this is important."

"Assistant Director Clemmons wouldn't have asked you to follow the case all the way to Michigan if it wasn't."

She surveyed the busy parking lot from her window. For a second, she debated what to say next and decided to go for it. "So … what is there about this Landon Jeffers case the FBI isn't telling me?"

"I'm not sure what you mean. You've read his case file and attended a briefing."

"Okay, but consider this. Mere days after my briefing on Jeffers, he, who has been in hiding for months, suddenly comes out in the open and heads north. Around the same time, somebody stabs his mom. Who else would be behind all this but the cybercrime network we've been investigating?"

"Probably. Why is any of that surprising?"

"It isn't, but I feel a little blind here."

"Blind about what? I've shared with you everything I have."

"Maybe everything *you* have, but there are more than a few loose ends, aren't there?"

"Like?"

Is he serious? Careful, Maggie. Watch your tone.

"Okay, for starters, what about this cop who was moonlighting for the crime network?"

"Ray Galotta is dead, Mags."

"Of course. But what happened to the investigation of his brain implant? Shouldn't we have heard something about that by now?"

"I'm afraid that's in the hands of another department."

Just like the investigation of Jade's uncle's mysterious death. Everything tangled in so much red tape. It's a wonder we get anything done.

Maggie rubbed her forehead. "That investigation is pretty critical. Determine who's behind the implant or who the implant was sold to, and we might be able to get some names and make a few arrests. Then this whole issue of Landon's safety, not to mention the safety of his mom, could go away."

"You know it's not that simple, Mags. Investigations take time."

"Of course, but it *has been* four months. Surely someone should be able to tell us something by now. Could you have somebody check on it and see where things stand?"

A pen scratched on paper. "Sure thing."

"Another thing. Are you familiar with an agent named Chad Moyers?"

"The name doesn't ring a bell."

"Somebody by that name called Jade Hamilton, Landon's former girlfriend, and said he was from the FBI. He told her it was safe for Landon Jeffers to come out of hiding. That's the event that apparently set these other events into motion."

Brad coughed, hinting that he might be struggling with springtime allergies again. "None of our people had the authority to tell her that."

"I would hope not. But because of that phone call, Jade and her dad went looking for Jeffers in Georgia without realizing somebody was tailing them. Next thing they knew, somebody was coming after Jeffers. Why would someone from the Bureau tell them that?"

"I have no earthly idea."

"Whoever this Chad Moyers is, Jade said he knew things about the investigation nobody but an FBI agent would. That was how he convinced her he was legit."

"Like I said, I don't know an agent named Chad Moyers."

"But you and I both know there are a ton of folks working for the Bureau."

A pause. "Next, you're going to ask me to see if there's anybody working for the Bureau by that name. You know, I thought you were my partner, not my boss."

Maggie laughed. "Oh, poor boy. Want me to send you a candy bar?"

Brad laughed back. "You know how much I love Snickers. Seriously, though, if somebody called Jade Hamilton, you can bet his name wasn't Chad Moyers from the FBI. But I can check the name anyhow."

"See if anybody from the Bureau called her, oh, about two weeks ago." She gave him Jade's phone numbers, home and cell.

"If somebody did, I bet he used a burner phone, unless he was stupid."

"Probably, but let's find out for sure. Because if somebody from the Bureau called her—"

"Then we've got a bigger problem on our hands."

That means this crime network has infiltrated the Bureau. Uh, yeah, big problem.

"Is there something else I can help you with?" he said. "It would be easier if I was in the field with you, but you know I've got stuff going on here with Cassie."

Maggie sighed, massaging her neck after the long drive. "Tell me what you've learned from the sheriff's office about this campground attack. We know two masked guys were after Jeffers. Any leads on their identities?"

"One of the assailants left a syringe behind, but as you know, no prints were found."

"The guy was probably wearing gloves."

"Probably. As for the other guy, there's only a dead end. We wondered if Gordon Hamilton drew blood on the knife wielder, but there's no evidence of that. We had several blood samples tested, but they all pointed to Gordon."

She sipped her coffee. "Well, we can only try, right?"

"What about this attack on Sandra Jeffers? Maybe *she* drew blood. I think it's worth checking into if the CSI hasn't already. You never know. We might get lucky."

"Will do. Talk to you soon. Oh, and I hope Cassie has that baby soon. Isn't she a week past her due date?"

"Yep, and she feels bigger than the Goodyear blimp."

"Oh, poor dear. I'll give her a call. Try to cheer her up."

"She'd appreciate that, Mags. You take care in the frozen north." A pause. "So how's Bill doing these days?"

Maggie bit the inside of her cheek. "The same old. My mom doesn't mind watching him full-time while I'm gone. At least he's alive and knows who I am. Things could be worse."

"You're right, Mags. Things could be a lot worse."

17

The lady at the hospital front desk gave Sandra's room number to Jade, and Jade, Henry, and Maggie grabbed the elevator. While gravity shifted beneath her feet, Jade took a deep breath, eager to see Landon again after his flight from the campground.

Henry clutched a spring bouquet of multicolored tulips, hyacinths, and daffodils. "Do you think Mrs. Jeffers will like these flowers?" he asked Maggie.

The agent smoothed his hair back with a motherly touch and gave him a wink. "I'm sure she will, buddy. Haven't met a woman yet who doesn't like flowers."

The FBI agent kept rubbing her hands together and smoothing them on her slacks. But what did she have to be nervous about? "I hope nothing has delayed Landon," Maggie said.

"If he was delayed, he would have texted me," Jade said. "He should be here. His mom almost died. I don't know where else he'd be at a time like this."

"Too bad Grandpa couldn't come," Henry said.

Jade gave him a squeeze. "It's better that he stays in bed and gets his rest, sweetie. He can catch up with Landon and his mom some other time."

Henry eyed Maggie, an eyebrow raised. "So you're an FBI agent for real?"

Maggie nodded. "Yep. For real."

"But if you're an FBI agent, where's your partner?"

"He's back in Georgia, but I don't always work with a partner. Sometimes it's just me, but I have plenty of colleagues I can call if I need help."

The elevator doors opened, and they followed the numbered doors until they reached room 226. The two stony-faced policemen flanking the doorway looked them over suspiciously until Maggie flashed her credentials. They gave her a nod.

Sandra Jeffers sat up in her hospital bed, face ashen and gray-streaked black hair unkempt. Iron bands tightened around Jade's chest. Somebody had wanted her dead, but why? Could the attack be somehow linked to Landon's coming out of hiding?

Pastor Mayhew sat beside Sandra's bed with an open Bible, which he'd apparently been reading to her. He rose with a smile, recognition pleating the wrinkles around his gray eyes. "Jade, you made it safely home, I see."

"Good to see you. So kind of you to sit with her for a while."

They shook hands, and the woodsy aroma of his aftershave enveloped her, so comforting and masculine.

"Hey, Mrs. Jeffers." Jade stepped toward the bed and reached for her hand; she gripped it tightly. "I'm so glad to see you. I heard you're doing well after your surgery. How are you feeling?"

A weary smile. "As good as can be expected, I suppose. I'm as weak as a newborn kitten."

Jade introduced Maggie to Sandra and the pastor, and they exchanged hellos. "Henry hoped you'd like these." Henry brought the flowers to Sandra, and her face lit up.

"Why, Henry, that sure was thoughtful of you," Sandra said. "You shouldn't have, but I'm glad you did. Thank you!"

"I'm sorry those bad men hurt you," Henry said. "I thought the flowers would help cheer you up."

"And they sure do, too," Sandra said with a smile. "You knew exactly the flowers I like best."

Henry glanced at his mom. "Well, I had a little help picking them out."

Jade placed the flowers, already in a pretty vase, on a side table near the window. "There," she told Henry. "Now whenever she wakes up, the flowers will be the first thing she sees. How does that sound?" Her words did the trick; the boy smiled.

Jade took in the rest of the room with a jolt of unease. "Where is he?" Jade asked Sandra. "Where's Landon?"

"He's sorry he couldn't be here to greet all of you," Sandra said. "He had an important visit to make." She handed her a piece of paper. "He left this note for you. He said you'd understand. Sorry he didn't text. He became suspicious of your phone and didn't want anyone to know where he was going."

Still so paranoid.

"Going where?"

"You'll see."

No, please. This can't be happening.

Landon's familiar but messy handwriting confirmed the note's authenticity.

I decided to visit my dad. I hope to see you all this evening. I knew Mom would be in good hands with Pastor Mayhew while I was gone. Sorry I missed you.

Weird.

First, Landon says something positive about prayer. Then he wants to visit his father.

When had he last given a care about his dad?

18

In a small room at the Marquette General Hospital's behavioral health unit, my father, Jacob Jeffers, sprawled across a narrow bed while his mind navigated drug-induced dreams. Visible footboard controls could lift, lower, and angle him anytime Mom or an aide wished to. Not wishing to disturb his slumber (but really, when was he ever awake?), I sat and initially left him undisturbed.

An old, beat-up fiberboard end table and a small blue recliner, where my mom sat during her visits and did only heaven knew what, flanked the bed. A silent TV monitor, attached to a swivel arm for convenient viewing, had been pushed toward the wall.

Unnoticed. Unwanted.

Which was how I'd felt during my last few visits to my father over the years.

Dad slept.

Once in a great while, Mom had told me, he woke and muttered a random burst of illumination (or absurdities), but mostly he slept the hours, days, and months away. His overweight body lay cocooned in white socks, black sweatpants, and a white crew-neck T-shirt stretched taut over a bowling-ball tummy.

His face was turned to his right, eyes closed. Yellowish skin stretched over a sharp nose, prominent cheekbones, and a high fore-head. Thick and curly salt-and-pepper hair fell almost to his black eyebrows. That thick hair, a trait I'd inherited, reminded me that I need never fear going bald.

Last fall Mom had practically begged me to visit my dad, but, drowning in resentment and self-inflicted lies, I'd declined. After all, the last time I'd entered these walls and sat with my mom, not knowing what else to do except stare at this mystery of a man who was my father, he'd briefly awoken and asked, apparently in a language only my mom could understand, who I was.

Me.

His own son.

Blame it on the prison beating and the related brain damage, Mom had said.

Thankfully, the Landon Jeffers of today no longer resembled the man who'd refused my mom's request last fall.

Sitting on the blue recliner, I grasped my dad's warm hand, longing to connect. But he gave not even the most infinitesimal of clues that I'd disturbed his slumber.

The profoundness of the moment prompted me to speak. "Hey, Dad. It's me, Landon, your son. Wow. It's been ... well, a long time."

No response. His chest rose and fell like bellows. The only sounds in the room came from his light snore and distant voices echoing through the open doorway from the hallway beyond.

"I haven't been here to see you in a while, but that's not your fault, Dad. I mean, it's obvious you haven't gone anywhere."

Lame joke.

The room waited in expectant silence for a reply. But not a sign of life, not even a twitch, came from my father.

"It's not your fault, Dad. It's *my* fault. Sorry I haven't come to see you." Invisible fingers wrapped around my throat and tightened. "I guess, to be honest, I didn't really *want* to see you. I know, that's a terrible thing to say, but I'm being honest. You didn't seem to know who I was the last time, so I figured, why bother?"

Only in dreams did Dad explore the great unknown, an adventurer in dreamscapes only fantasy writers could describe.

Okay, Landon, you know what you need to say. Stop stalling.

"But, I mean, you're my dad. So, I was just being selfish. I admit it. I'm really sorry. I should have come to see you anyhow. I had a lot of issues going on in my life at the time, but those are no excuse."

Mom could be longing to see you at the hospital. You're wasting time.

"And I guess I was angry. Okay, more than angry. I was furious. See, when you were in prison all those years for shooting those men at the school, you weren't around for me, Dad. I felt … I don't know … like I'd been cheated. I didn't have a dad around when I was growing up like my friends did. I'd missed out because you pulled the trigger. It was all your fault—or at least that's what I thought at the time. So yeah, I guess you could say I had a lot of anger issues I hadn't dealt with. But I'm dealing with them now, okay?"

If only he'd give me a sign that he at least heard part of my confession. Otherwise, what was the point?

The point is, Landon, God knows, even if your father doesn't.

What are you waiting for? When will you get this opportunity again?

A deep, cleansing breath filled my lungs. "But you know what? I can't believe I'm saying this, but none of that really matters now. We can't undo the past, right? What matters now is that I know your secret, Dad."

Couldn't he give me a sign? Just one glimpse of recognition? A small nod would suffice.

"See, I made a big mistake about you, and I'm so sorry. But then something weird happened. Surely Mom told you about my brain cancer, except it wasn't really brain cancer after all. Long story. And I don't really have time to go into all of it now. But …

"Anyhow, only recently, Dad, have I come to know the truth. Sure, some of my memories are still on the blink, but I know your secret. I know what really happened at the school on the day of the shooting."

He might as well have been encased in cement. Not a muscle twitched.

"Do you hear me, Dad? I know the truth now. I know you didn't shoot those men. In fact, I even know who did. *I* did it, Dad. *I'm* to blame."

The eyelid closest to me slitted to reveal an eye. A cattle prod couldn't have jolted me more. The other eye, never opening, had been blinded during a prison beating.

I swallowed. "Dad? Can you hear me?"

No response.

Could he be looking *at* me or somewhere *beyond* me? He didn't blink. Just eyeballed me.

Eyes stinging, I sniffed. "So, now that I know the truth, I just want to know one thing. Why did you do it, Dad? Why did you lie and say it was you when you knew it was me? *I* was the one who pulled the trigger. *I* shot those men in the back."

His gaze shifted almost imperceptibly. No mistake. Instead of looking *through* me, he now peered *at* me.

At my face.

At his son.

Our gazes met, and the connection made fine hairs on the back of my neck stand to attention.

I squeezed his hand. "Can you hear me, Dad? Could you give me a sign that you understand what I'm saying?"

No glint of recognition in that seemingly soulless eye, but something in that sage-like stare suggested untold wisdom.

"I wish you could jump out of that bed and tell me why you did it. Why you took the fall for me." I wiped my eyes. Wished for a tissue so I could blow my nose. "See, it doesn't really make sense, and I sure wish I had some answers right now. Because what really happened that day is just part of the craziness that's been going on in my life over the last few months. But I guess that's what God wants for me right now."

I sniffed. "Oh, yeah, I almost forgot to tell you. I've come to know God, Dad. Sure, I knew *about* Him before, but I don't think I ever truly *knew* Him. Pretty crazy, huh? And I guess I've got you to thank because those memories helped me realize who I was and how badly I needed God in my life."

Focusing on this man who had joined my mom in bringing me into the world, I resigned myself to the fact that this day would grant no answers. Only more mysteries.

"So anyhow, Dad, thank you. That's what I wanted to say."

The glassy eye reflected my image back but nothing more. Could anything be going on behind it? If only he could give me a sign.

The footfall of someone entering the room registered. I turned.

A woman appeared in the doorway, the redhead who'd led me through so much paperwork and so many doors before I could see my father today. Her name evaded me. June? Jean?

She smiled apologetically. "I'm sorry, but your time's up."

"Okay. Thanks."

Lingering, she waited to lead me back.

A sudden sense of urgency overcame me. There was one more task, the main reason I'd come. The other stuff had been part of the two-for-one deal.

Rising, I bent and whispered in Jacob Jeffers's ear the name Monty had given me. I'm not sure what I expected. That he'd suddenly snap awake and jump out of bed like Lazarus?

Seconds passed, and he gave not a clue that I could expect anything more than a repeat of the last half hour. Spirits flagging, I said, "See you later, Dad." I turned toward the woman waiting patiently in the doorway.

The name slid from his lips, issuing from little-used vocal cords, as if by magic. "So. No. Ra."

I whirled back. "Dad, can you hear me?" How many years had passed since I last heard his voice?

His gaze inched toward mine. A clue of recognition sparked.

"Dad, do you know that name?"

"Sonora," he repeated.

The redhead stepped closer and cleared her throat.

Ignoring her, I sank into the chair and gripped his hand. "What does the name mean, Dad? Is it important?"

A single tear welled in the corner of his eye and slid down his cheek, dampening his pillow.

"Dad? Can you tell me what it means?"

"I'm sorry," the woman said, "but you really need to go now."

Of course. Now that something mysterious had flung the crack of communication wide open.

"I'll be back, Dad. I promise. You hang in there, and we'll talk more soon."

———

"Sorry I had to interrupt you there," Jean said on the way back to her desk. "But we have strict rules around here that need to be followed exactly."

"I understand. It's just that he hasn't talked to me in years, and just now, right at the end—"

"You could always come back tomorrow and talk to him then. I'm sure he'd like that. He doesn't get very many visitors who want to talk. Mostly just your mom."

I caught her eye. "Mostly?"

She faced me. "Well, there are two men who visit him on occasion. One is a Pastor Mayhew, your mom's pastor. The other is a Catholic priest."

"A priest?"

"Yes, that's right."

"Are you sure? See, my dad isn't Catholic."

She frowned. "I'm sure your mom approved his visits, but I can double-check."

Strange just became downright weird.

I'd have to ask Mom about the priest. In fact, she might be frustrated that I wasn't there at the hospital to spend more time with her. I'd been away too long already.

I signed more paperwork and said goodbye. Jean apologized again for cutting my conversation short. "I'm sure your dad will be happy to see you. Come again soon."

If Dad hadn't known my identity during my last visit, why would I assume he'd remember today's connection? The visit would be like starting over with a clean slate.

Crossing the parking lot toward the Jeep, I slid out my phone and checked my messages. One from Jade said she'd arrived at the hospital to see Mom, disappointed not to find me there. Hadn't she gotten my message?

I texted back, "Sorry. Needed to see my dad. See you soon." My finger hit "send."

No matter. In less than two hours, I'd see her again and be able to fill her in on all the craziness over the last few days. The thought of connecting with her again put a bounce in my step. At Thanksgiving, her hand had slid into mine, the connection so natural and one I wouldn't mind experiencing again. Would we finally find a chance to deepen our friendship?

I pulled out my keys, only feet from the Jeep, when someone behind me, in a voice I didn't recognize, said, "Mr. Jeffers?"

No doubt a reporter had hunted me down. "Who's asking?" I turned, frustrated.

Before my brain synapses could even process his face and tell me whether I'd seen him before, the man in black plunged the needle into the side of my neck. The complete erasure of my strength and consciousness occurred in mere seconds.

PART 2

THE KILL ORDER

19

———

"**M**aestro, it's time for you to wake up."
A thousand butterflies had found their home on my head, tiny wings flexing in accord with cryptic insect murmurs. I brushed them away with one hand and struggled to open my eyes.

The butterflies alighted and drifted away like a cloud, in search of a new home. Cold air caressed my skin. Chilled me.

"Maestro, it's time for you to wake up," the familiar voice repeated.

Surely I must be dreaming. That can't be—

The splash of water on my face broke the spell, cold and jarring. I squinted to clear my fuzzy vision, temples aching, pulse thumping in my ears. My arms had been pulled behind me, secured by … something. My hands tingled and burned—whatever secured them was too tight. If I hadn't been tied to the chair, I might have listed to one side or even fallen with it.

Tied to the chair?

Peering through the drugged haze, I took in the room—gray cinder blocks, the outline of a distant closed wooden door, a single light bulb swaying above my head—and the woman standing before me. Amee Presley, my agent and manager, clutched an empty glass, no doubt the source of the cold water that had soaked the front of my shirt and now dripped down my chin.

In the left corner of my eyes, in the strange blindness the removed brain tumor from last fall had left behind, flashed an image of my dad's sleeping form. A single staring eye.

So. No. Ra.

She angled her head to one side, black hair brushing her tiny shoulders. Arms folded across a fuchsia blouse. "Landon, are you going to wake up?"

"I'm awake, Amee. What are *you* doing here? Where am I? What's going on? Why are my hands tied behind my back?"

My mind rewound to the parking lot at the psychiatric ward, to the man with the syringe. To the complete collapse of my defense mechanism.

Of course.

"One question at a time. At least you recognized me. That's a good start."

Why wouldn't I recognize her?

I shook my head to dispel the chemical haze wrapping my mind in a thick gauze. Who knew what she'd given me? "Is this some kind of joke?"

She shook her head. "No joke, maestro. We've finally got you, and you're not getting away from us this time."

Us? She'd been part of the Justice Club all along? Of course.

My agent, disappeared last fall, now appeared with clarity regarding which side she was on.

The pounding in my temples took a detour down to my right jaw. I clamped my teeth in a futile attempt to ward off the ache. Pressed my eyes closed and opened them, hoping I'd wake from this nightmare.

What time was it? Either way, I'd missed Jade and my mom at the hospital. They'd wonder why I hadn't returned and suspect something was wrong. That FBI agent would be looking for me, too.

The hot-poker sensation burning my right shoulder confirmed another fear. Monty's implant had doubtless been discovered and removed. The Justice Club had me in their clutches. Officially this time.

Gritting my teeth, I took in her smug expression. "I should have known you were mixed up in this business somehow. Clever of you to refer me to Dr. Korovin last fall just so he could put that implant in my head. How long were you planning that setup, huh?"

"Years, if you must know the truth. It took me that long just to worm myself into your life."

"So are they just using you? Or are you actually part of this silly game?"

"Maestro, surely by now you realize this is no game."

She ambled to my right, as if circling her prey, and ventured past my peripheral vision. Her voice behind me said, "There's no half way with the Justice Club, Landon. You're either all in, or you were never part of it to begin with. But then of course you'd be dead or soon to be. There's no hope of getting away once you know the truth."

The truth? The reality of a crime network that meted out justice wherever and however it saw fit? "Then why am *I* still alive?"

"Why indeed?" Now visible to my left despite my peripheral blindness, she leaned toward my ear until her lips hovered mere inches away. She trailed a finger across my beard. Toying with me or being seductive? Either way, not the Amee I remembered, but perhaps I'd never really known her.

Bending at the waist, she leaned close until her perfume hit me hard, an olfactory slap across the face. Her lips brushed my ear, voice low. "You, Landon, are somewhat of an anomaly. A pain in the neck, to be frank—I know that well enough—but you're apparently worth the trouble. They don't want to let go of you just yet, not while you still offer value."

They? Who were these people?

Faces flashed in my left mind screen: Dr. Korovin, Ray Galotta. Brady O'Brien. Puppets like me. Identities and free will stolen.

"What are their plans for me?" The question, of course, proved to be filler. She had no intention of revealing more than necessary.

She folded her arms. "All in good time. And then when they're done with you and your value has expired, guess who has been granted the honor of terminating you?"

Waiting, I feigned ignorance.

She cocked her head. "Are you surprised I asked for the privilege?"

"Very." Certainly she must be bluffing. Or could she actually have it in her? Nothing could surprise me now. Maybe she had a black belt in karate but had never told me.

"I'm trying to decide the best way to do it," she said, "and I confess that I find the possibilities intriguing. I know, for example, how much you love heights. Wouldn't it be killer to take you to the top of the tallest building in the world and watch you wet your pants before I give you the tiniest of nudges off the top?"

"Yes, I'm sure murdering me in cold blood would give you a rush, but I'm afraid it would take quite a bit more than that to fill that enormous black hole in your soul."

Girlish laughter rang out. "No, I have an even better idea. I'll wire a grand piano with a bomb and give you the hardest piano composition I can find. I wouldn't be completely heartless. I'd give you a full hour to practice it before our private concert. One little boo-boo, and ka-pow! You and the grand would be history."

"Sacrilege. The waste of a perfectly good instrument."

"I know how you'd practice like forever before a concert to be sure every song was *perfect*. How ironic it would be for you to die just because you made one eensy-weensy mistake. Death by a missed note."

"I was that bad of a client, huh?"

The smile vanished. "What did you do after your concerts, Landon? You certainly didn't want your Asian agent tagging along while you went on the prowl to pick up women."

The reminder of the man I used to be made my ears burn.

"Don't tell me you've forgotten how you used to send me packing without even inviting me out for a few drinks first. With me it was always all business. I was your personal grunt, wasn't I? Did it ever occur to you even once that maybe I had feelings too? That *I* would have enjoyed being picked up by the famous Landon Jeffers?"

"I'm sorry, Amee. I guess I was a pretty heartless guy back then." Shifting my hands improved the circulation a tad, but my fingers still tingled. Probably purple by now. "Make me your personal grunt for a decade so you can return the favor, but don't kill me."

One corner of her mouth hiked. "But it would be oh so much fun."

"But I'm not the person I used to be. I've changed."

She feigned a yawn only to smother it. "Yes, you've found religion, I hear. So pathetic. Landon has become a Bible-thumper and thinks a few little prayers will somehow free him from the big, bad monster." She sneered. "You're in a deep, dark hole, and you're never getting out, Landon Jeffers. Not even your Jesus can save you now."

"But He already has. And He can deliver you, too, Amee. I know they must control—"

Face reddening, she opened her mouth, and it became a gateway for the vilest things I'd never heard drip off her lips before. Spittle rocketed toward me, falling just short of contact. Finished and apparently satiated, she brushed the sleeve of her blouse across her mouth.

She regained her composure. "Before big plans, we have a small mission to make sure all systems are go, and there aren't any fancy gadgets to get you out of trouble this time. You can't escape, so don't even bother trying."

There's no harm in trying.

"What are you going to make me do?" I said.

She advanced a step. "When you wake up, instructions for your kill order will be obvious."

"What? You aren't going to just make me do bad things in my sleep?"

"You mean during 'daydream state'? That's what we call it—when you're in that sleep-induced trance." She shrugged. "You're not like the others, obvious from your troubled past. And you tend to go off script. Sometimes, as in your case, the old-fashioned way is best." She stepped back, pulling out a syringe.

What is it with needles lately?

"I have something important to show you," she said, "before you take another long, deep sleep."

Someone must have been listening in, because the back door opened on cue. A short, bald man in a blue jumpsuit appeared, pushing a large object on a dolly. As he drew closer, all moisture in my mouth vanished.

"I believe you know this woman?" Amee said.

Celeste Harding, mouth secured by duct tape and face streaked with mascara from her tears, had been tied to the dolly. Ropes had been wrapped tightly around her chest, waist, and knees, smirking at any fantasy of escape. She was a female friend from Denver; I'd been with her on the October night of my car accident at the beginning of this crazy journey.

Her eyes widened at the sight of me.

"I'm so sorry, Celeste. I had no idea they'd use—"

"Your kill order is very simple, Landon." Amee grabbed a fistful of Celeste's curly golden hair and pulled her head back, exposing her throat as if to slit it. Celeste whimpered. "We've got someone in mind for you in Dallas, but you can't mess up on this one. You do, and Celeste here will be fed to the alligators. And no, I'm not being metaphorical."

20

Saturday, March 26

At the first glimpse of dawn, my last coherent thoughts flashed back.

Amee, the traitor.

Celeste, the innocent.

Me, the assassin.

The kill order.

Amee's words: *You can't escape, so don't even bother trying.*

I rolled over in a strange bed, a chemical cloud cocooning my head and demanding extra effort to swim to the surface of full awareness. Silhouetting the edges of maroon drapes, sunlight gleamed.

Marshaling whatever gumption I could muster, I got up, aware of red pajamas that didn't belong to me. Feeling better than expected given the cocktail of drugs Amee had given me, I surveyed a typical hotel room. Corner chair and desk, armoire with wide-screen TV, small refrigerator. Hampton Inn by the looks of it. Even a Gideon Bible occupied its customary spot in the top desk drawer.

In the navy suitcase on the chair, I discovered blue jeans, a baby-blue polo, a belt, socks, undergarments, sneakers, a comb and two pens, and my wallet. But no cell phone.

Of course. I'd never see Monty's gift again. Maybe I'd never see him either.

What had he suggested? That perhaps I could help him in the advanced program, whatever that meant.

Almost hidden under the socks, I found an envelope stuffed with several twenty-dollar bills. But nothing more. No instructions.

When you wake up, instructions for your kill order will be obvious.

The butterflies in my stomach spun and capered.

I searched under the bed, in the desk drawers. Nothing but information about Dallas area attractions. At least I knew where she'd sent me.

A toiletries bag filled with everything I'd left behind in Iron Valley awaited me in the bathroom, even the same shaving cream. I slammed my fist down on the counter.

They still know everything about you. Did you really think this nightmare would just go away?

Of course not. Way too easy.

The nightmare had morphed into something else.

A daymare. A nightmare in daylight hours.

And I'd been planted smack-dab in the middle of the worst one in recent memory.

But what about the FBI? And Monty? He'd said he'd be watching out for me. Did he know about the Justice Club's plans?

If only I had a hint of what lay ahead, but with a name like "kill order," my next step could only be obvious. In the mirror, my gaze took in my worried expression while my stomach flip-flopped. Could I really pull it off—actually kill someone? Or, by not complying, assent to Celeste's murder?

Why not, Landon? You've killed before.

A knock on the door.

"Room service," an unfamiliar man's voice said. "I have your breakfast, sir."

But I hadn't ordered breakfast.

Surely someone at the Justice Club had scheduled everything, including my room reservations, to the letter. Maybe breakfast occupied a slot on my itinerary. Perhaps this man would give me more details about my next step.

The door yielded to a white-clad attendant pushing a white-tablecloth-covered cart on wheels. Black moussed hair, thick black-rimmed glasses. The chef had catered the food according to my new health-conscious regimen: cheddar and green pepper omelet with whole-wheat toast buttered with coconut oil. Colombian coffee with two packets of stevia and cream. Two large grapefruit, quartered.

Muttering my befuddled thanks, I handed him a perfunctory tip from the envelope of twenties and nearly missed eye contact. Monty, donning the employee disguise, locked his knowing gaze on mine.

I froze, but his quick head shake spoke. *Don't give me away.* He winked and exited, leaving the cart behind.

No dummy that Monty. Surely cameras somewhere captured every move I made, every word exchanged.

A search of the cart yielded nothing helpful beyond the food I now had no stomach to eat. Clever that Monty had somehow wormed his way into the role of a delivery boy under the very noses of the Justice Club.

No, not clever. Risky. What inspired the man to risk his life for such a cause? Surely there must be a story in there somewhere.

At least Monty was watching out for me, but why make an appearance at all? To dangle the carrot of hope before my eyes—*I'm watching you*—and then stroll away, taking it with him?

Illogical.

There had to be more, but so far, what it could be eluded me.

Having decided on a shower instead of food, I stepped into the hot jets. Soon I toweled off and found the fogged-up mirror and the message someone had fingered across the surface.

"Envelope under chair."

A white business-size envelope, taped under the office chair seat, hadn't been addressed to anyone. But the black text, printed on a white piece of paper, folded in thirds, wouldn't have made sense to anyone else.

Waldorf Astoria, Downtown Dallas
The mark: Leslie Neumann
Push off balcony by midnight tonight. It is imperative that the body be found on the street below.
Don't forget. We're watching, and the alligators are hungry.

Eyelids clamped shut, I crinkled the paper in my fist. Celeste had to be one of the sweetest women I'd ever met, though definitely not someone I'd entertain for serious romantic pursuits. She'd told me all sorts of things about her past. Her greatest fear: reptiles.

What's your greatest fear, Landon?

Killing Leslie.

With that name, the mark could be either a man or a woman.

Did it matter? It might.

After shaving, I got dressed and read the crinkled note again.

They'd taken me far from home. Nothing familiar could work in my favor.

Now what? Go in search of the Waldorf Astoria?

Push a woman I didn't even know off a balcony? Could I entertain the thought?

Even if I tracked down the hotel, how could I get into Leslie's hotel room without help? Did they expect me to figure this out on my own? A test to prove my worth?

Dropping the instructions on the desktop, I eyed the telephone. Could I call Jade? At least to let her know where I was and tell her I was okay? Nope. No dial tone. Surely all loopholes had been eliminated.

You can't escape, so don't even bother trying.

I swallowed hard. Shoved clammy hands into my pockets. They'd all be so worried about me when I didn't return to see my mom.

My tight chest prevented me from grabbing a full breath. I had to settle for shallow ones. Eyelids fluttered closed.

Oh, God, please deliver me from this day.

Perhaps, as Monty had said, I could be useful from the inside. But to continue on the inside—in fact, to graduate to the next level of trust —I had to pass this test.

Complete this kill order. Take Leslie's life to save Celeste.

The bed sank under my weight, the Gideon Bible heavy in my hands. Words in black type stared up at me. I'd come across Isaiah 26:3 during my idle days at the campground when I'd had so many hours on my hands to do nothing but fret about my loved ones and read the Bible. "You will keep him in perfect peace. Whose mind is stayed on You, Because he trusts in You."

Jesus, You delivered me once before. Because of what You did, I thought I was beyond their control, but here I am again. And faced with an incredible dilemma.

Now what am I supposed to do? I have no idea how to get out of this.

But isn't that what trust is? God has it all figured out. Depend on the One who already knows the outcome.

Another knock on the door. My pulse quickened.

Maybe Monty had arrived with my parachute. Hope propelled my steps to the door.

Nope.

Amee rushed in, chased by a whirlwind of perfume and frenetic activity. She clutched a sheaf of papers in one hand, a cell phone like a permanent appendage in the other.

How could I forget our last meeting? Amee with a syringe in hand. Celeste strapped to the dolly, blue eyes bugging above a duct-taped mouth.

Don't be fooled by any of this. It's all a masquerade.

My agent/handler grabbed a triangle of abandoned toast off the breakfast tray and bit into it. "Ew, what's with the coconut oil?" She slammed it down, shuddering, and surveyed my face. "You look so clueless, maestro. Surely you haven't forgotten about the concert in the park today."

Concert in the park? Today?

My best imitation of knowing rolled off my tongue. "Of course."

She tilted her head. "'Of course' as in 'I forgot all about it' or 'of course' as in 'I knew'?"

Surely she knew I hadn't a clue about any of this. "Of course as in I'm rolling with it."

She smoothed my collar in a motherly way. "That's good. I like your attitude. We expect a big crowd today." Crossing to the window, she yanked the drapes open, like a storm cloud rolling away from the blinding sun.

"Everyone's so happy to have Landon Jeffers back after disappearing for far too long. He just needed some downtime, that's all. We all need a break sometimes." She spun and faced me with a look of triumph. "But now he's back and ready to take on the world, right?"

"Right," I said, feigning confidence and enthusiasm I lacked. I sipped the lukewarm coffee and eyeballed the omelet, deciding I should probably eat something given her plans for this day.

A concert? Today?

When had I last even practiced my concert repertoire? More than five months ago. And what—she expected me to just wing it?

My mind whirled, the truth kicking me. The Justice Club wanted me back on the concert stage. But why? What did it all mean? Just a few days ago, I'd been hiding in the Georgia woods. And now this?

Landon, they want you to be an assassin.

"Yes, Landon, we have a whole concert schedule lined up for you. It took some doing on such short notice, so we took advantage of several cancellations. Then of course we had to blitz your e-mail list and hope for the best. Ticket sales are pouring in. Of course, some of the venues are smaller than you've done in the past, but hey, we've got you covered."

I just shook my head. "This is just a little overwhelming."

"Not to worry. The concert isn't until this afternoon, and there'll be plenty of time to rehearse and run a sound check. Then after the concert, you'll do a taping for *The Today Show*."

"What?"

A hand flutter. A rustling of the papers. "You know the drill by now —you just forgot. You'll be terrific. They love you. I've got a list of everything they plan to ask you, following by scripted answers, though you're free to revise anything you don't like."

She paused, hands on hips. "What's wrong with you? Aren't you excited to be back? This is the life you've missed for so long, maestro. And hey, we can even get that concert in Tokyo back on the schedule. What do ya say?"

Perks for rolling with it.

"Thanks, Amee." I *had* missed this life, but *surreal* didn't begin to describe my new reality. Returning to this life didn't seem possible, not while the Justice Club still watched me and Celeste's life hung at the end of a rope over a pool of hungry alligators. Not to mention my own life being in jeopardy if I failed my first kill order. And others possibly being in danger if I ran.

"Oh, and before I forget," she said with a scowl, "please shave off that ridiculous beard, maestro, before the concert. It just isn't you."

I gritted my teeth. "If you insist."

"After that taping," she said, as if not hearing me, "we're invited to a big party at the Waldorf Astoria this evening. Some Texas bigwig. It'll be just like old times. Mingling with the rich and powerful."

I nearly missed the last part. My stomach had plunged at the mention of the Waldorf Astoria.

She handed me a copy of the itinerary. At five o'clock, a limo would pick us up after my TV interview and convey us to the party downtown. Transportation would be provided to the location of my first murder.

21

S ettled in her chair, Jade nibbled on a fingernail while Maggie paced the small hospital room and talked on her cell phone with officials at the psychiatric unit. Meanwhile, Sandra Jeffers gave Jade an encouraging smile and squeezed her hand. "I'm sure Landon is probably fine somewhere. He couldn't have just disappeared."

Maggie clicked off and faced them. "Yep, Landon visited his dad yesterday around two thirty. He left shortly after three thirty. Hospital security has surveillance video of him in the lobby, talking to the receptionist and then exiting the building. Unfortunately, there's no video of the parking lot."

Jade spread her hands. "And then he went—where? He didn't mention going anywhere except to see his dad. I can't believe he'd have any other plans except to come back here ASAP to see his mom."

Maggie nodded, tapping a pen against her lip while she paced. "What about his vehicle? Any idea what he was driving?"

"A Jeep. He said that friend of his in Georgia, Monty, gave it to him."

"My son has a Jeep?" Sandra said.

"Any idea what color?" Maggie said.

Jade shook her head.

"Then it probably has Georgia license plates," Maggie said.

Jade shrugged. "Maybe. I don't know."

"At least it's possible. I'll ask the hospital security to check for a Jeep in the parking lot, possibly with Georgia license plates. His vehicle may still be there."

"But I don't understand," Jade said. "You just told us they have video of him leaving the psychiatric unit."

Maggie nodded. "Yeah, but maybe he never drove away. Maybe somebody was waiting for him in the parking lot beyond the cameras."

Jade pressed her palms against her stinging eyes. "You think someone might have abducted him from the parking lot in broad daylight?"

"I'm just saying it's possible."

Jade sat up straighter. "Hold on. What about Sandra's house? Where did Landon plan to stay when he wasn't here? Could he have gone there?"

Sandra perked up. "Yes, he could be at my house."

Maggie shook her head. "Nope. I checked your house earlier. There were no signs that he'd slept at your house last night or spent any time there."

"Maybe he's there now," Sandra said. "Could you have missed him?"

Maggie shook her head. "Sorry. Cops have been watching the house. So far there's been no activity. And if he had a flat tire or engine problems that delayed him, he would have called, right?"

"Absolutely." Jade leaned forward and rested her forehead against her hand, a dull ache pulsing at the base of her skull. "Oh, this can't be happening. Someone must have taken him."

"We don't know that for sure," Maggie said.

"What other explanation could there be? He loves his mom," Jade said to Maggie. "If he could be here with her now, you better believe he would be. I think I know who's responsible. The Justice Club."

Maggie's eyes narrowed. "Where did you hear that name?"

"Landon mentioned it on the phone."

"I wonder how he knew. The name's been pretty hush-hush within the Bureau."

"Landon said his friend in Georgia, Monty, mentioned the name to him."

"Monty. There's not much to go on. If it was somebody from the FBI, surely I'd know about it."

Jade ran her fingers through her hair. "So what do we do now?"

"Give Landon more time to show up, I guess," Maggie said. "Maybe there's a logical explanation."

"More logical than being by his mom's side after somebody almost killed her?"

Maggie cast a grim look. "You've got me there." Her phone rang, and she pulled it out. Stepping a few yards away, she spoke in a hushed tone.

When she rejoined them, her eyes blazed with new energy.

"What?" Jade said. "You know where Landon is?"

"No. It's something else. That was the sheriff here in Iron Valley." She turned to Sandra. "A forensics team examined your bloody clothes from the attack."

"And?" Jade said.

"They found blood from someone else. We've got a DNA match on one of the attackers."

22

Amazing how quickly the songs came back to me, note upon note, chord upon chord. Amee had chosen the package of songs, and though my stomach tightened due to the cloud of anxiety under which I found myself, I played and sought to smile my way through them with the greatest of ease. Until I began to wonder whether the Justice Club had programmed the songs through the implant so I could play them flawlessly despite not practicing for months.

But didn't this influence usually begin during a sleep cycle? And if the Justice Club exerted control beyond sleep, wouldn't I be aware of it? It was a disturbing thought but a possibility I couldn't deny.

At Strauss Square, beautiful and immense, the sun smiled down through the massive glass ceiling. Beyond the stage, the tile floor, crammed with fans on bring-your-own lawn chairs, merged into a plush lawn with barely a hiccup. Wow, I guess folks *were* eager to hear me play after so much in the entertainment news about my cancer scare, hiatus, and sudden appearance.

Afterward, I met Savannah Guthrie, and we taped a soft interview for *The Today Show* about my brain cancer scare and the lessons I had learned along the way, mostly vague statements about family and friends being there for me—and they had been. But I could hardly tell millions on TV the truth about my brain implant, though the possibility tempted me. Despite my stress-induced upset stomach, Savannah stroked my ego like good interviewers do and mentioned that she played my albums around her house all the time. What a flatterer.

Then we were off to the dreaded supper party at the Waldorf Astoria, hosted by some mover-and-shaker Dallas bigwig. I assumed he'd made it big in Texas oil; wasn't that how most big-shot Texans had become wealthy? The wince from his tight handshake reached my eyes, but several gussied-up females strolled by, distracting him too much to notice.

One would have thought we were attending some Academy Awards post-show party, not some meet and greet with Dallas's finest. Either way, the man with the bucks had spared no expense on the invitation-only party with more seafood appetizers and entrees than I knew there were fish in the sea.

Amee steered me to a round table, overly decorated with aquatic ice sculptures, and took a chair across from me. There I came face-to-face with movie star Clint Robson, who'd experienced recent success on Broadway. In the taxi on the way, Amee had suggested that he might be persuaded to sing a song for the next studio album—with me accompanying him, of course. Time to pour on the charm. Duets with big names like Clint always guaranteed good sales. Such arrangements proved to be the biggest form of name-dropping in the recording industry.

Sharp guy, Clint. Every bit as nice off camera as on. And quite the imposing figure; he rose taller than I expected compared to my five eleven. Surely he must pump iron a few hours daily to sport a physique like that, obvious due to his tight dress shirt.

We had barely gotten past his compliments about my latest CD when a heavy-set woman, hinting at her sixties and wearing a sequined purple dress, barreled toward us. She interrupted me mid-sentence by inserting her substantial bulk between me and Clint and pouring on endless words of adulation.

"I'm sorry," I said. "Did I miss your name?"

"Leslie Neumann." Brown eyes, twice their normal size, ogled me through thick, silver-framed glasses, which went well with her shoulder-length salt-and-pepper hair. "I must be one of your biggest fans," she said with the cutest Texas drawl.

She towered over us, since Clint and I sat, then grabbed the empty chair on the other side of Clint and leaned across the table to focus on me like the actor didn't exist. Perhaps Leslie didn't realize the diss, though how she'd gotten into this party without at least some understanding of decorum bewildered me. Clint forced a smile and focused on his food with merciful patience.

Leslie Neumann.

I swallowed, but nothing went down except my heart, which got stuck somewhere between my knees. "So you like my music, huh?" I said in something more like a croak.

She waved a well-practiced hand. "Honey, you have no idea. Saw you in Orlando about five years ago with my son, Danny, and we became immediately obsessed. Then we saw you in Atlanta two years ago when you were doing your Private Island tour. Couldn't get enough, so Danny and I headed to Montreal to see you again a year later. We still couldn't get enough, knew we had to see you in Detroit. Then after Detroit, I heard you'd be in Dallas, my hometown, and here I am." She spread her hands and angled her body as if posing for a photo, bleached teeth gleaming.

But her obvious need for oxygen barely registered due to the honking of her name in my consciousness. My gaze flicked to Amee and took in her knowing look. The mark—this woman? Surely she had a grandchild or two, but within a few hours, she was destined to lie dead on a sidewalk after a great fall.

Swallowing hard, I let the realization hover somewhere in my midbrain. What on earth could she have done to deserve such an end? Could the Justice Club have made a mistake?

Didn't matter. I had my orders.

While Leslie gushed on and on, with my pitiful smile frozen to my face (hopefully it looked genuine), my stomach soured after supping on too much shrimp scampi and buttery lobster tail. My gaze slid away from her transfixed, unblinking expression and froze.

In the distance Monty, now blond haired and goateed, served hors d'oeuvres from a silver tray. He swiveled toward me with a full connection of the eyes.

Did he know what I'd been tasked with before midnight? Of course. Why else would he be here?

C'mon, Monty. Do something. Save me from my mission of violence.

"What a magnificent concert you did in the park today." Leslie layered her hand on top of mine, warm and intimate. If her age didn't come close to that of my mother, I'd wonder if she was hitting on me. "Those glissandos look so effortless when you do them. How in heaven's name do you pull them off the way you do?"

"Practice, I guess." Sipping my water, I hoped it would calm my upset stomach. Nope. Perhaps some ginger ale would fare better. If I signaled Monty, maybe he could bring me some or pretend I had a phone call and shuffle me off to a dark corridor somewhere and deliver much-needed advice.

I cleared my throat. "You seem to know a thing or two about music."

She beamed. "My Danny could do glissandos, too, though not as well as you, of course. My son worshipped the ground you walked on and never ceased to look to you for inspiration."

Past tense. Careful.

"Is Danny here? I'd enjoy meeting him."

Her smile faltered, her gaze nose-diving to the dolphin ice sculpture in the table center. "No, unfortunately, he's not. I'm afraid he—he died."

Clint took advantage of the awkward conversational pause to excuse himself, muttering something about finding the men's room. He exited, and Amee scowled at me, our opportunity with Clint lost. But surely she couldn't be too upset. Leslie, the mark, had essentially beelined straight to me. Making the connection couldn't have been easier.

"I'm so sorry for your loss," I said.

Leslie snatched Clint's seat. "He was only twenty-two years old. Practically lived on his piano until pancreatic cancer took him about four months ago."

"That's terrible. I'm so sorry."

"You don't need to be. If anything, I should be grateful." A shaky hand pressed to her chest, her soulful, owlish eyes connecting with mine again. "When Danny heard about your brain cancer story, he refused to lose hope. After all, if you could fight your cancer, he could fight his too. He even started eating grapefruit when he read in *Rolling Stone* that they were a regular part of your diet. He was a fighter all the way to the end. Refused to stop composing until the day he died."

"So he liked to write songs?"

"Oh my, yes. He cranked out a new song practically every week during those last few months. Amazing what humans can accomplish when they are on a deadline. He wanted to make the most of the time he had left."

"Did he publish any of them?" Amee said.

Leslie wagged her head, regret heavy in her eyes. "He was too sick at the time. But lately, I'm afraid it's been my fault. He left me with pages and pages of songs written in longhand, but I frankly have no idea how to go about getting them published. Who on earth do I send them to? I'm afraid it's all beyond me."

"I see." No mystery where this talk was heading.

Leslie leaned toward me flirtatiously. "But surely someone like you —I mean, if you took a look at them—could tell me if they're worthy of being published."

I looked away. "I don't know ..."

"Forgive me. I didn't mean to be so presumptuous." She leaned back in a clear retreat. "I mean, you haven't even seen the songs. But if you did, you could tell me whether they're any good, couldn't you?"

Amee, who'd been focusing on her food since Clint no longer gave her someone to flirt with, spoke up. "Why not, Landon? After all, he *was* a fan." Fans never exited Amee's universe. Once she'd pressured me to kiss the forehead of a stranger's child just because the mother was in my Facebook fan club.

Leslie breathed on me, a garlicky gust swimming in something alcoholic. "And wouldn't you know it? I just happen to have his songs with me. Well, not right here, right now, but they're in my suite up on the fifty-third floor."

While her invitation blazed in virtual neon, my knocking heart picked up speed at the mention of her room. If I didn't go to her hotel room to look at the songs, I'd never have to push her off her balcony.

She patted my arm. "Would you at least look at them? Providence must have arranged this meeting."

Don't pin this on God, lady.

"Well, I don't know." I turned to Amee, broadcasting an articulate *Get me out of here* look. But what foolishness on my part. Of course, Amee's agenda couldn't have been clearer: babysitting me all the way to Leslie's balcony.

Amee rose and pushed her chair back. "C'mon, Landon. Why not now? Let's take a look at those songs—that is, if you're okay with that, Leslie."

Behind me, a familiar voice tickled my ears. Monty hovered behind Amee, as if on cue. Several filled champagne glasses crammed the tiny tray positioned on his hand. With his other, he patted Amee's hand, raised while holding her wine glass, as if to warn her not to back into him. "Excuse me. Right behind you," he said and vanished.

"Oh my goodness!" Leslie clutched my arm. "Would you really do that? For Danny?"

Did I have any choice? I forced enthusiasm into my vocal cords. "Of course." My gaze scanned the room, searching for the wig-wearing waiter. No sign of Monty now. He'd swept by but offered no parachute.

Clearly, Amee had been ordered to tag along to make sure I did as ordered; after all, I'd run before. With her presence practically glued to my side, how could I possibly find an exit from this situation?

WHILE THE ELEVATOR lifted us toward our doom, Leslie's and mine, Danny's mom prattled on endlessly about him: his amazing childhood as a prodigy, his forsaking all pursuits for his one love, his piano. I nodded, not missing the parallels between Danny's background and mine. We all must make sacrifices for our choices in life.

And I had a choice doing a stare-down contest with me at this moment. Could I really go through with this kill order? I had no desire to hurt this woman.

Celeste or Leslie?

Someone had to die.

What an incredible dilemma.

Amee scratched the back of her hand, where Monty had touched her. The skin had turned an angry red. From her scratching or something else?

23

My mouth turned dry, and I took a deep breath, trying to keep my head. There had to be a way out of this situation.

Think, Landon. Think.

Leslie studied me, her wrinkles deepening. "You poor dear. You don't look so well. Are you afraid of elevators?"

"No, I'm just—"

"He'll be fine," Amee said, patting my arm. "Maybe it was too much lobster."

Leslie unlocked the door and ushered us in. "Here we are."

What else could I expect but an impressive suite at the Waldorf Astoria? The glass, the chrome, the detailed moldings—clearly Leslie lacked nothing in the financial realm. The view of the city from the floor-to-ceiling windows and wraparound balcony made my palms sweat. The sun had begun setting past the Dallas skyline, the nearest skyscrapers looming like dark silhouettes.

I gladly accepted a seat beside Amee on the posh sofa while Leslie went in search of the music. The small but adequate digital piano stationed beside one window cast her coincidental bumping into me in a new light. This meeting had surely been planned. Why should I be surprised? She must have done her homework and knew I'd be at the party, making my need to locate her obsolete.

Leslie had been cleverer than I expected. Perhaps that character trait had something to do with her name appearing on the termination list. But what could this grandmotherly type have done to deserve such a twisted form of justice? She must have done something truly treacherous to deserve a visit from a hit man.

I rose. Weighted keys depressed beneath my fingertips, delivering one of the best digitized piano sounds I'd ever heard. Amazing what money can buy, but I could hardly concentrate. Just beyond the window glistened the balcony's chrome railing and the sweaty-palm-inducing plunge beyond.

Perhaps this test had nothing to do with Leslie. Maybe my fear of heights was the real test here. Given my past, Amee knew my venturing onto the balcony would be no small feat.

Oh, the choices we make.

If I didn't push Leslie off the balcony, Celeste would die, but it wouldn't be at my hand. Nor would I be required to see her demise. But did that fact make her death any less important?

If I did push Leslie to her death, I'd be solely responsible. The fate of both lives depended on what I did next, but my participation could hardly be called parallel.

One died if I committed a murderous act. The other died if I simply did nothing. Commission versus omission.

Do or don't do?

Either way, someone died, but would I be involved to the same degree?

Leslie appeared with a brown leather valise crammed with hand-written sheets of music. Behind me, Amee touched my shoulder and muttered something in a weak voice about needing to use the restroom. She vanished.

Could this be my cue? She trusted me to do the deed in her absence?

Somehow I had to get Leslie on the balcony.

I froze. How could I even be plotting her death?

"This is his best one, I think." Leslie handed a few pencil-scrawled sheets to me. "He played this song more than the others. I hope you like it."

Yikes.

Imagine the expectations of a mother who'd lost her son and had only memories and the songs he'd left behind.

No pressure, Landon.

While Leslie went in search of the switch to control the canned ceiling lights, now that the darkening sky cast a shadow across the room, I played through the first page, jaw tightening. So genuinely I wanted to like the song, but in short order it proved to be little more than drivel. The pages offered no hint of originality, never mind something suggesting they belonged anywhere other than the nearest trash can. But how could I break this news to Danny's mom?

Peering over my shoulder, she hovered so close her acrid breath made my neck tingle. "So what do you think?"

Groping for kind words, I came up with, "I've heard worse." At least I didn't say the song was the best thing since "Somewhere over the Rainbow."

Leslie handed me the full valise, and I played through several more songs. At least Danny knew how to get the notes down on paper; his persistence and his music theory classes deserved credit for that. But nothing here suggested that the first song had been a one-off; nothing rose above the label of hackneyed. Not a single catchy, original tune to be found.

Well, not exactly. The last song sounded like such a copycat of my "Snow Serenade" that had Danny lived, I could have sued his socks off.

Fingers dug into my shoulder. I turned.

"Landon, I gotta go." Amee pressed a red hand to her mouth, face flushed. "It must be something I ate. I seem to be having some sort of allergic reaction."

Leslie turned to her, forehead pinched with concern. "Should I call an ambulance?"

"Oh, no. Definitely not."

"I've got some antacids. Would they help?"

"That's very kind of you, but I'm afraid I'm past those."

Could this be Amee's way of isolating me with Leslie so I could do the deed? No, her pallor didn't appear to be a put-on, and she'd already given me sufficient alone time with Leslie.

"You don't look so good," I said. "Maybe it's food poisoning or something."

At the mention of food, her face spasmed, and she bent, clutching her stomach with both arms. "I gotta go. I'll catch you downstairs. If you don't see me, I'll be in the ladies' room."

Before I could argue with her, she hustled to the exit and disappeared, the door clicking shut behind her. The video clip of Monty touching her hand flashed in the left corner, the private theater, of my eyes. Had he poisoned her to get her out of the way so she couldn't observe what happened next?

He must have. But why?

Leslie managed her most solicitous voice. "I'm so sorry about your friend."

"I'm sure she'll be okay. Some people just can't handle seafood."

"So what do you think of Danny's songs? Will you publish them?"

A Bible quotation hummed across my synapses, a gift from Sunday school classes I hadn't appreciated at the time. *Out of the abundance of the heart, the mouth speaks.*

"I'm not a publisher, Leslie. I only agreed to look at them."

Her hands fluttered like a bird on LSD. "Of course. I'm sorry. I didn't mean …"

But she was no fool. Surely she knew that if I could be persuaded to use just one of Danny's songs on my next album, no matter how unworthy, its spot on the top-twenty contemporary instrumental charts would be guaranteed. My stamp of approval equaled instant notoriety for the late songwriter.

"What I mean is," she said, pausing to choose her words, "do you think they're good enough to be published?"

Sucking in a deep breath, I braced myself. She'd prematurely lost her son, a major blow to any parent; surely some good news after his death would be welcome. But didn't I have a reputation to protect? She could run to a reporter with her sob story and say I'd discovered the musical genius of her dead son. Then I'd be in trouble once music critics heard the truth.

Swallowing, I searched for a creative way to frame my answer. Finally: "I see potential here, but … I must be honest. I'm sorry to tell you this, Leslie, but unfortunately these songs just aren't ready for prime time."

Her face crumpled. "You mean, you don't like them?"

"It isn't a question of *liking* them. You asked me if they were good enough to be published. I'm sorry, but that's my professional opinion."

She squeezed my arm, hope flaming in her brown orbs. "But you said you've heard worse. Maybe you see potential. They just need more work, that's all. Nothing Landon Jeffers couldn't handle. You could work your magic and bring them up to snuff, couldn't you? You could *cowrite* them. I know you could."

I closed the piano lid and plunked the overstuffed valise on top. "No."

"No?" Her befuddled tone betrayed the rareness of this word in her vocabulary.

Rising, I faced her. "I'm sorry. I'm not in the business of rewriting songs for others. There are people you could pay to do that." I eyed the door to the balcony.

The stress of my choice hit me again. I swiped droplets of sweat off my forehead.

Now's your chance, Landon. Remember Celeste. Say you need fresh air to clear your head. Lure her out to the balcony.

But this woman didn't deserve to die any more than Celeste did. How could I choose between the two?

No matter what use I could be inside the Justice Club, could I really pay this price? Become like the murdering operatives I was determined to stop? Stop them by becoming as evil as they were?

"Thanks, Leslie, for inviting me up here. I'm very sorry about Danny. Thank you for sharing his music with me. I'm sorry I couldn't give you good news, but I'm so glad we met."

I eased toward the exit, longing to be gone, but she dashed toward the door and blocked my path, checkbook in hand. "Tell me how much. If it's a question of money, I'm happy to pay. At whatever price you think is fair."

"I don't want your money."

"But can't you just do this one thing for me? For the sake of my son's memory?"

"I'm very sorry you lost your son, but long ago I promised myself I'd never let a fan manipulate me to do something I didn't believe was right. I'm sorry."

Two steps bridged the distance, and I escaped to the hallway beyond. The door whooshed closed behind me, just shy of cutting off her whimper. I leaned against the door, heart hammering, knowing I should leave but fearing to.

Could cameras be watching me right now? Did the Justice Club know what I'd decided? But the deadline was midnight. Perhaps they allowed time for me to reconsider.

Maybe Celeste was dead already.

But what choice did I have?

Wait.

If I didn't perform the kill order, wouldn't another operative just take my place? Kill Leslie anyhow?

Yes.

Unless she was only a test. A test to prove my worth. The entire situation manipulated just to reveal whether I'd make the terrible choice and do what the Justice Club had requested.

No.

She'd been chosen for termination. Walking away wouldn't change her fate one iota. Someone would still terminate her, just not me. If they knew my decision, another operative could be on his or her way here right now to succeed after I'd failed.

But you can stop it, Landon.

Maybe I could run and take Leslie with me. If I left her behind, she'd soon be dead.

She *and* Celeste.

And you, too, Landon. Do you think they'll let you live if you fail your mission?

At least if we were on the run together, we'd have some sort of fighting chance. I'd rather die while bucking the system than stay and be forced into their mold and lose my soul.

Do it now. Tell Leslie the truth and take her with you. Get out of here. There might still be time.

And then what?

Find a way to get off the grid.

Why not? I'd succeeded before.

The unlocked door yielded to my touch, and I entered. No sign of her in the great room. Where had she gone? She couldn't have left without my seeing her.

"Leslie?"

Her faint whimpers lured me toward the glass windows.

On the balcony she stood, back facing me. Her shoulders shook.

She tossed something into the wind, sheet music from Danny's valise. One song after another fluttered like birds before spiraling, wounded and dying, toward the street below.

With wails that pierced the plate glass, she chugged the whole valise over the edge, songs avalanching into space. Tossing the valise after them, she buried her face in her hands.

"Leslie!" I called.

No response. Couldn't she hear me? Perhaps the thick glass prevented—

Leslie leaned on the railing and lifted one leg as if to climb over it.

"No, Leslie. Wait!"

My legs spanned yards in mere seconds.

Her leg slid over. Now she straddled the railing.

Despite my acrophobia, I shoved the door open and sprang onto the balcony.

"Leslie! No!"

The seafood that had soured in my stomach earlier now scalded my throat. Backing against the plate glass windows, I cradled my head in my hands.

And gaped at the empty balcony.

24

The wail of approaching police sirens slapped me out of my sick stupor on the balcony.

My fault.

They'd wanted me to kill Leslie, and I'd succeeded. I'd done so by crushing her spirit. If only I'd come a few seconds sooner ... Leslie's voice drifted to me.

But can't you just do this one thing for me? For the sake of my son's memory?

I shakily rose to my feet and avoided the mess where I'd thrown up. Wiping my mouth on my sleeve, I shivered in a cold sweat and eyed the railing. No need to look at the street below. My imagination painted pictures I had no desire to see, enough to twist my already-upset stomach.

Besides, surely a crowd had gathered around Leslie's body below. If they glimpsed me peering down from above, I'd be implicated. But surely I must be already. No doubt cameras in the hallway and elevator had recorded my visit to her suite.

Go, Landon. Run. Get out of here.

But why run? I hadn't pushed her. Wouldn't running make me look like I had something to hide? An innocent man would find the nearest cop and describe what had happened.

But my instincts goaded me to flee the scene. And fast.

Back in the suite, I glanced around to ensure I hadn't left anything behind that might identify me. Could they lift my fingerprints off the piano? No time to clean it. If the police saw a clear case of suicide, why would they dust for fingerprints? But I'd been the last to see her alive; they'd have questions for me before accepting the suicide story. What else could I do but tell the truth?

Heading out the door, I hustled down the hallway and found the elevator. Inside, I hesitated.

Go back to the banquet room and find Amee?

Or run?

So badly I longed to hightail it out of this place. But if I returned to Amee and told her Leslie was dead, Celeste might still live. If I ran, surely they'd kill her.

I punched the symbol for the lobby. On the forty-ninth floor, the elevator stopped, and the doors slid open. Monty pushed in a wheeled cart with the remains of someone's room service meal. A T-bone by the looks of it, along with a half-eaten baked potato with sour cream and a wilted, uneaten salad. He still wore his waiter's getup, his face expressionless.

The doors whooshed closed, and the two of us stood side by side, facing the door, the descending floor vibrating beneath our feet. We marinated in silence while I waited for words of encouragement, for something to make the loss of this woman's life somehow worthwhile.

He punched the button to stop the elevator and turned toward me. "We've only got a few minutes to talk." He reached below the cold meal to a hidden space and pulled out what resembled a green smoothie with a blue straw. "Drink this."

"What is it?"

"Something to help you. You'll thank me later."

"I'm sick. I won't be able keep it down."

"No, it'll ease your stomach. Trust me."

The flavor reminded me of a combination of bananas, mowed

grass, and black licorice. Repressing my gag reflex, I downed half of it within seconds. Just about anything tasted better than stomach acid.

"Okay, talk to me," he said.

"But isn't someone watching and listening?"

He panted, suggesting he'd run to time this meeting to precision. "No, the elevator's clean. Take some deep breaths. Trust me. You'll feel better."

I did as instructed and downed the rest of the smoothie. Monty accepted the empty glass, then whisked it out of sight like a magician. "Don't feel bad," he said. "You couldn't have known she'd jump."

"How do you know what happened?"

"You think Justice Club operatives are the only ones watching you? It's not important. What *is* important is that you passed the test. They think you pushed her."

"But why would they think that? I didn't."

"Doesn't matter. They've got a dead woman on the sidewalk. Congratulations."

"Goody for me."

His gaze bore into me. "Maybe you don't understand what this means. The more access you get, the more we can learn to shut these people down for good."

"Forgive me for not feeling overjoyed."

"You're letting your emotions control you. Think, Landon. Be rational."

"I can't. She jumped because I stole her last hope. It's my fault."

"You have every right to be upset. Perfectly natural. Her death was … unfortunate."

My glare refused to be tempered. "Unfortunate?"

"Lest you think I sound callous, consider the bigger picture. Think of the lives you'll be able to save because of your privileged position."

"And how exactly will this 'privileged position' help me do that?"

"Just give it time. You'll find out."

"What's *that* supposed to mean? I'm in no mood for riddles."

"We have an inside track on their plans for you."

"Mind sharing?"

He shook his head. "Too much too early would be a mistake, but there are some big plans coming. You need to stay put. We don't want you to try running and getting yourself killed."

"I already want to run."

"I know you do, but you can't. You do, and you'll jeopardize everything we've worked so hard for."

"We?" I said, locking gazes with him. "What are you talking about? I hardly know you."

"Sure you do. You're just upset."

"You're right. I *am* upset."

"Don't forget who your allies are. I'm the guy who saved your life when operatives were hunting you in the woods, remember?"

"And you're the guy who told me to visit my mom. Something bad was about to happen to her. How did you know?"

"We suspected something, partly due to our sources, people like you working for us on the inside. We also have computer algorithms that study events and predict what *might* happen next. But I didn't want you to panic. That wouldn't have been helpful. As it turned out, you showed up in the nick of time."

"Yes, how convenient. She nearly died. You could have prevented that."

"You don't understand. We got a tip that plans to hurt your mom were being considered, but we didn't know anything for certain. Certainly not when."

I remained silent.

"Landon, I saved your life in the woods, and you saved hers by showing up in time. Isn't that what's important?"

Finding my hands more steady now, I unclasped them and allowed his words to sink in. "I guess I should be grateful right now."

"I don't need your thanks. I just did my duty. But some trust would be nice."

"Okay."

"So what other resentment is festering inside you? C'mon, out with it. Confession is good for the soul. Better in the long run if you spill the beans now."

"I went to see my dad and did as you instructed. Was there a point to it?"

"There's always a point to what we ask you to do. Trust me, Landon, your father is an important piece in this puzzle. That's all you need to know right now."

The chuckle came unbidden. "Riddles. Is that all you're good at?"

The almost-imperceptible shake of his head complemented the tight seam of his mouth. "I dropped by to encourage you, but I see we have some trust issues."

"Can you blame me? I just saw a woman jump to her death. I thought you'd show up and prevent it."

"Prevent it. Haven't you heard a word I've said?" He sighed, the first sign of frustration I'd detected in him. "There isn't time for this."

He glanced at his watch and whistled softly under his breath. "You may have noticed a peculiar rash on Amee's hand. I gave her a little bio irritant to get her out of the way. If Amee had been there, she would have made you push Leslie. Oh yeah, she's one nasty customer."

"What does it matter? Leslie is still dead."

"But you didn't push her, Landon. Your hands are clean. That's perhaps more important than you realize. I know you're blaming yourself, but you shouldn't. Leslie was an unknown variable who chose to die. Her death is a tragic loss, yes, but in this business, we never let a setback or tragedy go to waste if something good can come from it."

He punched the button to resume the elevator's descent. "Just roll with Amee for now, and you'll be fine."

"The nasty customer. Quite the babysitter."

"I'm concerned you're not taking this seriously."

"No, I am. I just get sarcastic when I'm upset."

When I closed my eyes, a full-motion memory flared in my blind left corners: Leslie deliberately climbing over the railing. Not a trace of indecision. Like she'd known exactly what she should do.

I fought a moment of dizziness and staggered, hand reaching for the wall, eyelids fluttering open.

"Are you okay?" he said.

"Still a little queasy."

"Delayed reaction."

"I'm okay now." A deep breath lingered in my lungs a moment before I released it. "One more thing. The police will know I visited Leslie. They'll want to question me."

"No, they won't. Amee will hide your tracks."

"How do you know?"

"I just know. When you see I'm right, maybe you'll learn to trust me a little more. I have been involved in this business for a while, Landon. How long have you been doing it? One full day?"

Touché.

"That thing you put in my arm to block their signal," I said. "They found it in no time and removed it."

"Of course. Otherwise you wouldn't even be a blip on their radar. And you're more than that now."

"Couldn't you give me another jammer? I don't know if I can take much more of this."

"What do you mean? We're just getting started."

"I could find another woods to disappear into."

"And what good would that do? You wouldn't be helping anybody but yourself. Besides, they'd hunt you down. In the Justice Club, you're either all in, or you're dead."

Just like Leslie.

"Hang in there, Landon, and together we can shut the Justice Club down for good. Isn't that what you want?"

My gaze connected with his. "Of course. Otherwise, what's the point?"

"Exactly. Be patient. Work with me here."

But for how long? What else will they pressure me to do?

A few more floors to go. I waited for the rest of his lecture.

"With the exception of this elevator ride, Amee and her buddies are always watching you, but we're watching you too. Don't forget. You're never completely alone." He patted my back, like a nurturing father after some tough love.

Nope, no ticket out of this place. I had no choice but to stay put where I'd been parked. I took a deep breath. "If something comes up, how will I find you?"

He hiked an eyebrow. "Don't you remember? You won't. I'll find *you.*"

The door slid open, and he whisked the wheeled cart around a corner and out of sight, the aroma of steak following his wake.

25

Amee grinned excitedly. "Congratulations! You completed your first kill. Aren't you proud?"

Pride didn't register in my mind. *Sickened* and *disturbed* ranked much higher in my troubled thoughts.

At a bar near the hotel, I nursed a Pepsi while Amee sampled something stronger with a basket of onion rings. In the blind corners of my eyes, a video clip looped. Leslie throwing the sheet music into the wind, shoulders shaking with sobs.

She died because of me. I didn't push her, but I still killed her.

Oh, yes, I did.

If only I'd gone to Leslie a few minutes earlier ... we could be on the lam right now. Most likely running to our graves.

And then what a waste that would have been for the resistance. Monty was right.

Amee bent into my line of sight, her eyebrows knitted. "Hello, I asked you a question. Well, aren't you proud?"

"No, Amee, I'm exhausted."

Why can't she just go away and leave me alone? She knows none of this is my cup of tea. Why keep up the false pretense? She knows I'm playing along because if I don't, those I love will die.

She'd nagged me all the way here to have a drink with her, and I'd sought to beg off. My only desire at the moment was to chill in my hotel room and not have to endure more fans and give the perfunctory thank-yous and autographs. Not while Leslie's death pressed on my mind. Along with this otherworld feeling of being yanked out of Upper Michigan and forced on a journey I had no desire to take.

"Of course you're tired," Amee said. "You had a big day, but my superiors are very pleased. You should be happy too. You passed your first test."

Only the first one, huh? How many lie ahead? What will they require of me next to keep the all-important superiors happy?

I took another sip of the soda, the carbonation tickling my tongue and throat, the sugar helping to chase away the lethargy from my adrenaline crash.

"You should have something stronger," she said. "Oh yeah, that's right, you already told me. God took your liquor craving away."

I nodded. "Last fall I called on Him to save me. He did and also gave me a loathing for the stuff. You wouldn't understand."

"I can't even tempt you with a Jack Daniel's?"

"*Especially* not a Jack Daniel's."

She shrugged and nibbled on an onion ring, then licked her greasy fingers. "You'll be happy to know your friend, Celeste, is in the process of being returned to her life, safe and sound. Just as we promised."

At least somebody's alive because of me.

One life snuffed out. Another preserved.

Did they somehow cancel each other out in this bizarre grand scheme of things?

"Think of her restoration as a—well, as a reward for a job well done," Amee said. "She won't remember anything about her abduction."

"And how exactly will you pull that off?"

"She will wake and find herself in the hospital with a concussion. The engineered story will be that she had a car accident and hit her head, and that's why she can't remember what happened."

I studied her with a raised eyebrow.

"The human brain is our specialty, remember? We have our ways to tinker with the greatest CPU known to humankind."

"Yeah, like making someone *catch* a brain tumor as if it were the common cold. Was that how you gave it to me?"

Smirking, she remained silent. I didn't yet rank high enough on the food chain to know trade secrets. But now that I'd passed my first kill order, perhaps I'd learn new things about this secretive organization.

When she obviously wouldn't answer my question, I said, "How are *you* feeling, Amee? The last time I saw you, you were pretty sick." A bandage secured her hand, where the nasty rash had been.

She shrugged. "Bad clams, I expect, or an allergy to seafood I didn't know I had. I feel fine now. But it's very thoughtful of you to ask, maestro." The lilt in her voice tossed a question in the air. She wanted to know what game I was playing without outright saying so. Her plan to kill me once I no longer proved useful to the Justice Club hardly made us bosom buddies.

So why my gesture of thoughtfulness? She probably ached to know but chose not to ask.

Wait, and you'll find out. This is how I'll slowly drive you mad. If it's possible to drive somebody mad who already is.

What did she want anyhow? Couldn't she give a guy some peace? I'd just watched a woman close to my mother's age jump to her death. Maybe this was standard fare for her, bodies lying on the sidewalk, all part of a hard day's work.

She leaned her head to one side, perhaps to be alluring. "So tell me, what was it like to push Leslie to her death? How did that make you feel?"

So—what? Now Amee was a shrink?

"I must confess that I don't remember pushing her, but I guess I must have, right? It was like watching her go over the railing and knowing I couldn't do anything to stop her. As if fate had written this end for her long before she'd been born."

"Wow. Landon, the philosopher. A whole new you." Her playful expression sobered. "At the beginning, the stage of denial isn't so unusual. In time you'll remember everything you did. I'm quite impressed. For a while there, I thought you were going to spare Leslie instead of Celeste. I could sense your struggle, but you made the right choice in the end. I knew you would. Even your God couldn't save you this time."

She fancied she had everything figured out, didn't she? Could this overconfidence be a weakness for me to later exploit? "I suppose the police will want to interview me."

A smug smile. "No, there won't be any need for that."

"What? But I was there—we both were. We put fingerprints all over her—"

"Don't worry about it. Video feeds, fingerprints. I took care of everything."

Score Monty.

I splayed my hands. "So that's it? We just walk away?"

"We just walk away," she said, and with the faintest of smiles, the queen of ADD struck again. "Hey, I was able to chat with Clint Robson later after Leslie snubbed him. He might still be persuaded to do a song on the next album."

Amazing how effortlessly she juggled both hats with barely a pause. Agent one minute. Assassination coordinator the next. I stared into the eyes of this sociopath and buried my amazement deep.

"We could probably coax him to do a favorite from his latest Broadway show," she said. "Your keyboard genius as backup, of course. Something spectacular from the creative team to guarantee lots of likes on YouTube."

"Good work, Amee," I said, pretending to care.

"I have my uses. I also called a journalistic contact. Tomorrow there'll be a story in the *Dallas Morning News* about your new tour with a review of your concert in the park today. I saw a preview of it. You'll be pleased."

That was all she wanted to talk about now—the concert scene? "So where are we off to next?"

"New Orleans. Then we head west to LA, San Francisco, Seattle."

"This is all so surprising. What on earth does another concert tour have to do with the Justice Club's plans?"

Her mouth pulled to one side. "Do you really think I'm going to answer that?"

"No, I guess that would make life way too boring."

"There are, however, two important news items I *can* share. First, your mother is doing fine and went home from the hospital."

The lifted weight tempted me to leap from my chair. "I want to call her."

"Of course you do. You have permission with the new cell phone I'll be giving you tomorrow. Understand we'll be listening in on everything you say."

"I would have expected nothing less."

"Keep in mind that your mom's health status, not to mention that of your friend Jade is entirely up to you. The wound wasn't mortal ... this time."

My pulse accelerated. "So the men in her house—"

"—were our operatives, of course. Did you really think the attack was an unrelated matter? We needed a way to flush you out. We succeeded."

Confirmed. They'd hurt my mom to get to me. My fists balled beneath the table, and I wanted to hit somebody. Hard.

Save your anger, Landon. Store it up for the right time.

I said, "So whatever you have to do—as long as you achieve your goal, that's all that matters, huh?"

"Hey, you're starting to catch on. But something in your tone tells me you don't approve."

"Does it matter whether I approve?"

"I guess not, but it would make life a lot easier for everyone if you did."

So not happening.

"So what's the second news item?" I said.

"You have a new addition to the band, a woodwind virtuoso named Cynthia Lemke. She's excellent. You'll like her."

In the past, since this was my band, I'd had a major role in doing interviews and deciding who made the cut. But now I was notified after the fact.

She must have sensed my frustration. "I realize this isn't how you ran things in the past, maestro, but we needed a way to bring her on board. I think you and Cynthia are going to get along really well. In fact, you may want to think of her as your protégé."

"And why would I do that?"

She wiped her mouth on a napkin. "About three months ago, Cynthia was riding a motorcycle with her fiancé, Lee, on a road trip through the Midwest. They were going too fast. Somewhere near Indianapolis, they came upon road construction too quickly and lost control. Lee didn't make it. Cynthia did but had to have brain surgery." She shot me a meaningful look.

"I see."

"The Justice Club's protocol has expanded. We now find operatives beyond brain cancer patients. But don't worry. The surgery didn't affect her musical ability."

"And my role relates to Cynthia how?"

"She's often a troubled soul. Seems she wakes up in strange places with blood on her hands but no memory of what she did."

"That sounds oddly familiar."

A cruel smile. "I thought you of all people might appreciate her situation. She's a malfunctioner like you."

"A what?"

"A malfunctioner. In spite of your implant's programming, you sometimes go off script for some unknown reason. Fail to clean up after yourself. Our experts haven't yet figured out why," she said, suspicion glinting in her eyes, "but the glitch makes you unpredictable, a problem warranting further study."

Maybe God has something to do with it.

"Why go to all the trouble?" I said.

"Big plans are in the works, maestro, the kind that will make major headlines, and you'll be a key player."

Interesting.

"What does this have to do with Cynthia? Don't tell me I'm going to be her babysitter."

"Something like that. Since the cop Ray Galotta is dead, we thought it only fitting that you should take his place, learn to watch malfunctioners and guide them along like he did for you."

She must have a short memory. Galotta may have done a good bit of watching, but he'd been too busy with my going rogue to offer much in the way of guidance.

"So about Cynthia ... does she have any clue what's going on?" I said.

She stirred a straw in her drink, clinked ice cubes. "Nope. She's at square one, just like you were not so long ago, so you probably know what must be going through her mind right now. Your empathy should help. Track her down and fill her in on how the system works. Both of her retiree parents are expendable if she decides not to cooperate."

This unexpected job description gave me something unsavory to chew on. Amee had mentioned the first of several tests, and I'd passed it. Might my response now be a second test on my path to greater things?

In other words, Cynthia likely wasn't the only one being watched. Unpredictability had become my middle name. And they didn't like it.

And yet they had me in mind for big plans. Oh yeah, they had their sights on me, all right.

Amee downed the rest of her drink, rose, and tossed a tip on the table. "Look, it's getting late, and you need some sleep from the looks of it. Let's go."

Yep, my babysitter all right.

Once in a cab, she took a phone call, then said, "Since you do better when you're not totally surprised, tomorrow's plans have changed. We're heading to Houston for the next concert. We have a regional center for operatives outside of town. There, before the concert, we'll meet a guy named Stu. He'll talk you through the protocol of shadowing another operative, and he'll show you how to use all the gadgets you'll need to surveil Cynthia and keep her in line."

She angled her head to one side. "Just remember, if she runs, it's up to you to track her down. And if she successfully evades you, guess what happens, maestro? The same thing that happened to Galotta. The end of the line for you."

While I tried to swallow the bad taste in my mouth, we exited the cab and took the elevator to my room. What—she planned to tuck me in? If she expected more, she didn't know me well enough.

In my room, she pulled out a syringe. "I want to give you this to help you sleep."

"Oh, c'mon. I've had several of those lately. Can't I get my rest the old-fashioned way?"

"But you won't get much sleep. I guarantee it, not after your first kill. Believe me, you need this." She stepped closer, spraying some of the amber fluid in the air. Jabbing people with needles had apparently become her new favorite pastime. "And if you're really nice to me, I could accidentally give you too much, and then you'd never wake up at all. How would you like that?"

A suspicion nibbled on the edges of my answer-seeking mind. How expertly she handled that syringe. Maybe she'd done this before, putting people out of their misery with needles. If only I had the means to research her past … find some useful information I could use for leverage.

"If I'm really nice to you?" I said. "Why would I want a mercy killing?"

She nodded. "Remember, maestro, there are only two doors in the Justice Club. Door number one—you're all in and going with the program. The future is an open door to greater things. Door number two—you run or prove to be more of a liability than you're worth. If you ever get trapped behind door number two, believe me, you'll be begging me for a peaceful end instead of what they have planned for you."

26

Gavin Dane Morrison took a cab to the Sportsman's Club near Humboldt Park, where Father waited for him in a room that could have been called "Taxidermy Paradise." Antlers sprouted from everywhere, even from the ceiling. The dark walnut table had been stationed in a remote corner, more at home in shadows than near listening ears. They alone, except a waiter, occupied the room.

"What should I get you?" Father said.

Gavin slid into the chair across from him. "I'll have whatever you're having."

An eyebrow lifted. "It was a bit strong for you last time, if I recall correctly."

"I can handle it. I'm more experienced now."

With a shrug, Father signaled to the waiter with two fingers and pointed at his drink. The ponytailed man nodded and left.

"Thanks for getting back with me so soon," Gavin said. "It's nice to see you, Father. It's been a while." Father had never liked the name Dad, said it was too low class for his taste.

Sporting a handsome, tan face, Father had the rugged good looks of a fashion model in his sixties, with his toned body, full head of thick, graying black hair, and Hollywood cleft chin. The salt-and-pepper beard had been professionally manicured to accentuate the manly contours of his face.

When Father took a drink, he studied Gavin over the rim with keen, even wistful eyes. But the charm ended there. Gavin had no delusions that his father wasn't one cold, hard customer. The man could reach across the table and break Gavin's neck before Gavin's heart considered its next beat.

Gavin wished the DNA had been passed down. He'd once hoped to find the father who would show him what it meant to be a man, to help him attain what he apparently lacked. Instead, he'd learned that Father ranked in another class of men, and nothing Gavin did would ever be good enough to garner a membership in that secret society.

But that didn't stop him from trying.

Father wiped his mouth and set the cloth napkin down, well into his first drink. "I heard about the bloody clothes in your closet."

"You don't waste time, do you?"

"No, not when there is not time to waste."

"You know, Father, most civilized people start a conversation by saying hello when they greet somebody they haven't seen in over six months."

A cynical smile. "Fine. Hello."

"See, that wasn't so hard, was it?"

A warning flashed in the unblinking glare. The man could be pushed only so far before he snapped. Gavin had long mastered the tightrope.

"Look," the submissive son said, "I'm not here to spar with you. I can have a civilized conversation."

"Glad to hear it. Otherwise I would not have invited you here. We could have done business over the phone, but this seemed like more than business. It seemed … personal."

"You work too hard, Dad. You need to get away. Have some fun."

Blue eyes fastened on Gavin's face, the gaze so piercing Gavin couldn't help flinching.

"When there is a world in need of being saved from itself, I forget about how hard I am working." Father waved a dismissive hand. "About the bloody clothes ... I am sorry you had to see something like that."

"Yeah, well, it's easier to deny what you've made me do when I don't have to see the reminders of what I've become."

"And what is that?"

"Do I really have to say it?"

The waiter arrived and delivered two glasses of something exotic: amber with a hint of red. Gavin couldn't recall what it was called, but he'd requested this meeting, so he would be drinking every drop.

Father dismissed the waiter with instructions to close the door on his way out, then leaned back with a sigh, arms folded. Dressed for success in his crisp white dress shirt, purple silk tie, and gray herringbone jacket. "It was a malfunctioner who bloodied your clothes. He will be dealt with. The episode won't happen again."

"You told me something like that would never happen."

"Sometimes when you are forced to work with buffoons, things happen beyond your control."

Unfathomable. Being out of control didn't exist in his father's vocabulary. Gavin said, "Why Iron Valley? I thought I was never to go back there."

Father winced. "The operator should not have disclosed the location. She will be reassigned."

Gavin took a sip, struggled to keep the grimace from reaching his face. "You didn't answer my question."

Father splayed tan hands, expensive rings glinting. "It was just a job. The location is not important."

"It's only a coincidence that that's where I grew up?"

"Why should it be a big deal? You had a mask on. Left no DNA. You have nothing to worry about."

The silence lingered between them. Father drained his glass and started on his second.

Gavin took another drink, the liquor quickening his blood. "I know it was Sandra Jeffers." When Father's gaze lifted in unveiled surprise,

Gavin added, "I did a little research. Not too hard to find a stabbing in a small town like Iron Valley."

"I thought you did not like reminders of your missions."

"What if she'd pulled off my mask? What if she'd recognized me?"

"But that did not happen. And even if she had seen your face, she probably would not have recognized you. We are talking a lot of years, Gavin."

Decades had passed since he was declared missing after telling his adoptive mom he needed to meet a friend at the library. For months, he'd stayed in hiding, trusting that Father, who'd charmed him with a lavish lifestyle at his Chicago penthouse, knew best. All the while his adoptive family had scoured the nearby woods and ravines for him until the grisly discovery. How Father had arranged all the details, especially the body and DNA, still amazed him.

"I just have one question," Gavin said.

An eyebrow lifted. "Only one? And this from the boy of a thousand questions." An endearing nickname from years gone by.

"You told me never to ask, but I'm going to anyhow."

Already Father began shaking his head. "Gavin, no—"

"Whose body is buried in my grave?"

Fire leaped into those eyes. "I said, no."

"Was he murdered for me? Tell me the truth, and I'll never ask again."

"You will never ask again because I said so!" Father slammed his fist down on the table, jostling their glasses. He breathed hard for a few seconds before reining in his anger, lowering his voice to a conspiratorial whisper. "All you need to know is that the exchange bought your freedom. Without an ID, you were able to do all sorts of missions behind the scenes, like a phantom, and nobody knew who you were. You were absolutely indispensable to our program."

Father's answer told Gavin everything. If the boy who'd taken his place hadn't been murdered, Father would have insisted on his innocence. But he hadn't.

Only weeks after his own funeral, Gavin had woken one morning with a headache and blood seeping from a head wound. When he complained to Father, the truth had emerged. The brain implant had been administered while he slept without his consent, but he had little reason to complain. It transformed him into a super soldier of sorts—with his dad's computer programing, of course. Without any training, Gavin had been able to execute martial arts moves to rival the most recent Marvel flick.

"I want to be in the uncloaked program," Gavin said.

Father shook his head. "You think you can execute a hit by following directions to the letter without wireless interference beyond enhanced skills? You are not ready."

"Yes, I am."

"No. You have not been hardened sufficiently. You have been in the cloaked program too long."

"What do you mean?"

"Do I really need to say it? Yesterday, you found blood on your clothes and freaked out."

"That was only because you had given me your word that something like that would never happen. The DNA in my apartment could have linked me to the hit. Blood and killing don't bother me, as you well know. Enemies are like bugs underfoot. Better to squash them before they squash you."

A slight smile, only the second to emerge. "You know my manifesto well."

Gavin smiled back. "You don't think I read it? Anything to please Father."

Father glanced at his watch. Finished off his glass in two gulps. "I will consider your proposal. We may need to run you through a few real-time scenarios first to be sure you are ready."

"I'm ready now. Whatever you want, I can do it."

A full meeting of the eyes. "You really think you have it in you?"

"I wouldn't have said so if I wasn't sure."

Father got up, tossed some money on the table. Met his son's gaze. "We do have a rather important job coming up, and you *could* play a key role, though doing so uncloaked is doubtful. There are no guarantees that you are the right person or that you'd even walk away from it alive."

Gavin rose and faced Father, puffing out his chest a bit. "I hope you'll consider me for the job."

A brief hesitation. "We will see. Until next time."

Frederic Samuels shook his son's hand and moved toward the door with the agility of a tiger. Then, as if remembering something, he stepped back and lowered his voice. "Nicki is asking too many questions about you and cannot be trusted. You kill her quietly, uncloaked, and I will take your offer seriously."

27

Sunday, March 27

A h, the tour bus. How could I have forgotten my private oasis,
where I could while away my time between destinations by
entertaining, talking business, or doing some serious song-
writing? But before checking out my much-missed domain, I headed to
breakfast in the hotel's lower-level restaurant.

Naturally, my situation hadn't changed, but I had every reason to
roll with it and make the best of my difficult circumstances. Even
pretend I was enjoying myself when I'd rather be back in Michigan
with Jade by my side.

Everybody was there: Amee, of course; Stacey, my makeup artist;
Kim Ono, my cellist; Zeek, my percussionist; Yearik, my sound guy
extraordinaire; and of course Ted, the moody bass player who sometimes rubbed me the wrong way. They were all so happy to see me
again after my hiatus, and we paused between mouthfuls for hugs,
well-wishes, and chatter about what had been going on in their lives.

And then I met Cynthia Lemke, my supposed protégé. Straight
brown hair hanging to her shoulders. An almost ghostly white face.
Not a hair over five foot two, she was a slim, lithe wisp of a woman.

Demure to a fault but downright pretty with those sparkling brown eyes. The type who left you wondering whether she was flirting or just being friendly.

Did she even meet my eyes when I said hello? Barely. And from what I'd been told, this girl from some tiny town in Indiana could play the flute, not to mention pennywhistles and recorders, nearly as well as Sir James Galway. Yep, hard to imagine she had enough wind in those tiny lungs to play a kazoo.

Her playful eyes twinkled, her fishy handshake barely existent. "I'm so honored to be part of your band."

It was hard to imagine this woman getting a speeding ticket, never mind waking in the dead of night with blood on her hands.

Could looks be deceiving?

WE HAD to pack the tour bus and hit the road after I signed a few CD jackets on the way to the bus, where a crowd, hearing about the famous people staying at the restaurant, gawked. Then the highway rolled away beneath us like a ribbon, and the miles spun the odometer. In my suite, as if nothing were unusual, Amee and I chatted about the next show and my next interview before I cherished some alone time and found a moment for that long-awaited call to Jade and my mom.

Inputting Jade's number on my new phone, I rehearsed my answers to inconvenient questions. How much could I say?

"Landon! Oh my goodness. Where are you? We've been so worried."

"I'm near Dallas, Texas. We're on our way to our next concert in Houston."

"We?"

"Me and my band."

"What? You're touring again?"

"That's right."

Pause. "But weren't we supposed to meet at the hospital in Iron Valley, like two days ago?"

"I'm sorry, Jade. Something came up."

"Something came up. Are you okay?"

"Sure. I'm fine."

"You're fine." Seconds ticked by, and I imagined her creased brow. "Landon, the local police and FBI have been looking everywhere for you. We didn't know what happened. Why didn't you call?"

"I, um—"

"Are you having memory issues again? Do you mean to tell me you actually *forgot* about your mom being in the hospital?"

How could I talk myself out of this one? No bother trying. "How is she doing?"

"She's doing great. She's out of the hospital and living with us now. She's staying in our guest room."

"Why would she do that?"

"She didn't feel comfortable going back to her house, not after being attacked there."

My cheeks warmed. "Oh, of course. Thanks so much for taking her in."

"And don't worry about her. After everything that's happened, Dad installed a top-dollar security system. She's safer than in the county jail." She paused. "She's been asking a lot about you."

Mouth dry, I reached for my bottled water and took a swig. "I'd love to talk to her."

"That lady from the FBI I mentioned to you—Maggie—she's hoping to talk to you, too."

"What does she want?"

"What do you think? We were hoping the FBI would catch those crooks who gave you the implant so you could go home, remember? Or did you forget about that too?"

"No, I remember, but it doesn't matter anymore."

"It doesn't matter?" Another pause, this one longer than the first, stretched the awkward silence. "Landon, you're not making any sense. We've been worried sick about you."

"Why? What's up?"

"Are you serious? You disappeared—that's what's up. We found records at the psychiatric ward that you visited your dad. The police found your Jeep there but no sign of you anywhere or any clue about where you'd gone. It was like—like you'd vanished off the face of the earth. We thought you'd been kidnapped or worse."

When Jade got riled, all you could do was step back and behold.

"But that's why I called. So you'd know there's no cause to worry. Feel free to have the Jeep towed to my mom's place—at my expense, of course. I won't be needing it anytime soon."

She breathed across the line. "That's all you're going to say? Are you kidding me? You never stopped to consider that maybe you should have let us know before now that you were okay?"

"You're right. I'm sorry. I messed up."

Actually, I had no way to call you.

"I was afraid the puppet master had abducted you this time."

Smart girl.

"Don't worry about the puppet master. That's all in the past. I've decided to move forward with my life." Surely she realized how fake I sounded and that I must be saying these words because I had no choice.

"Okay. I'm just … surprised that you're touring again. I mean, with everything that's happened over the last few days and everything you've gone through, including your mom. Well, it seems pretty odd."

"I met with my agent and manager, Amee, and she persuaded me that it was a good idea."

Yep, good, old selfish Landon is back, sweetheart. Better get used to it.

"I see." Her disappointment translated into stark silence, as if she needed time to process all this. She probably nibbled on a fingernail. "And how exactly are you moving on? You're not concerned about the puppet master tracking you down? Landon, you're still not making any sense. You hide out in the Georgia woods for four months to keep us all safe, and now—what—you don't care?"

Of course I care. She doesn't understand, and I can't explain it to her. This is going nowhere and will only get harder.

"Like I said, that's old news. Can I talk to my mom?"

No doubt mad, perplexed, or both, she said, "Yeah, sure. Hold on."

Be positive. Act like you're fine.

Some muffled voices. Then: "Hey, where have you been? You said you'd be back, and then you were gone."

ADAM BLUMER

My throat tightened. "Sorry, Mom, I had a change in plans. I'm so glad you're doing okay after what happened."

"I guess the good Lord has more for me to do here."

"So, the guy who hurt you ... what happened?"

"I'm not sure. I don't remember much beyond a masked man. I guess I must have blacked out after I scratched the guy. The police say I must have drawn blood, but I don't recall doing that. The doctor says the memories may return in time, but there are no guarantees."

"I know the feeling." After I was traumatized by a school shooting, an event I couldn't remember for years, doctors had told me the same thing.

"So what's this business about you touring again? I thought I'd get to see you for a while. You're my son, and I've missed you. When are you coming home?"

"Sorry, Mom. I've got a full concert schedule now, at least until the end of the summer."

"Oh, that's too bad."

The disappointment in her voice made me wince. "Maybe in the fall I could take some time off and head to Iron Valley for a few days."

Pause. "Landon, are you okay?"

"I'm doing fine, Mom."

"I mean, really okay? We've been pretty worried about you. We thought something terrible had happened."

"I'm sorry, Mom. I should have called earlier."

"Nobody knew where you were, and we feared the worst. The last time you ran, we were there with you, and we all knew why. Remember?"

"I'm not running anymore, Mom. I'm just making music again. I apologize. I should have been better at communicating."

She snorted. "You can say that again. I'm still not sure I understand. I mean, a few days ago you were running for your life through the Georgia woods. Now you act like nothing's wrong. What's going on?"

I searched my brain for something to say. Before I could, she said, "The puppet master got to you, didn't he? He's got you under his thumb, and now you're afraid to say too much out of concern for my safety."

144

Grappling for words, I said, "It sure is nice to talk to you again, Mom. I've missed you so much. I wish we could have talked more before I had to go."

"I see. And they're probably listening to every word we're saying right now, aren't they? Well, Mr. Puppet Master, if you're listening in, I've got a few things I want to say. You can just get your big, slimy hands off—"

"Mom, don't."

"—the dearest person I have left in this world, apart from my husband." A sob made her voice teeter. "How dare you think you can just steal—"

"Mom, please don't. You're not helping anything."

I imagined her wiping her eyes. She would have said a lot more if she had any clue that the same people who had me under their thumb had nearly gotten her killed. She drew a deep breath and turned silent.

Change the subject.

"Dad and I had a good talk at the psychiatric ward. Well, really I was the one doing the talking, but there was a moment at the end when he seemed to understand me. How's he doing?"

"I don't know what you said, but he's changed."

"Changed? What do you mean?"

"It's like something woke him up. He's sitting up and jabbering all the time. They can hardly get him to quiet down. It's amazing."

Monty was right. Again.

But how could a single name spoken in his ear cause such a transformation?

"What's Dad saying?"

"Not much that makes any sense, I'm afraid. I suppose that's because of his brain damage. But he sure is trying to communicate, which is good."

"That's amazing."

"Maybe in time he'll make sense."

"Mom, about Dad. Has he had any unusual visitors?"

"Just Pastor Mayhew."

"Not a Catholic priest?"

"Why would he have a visitor like that?"

"I was hoping you could tell me. Some priest is listed on Dad's visitors' log. You might want to check that out." *Uh-oh.* Others listened in on the conversation. Had I said too much?

"I will, Son. That's pretty strange."

Time to go before I said more than I planned to. "Hey, Mom, I need to go."

Her voice turned shaky with emotion. "Thanks for calling. Stay in touch, okay? I'll be praying for you."

"Please do. I'll be in touch. Love ya."

"Love you, too, Landon. More than you'll ever know. Remember, even though your father wasn't around much after the school shooting, he always loved you. I hope you believe that."

"I do, Mom."

"In spite of everything that's happened, I'm so glad you see that now."

28

Shortly after returning home from church, Jade greeted Maggie at the front door, pleased the agent had accepted her lunch invitation. They had so much to discuss since Maggie's interview with Sandra's alleged attacker.

"Welcome to our home." Jade locked the door behind Maggie and pushed a few buttons on a wall keypad to engage the security system.

"Thanks for the invitation," Maggie said, eyeing the keypad. "My, is that a beef roast I smell?"

"Yep, it's been in the slow cooker all morning. We've got some mashed potatoes, carrots, gravy, and a few other side dishes too."

"Oh, you shouldn't have gone to so much trouble."

"It's no trouble at all. Interested in a cup of coffee? I just made some in the French press. It's called 'Heavenly Caramel.'"

"Sounds lovely. Thanks."

"You just make yourself at home while I check on a few things in the kitchen. Sandra's helping me with lunch, but we should be able to join you soon."

Maggie sauntered into the living room and collapsed on the couch. A few minutes later, Jade brought the steaming mug, remembering to offer plenty of cream and stevia. Maggie thanked her and accepted the joe, smelling it with a wide smile and closed eyes.

Sandra entered the room and greeted Maggie, taking a seat. "So tell us about your interview. Did it go okay?"

"We'll talk about that soon."

Jade sank into a wingback chair across from Maggie. "I just put some rolls in the oven, so we've got some time to talk. Guess who called me and Mom before church this morning? It was Landon."

Maggie nodded. "Oh, so he finally called you, huh? Yeah, I found out yesterday that he's in Texas, back on the road and doing concerts. I was going to let you know this morning. Crazy, huh? So what did he say?"

Jade filled her in, with Sandra adding details here and there.

"Thanks for letting me know," Maggie said.

"Landon seemed pretty evasive. Sandra and I are concerned that he may be under the control of the Justice Club," Jade said. "Otherwise, he'd still be on the run, wouldn't he?"

Maggie nodded. "One would think so, unless the Justice Club simply lost interest in him, but that wouldn't make sense, would it?"

"So how did the interview go with that suspect?" Jade said.

Sandra asked, "Is he the guy who attacked me?"

Maggie tore open a packet of stevia and poured it into her coffee. She added cream and stirred it in, taking her time. "Oh yeah, it's him all right. Well, at least he's one of them."

She looked at them and hesitated. "Look, before I go any further, I need to make something clear. I don't typically discuss pending investigations, but because you, Sandra, were attacked and are logically concerned about your safety, I'm going to share a few details to hopefully put you at ease. Besides, if I were in your shoes, I'd want to know if the guy who stabbed me had been caught. But I'm going to withhold some details, such as the man's name. We'll call him 'John Smith,' okay?"

Sandra nodded. "Thank you. I appreciate that."

"We believe two men were working together in the attack," Sandra said, "but we've been unable to identify the second suspect yet. He didn't leave any DNA at the scene."

"So this guy you talked to, this John Smith," Sandra said, "how do you know for sure it's him?"

"We have his DNA. The police found his blood on your clothes, even some of his skin under your fingernails."

"As far as physical evidence," Jade said, "that sounds like a slam dunk."

"You bet." Maggie paused. "Actually, I feel sorry for this guy. He has no idea what he did or why."

Jade nodded. "That's exactly how Landon felt when someone was controlling him through his implant."

"I'm perplexed though," Maggie said, then sipped her coffee. "John Smith has never had brain surgery, but somehow he has a brain implant. I took him to the hospital for a scan to confirm. It's there all right, though closer to the surface than Landon's. He couldn't believe it. The only head injury he could remember going to the ER for was from a bicycle accident. It was after that that he realized he was doing odd things during his sleep."

"So did you arrest this guy?" said a voice from the hallway. Gordon Hamilton ambled in and took a seat next to Jade, draping his arm around his daughter.

"How much did you overhear of what I just told Jade and Sandra?" Maggie said.

Worry lines traced the edges of his mouth. "Enough. Please tell me you put this guy behind bars."

Maggie took another sip of her coffee and put it down. "Actually, no."

Sandra stared at her. "What? You didn't arrest him?"

"Why not?" Frustration simmered in Gordon's voice.

"You just said you had his DNA," Jade said. "So there's no question he attacked Sandra, right?"

"DNA never lies. There's absolutely no question he's our man."

"So you're going to just let him go?" Gordon said, spreading his hands.

Maggie held up a hand, palm out. "Now hold on. Did I say anything about letting him go? I said we haven't arrested him yet. That's not the same thing."

Jade rested her chin on her upraised fist. Gordon folded his arms, and Sandra waited.

"Did you really think I'd interview this guy," Maggie said, "without a plan?"

"What plan?" Gordon said, voice tight. "Remember, my brother, Jed, is dead because of these sick people. I almost bled to death because one of these operatives stabbed me, and Sandra got the same treatment and could have died, too."

"Look. I know this situation has been tough on everybody," Maggie said, "but don't worry. We've created a task force with FBI agents and local law enforcement. Folks will be monitoring Mr. Smith around the clock and watching what he does next, where he goes."

"But what if he tries to hurt somebody like he hurt me?" Sandra said.

Maggie shook her head. "He won't. If he even looks at a knife, they'll be all over him."

"But what's the point?" Gordon said. "Wouldn't it make more sense to simply arrest this guy before he hurts somebody else?"

Maggie enjoyed a last gulp of coffee and set the empty mug on the coffee table. "There is some method to our madness. Remember, I said we have a plan. Since this situation has hurt all of you to some degree, I'm going to tell you more, but what I'm about to share doesn't leave this room. Got it?"

Everyone nodded.

"Remember, the FBI's original plan with Landon was to do reverse tracking."

"Oh yeah," Jade said. "I forgot about all that."

"Unfortunately, due to the escalation of his situation," Maggie said, "the strategy never panned out. But now we have a chance to try it again."

Gordon shook his head. "Reverse tracking? Sorry, but some of us aren't as familiar with the lingo as you are. Care to fill us in?"

"Sure. Remember, the Justice Club controls operatives through wireless signals to their brain implants. If our techs are able to isolate the signal controlling John Smith, they can track it backwards to its point of origin, right down to GPS coordinates on a map."

"So you can figure out where the bad guys are operating from?" Jade said.

"Absolutely. Now do you see the bigger picture here? Sure, we could march into John Smith's house and arrest him right now, but why settle for a minnow when we can go after a whole school of fish? If we're patient, perhaps we can track down whoever is using John Smith and make an arrest."

Gordon nodded. "Impressive. Now, guys like John Smith—you think he's only one of many across the country?"

"I know it's chilling to consider," Maggie said, "but we believe most communities have some type of regional control center through which the Justice Club is calling the shots. But theoretically, if we can track the signals and determine a control center's GPS coordinates, we can put these guys out of business."

"And you've done this successfully?" Gordon said. "Shut them down, I mean."

Maggie grimaced. "Actually, no. Not yet. But there has to be a first time for everything. If we're successful in Iron Valley, our techniques could be replicated across the country."

"You said 'most communities,'" Sandra said. "Just how many operatives could there be?"

The agent's face turned grim. "In heavily populated areas like Chicago or New York City, you really don't want to know. Up here in the woods, the situation is more manageable if we can get our finger on the pulse of it."

Gordon scratched his whiskers. "Hmm. Makes you wonder, doesn't it? Consider all the unexplained mass shootings we've seen over the last few years. Some people blame them on a radicalized American Muslim, but what if they're really just the work of the Justice Club?"

"Pushing some sort of agenda," Jade said, shaking her head. "Who are these people who mete out justice as they see fit?"

Gordon snorted. "*Injustice* more like."

Maggie's phone rang, and she rose, fishing it out of her pocket. "Songbird here." She stepped toward the kitchen and paused, while they looked on. "Oh, really ... And how long ago was that? ... Okay ... well, keep me in the loop if anything develops, even if that means calling me in the middle of the night. Okay, thanks. Have a good one."

She clicked off and turned toward their expectant faces. "John Smith had a fight with his wife and stormed off. Now he's driving who knows where, but one of our guys is tailing him."

Jade said, "So if he tries to hurt anybody—"

"We'll arrest him, but he's probably just blowing off steam. What will be telling is what he does tonight if he's in sleepwalking mode."

"Sleepwalking mode?" Gordon said.

"Yeah, that's our code phrase for when operatives are performing while under control of the Justice Club and unaware of their actions. Because the controlling signals tend to correlate with sleep cycles, nighttime is prime time. Tonight may be revealing."

"So what now?" Jade said.

"Now we can enjoy lunch. I doubt much will happen this afternoon. My colleagues and I hope the Justice Club has plans for John Smith tonight. If they do, we'll be ready."

29

"I killed her," Gavin Dane Morrison said.

Father nodded, face impassive. He peered at his son across the table at the same bar they'd visited yesterday. "Good. I am pleased. Tell me how you arranged it."

"Gas leak. It was simple. She went to sleep and never woke up."

"Clever. Bloodless and very hard to prove anything other than an accident."

"Exactly. It was easy enough to meddle with her furnace so it wasn't venting properly. She never knew anything was wrong."

Father leaned back, eyes calculating. Left his drink untouched. "So how did it make you feel? To kill her, I mean."

"I didn't feel anything. She didn't mean anything to me."

He paused, his look appraising, skeptical. "Is that so?"

"You don't believe me?"

"What I believe is that you would do just about anything to impress me. And that's good, because that desire to meet expectations pushes you out of your comfort zone and stretches you in new ways. You wonder why I have such high standards? Why I cannot tolerate failure? The product is a better, stronger you in the long run, and that pleases your father."

"Anything for Father."

A pause. "Is that sarcasm I hear?"

Gavin kept his spine straight, his face expressionless. "No, I mean it. Every word."

Father sipped his bourbon. "Be aware that others will confirm everything you've told me."

Gavin shrugged. "Be my guest."

"Remember, we have multiple cameras watching your every move. We even know how many hours of sleep you get each night, how much you eat, how often you visit the toilet. Strains from this experience will be evident in loss of sleep, change in appetite. We'll be able to tell if you've passed this test as well as you say you have without the emotional stress you claim."

Gavin remained silent.

"If you pass the test, you *may* be called on to execute a mission, as I said before, that could require the ultimate sacrifice. If you want to please Father, you may be called on to die for him. What do you think of that?"

Gavin kept his expression stony, though his heart hammered. "If that's what you think is best, Father, you can count on me."

"A certain former president promised to fundamentally transform the United States of America. Be assured that if you are chosen for this mission and are successful, you will, in fact, do just that."

Father drained his drink and rose, pulling something from his pocket. He slid a music CD across the table toward his son. "I want you to listen to that."

It was a Landon Jeffers greatest hits CD. Gavin recalled Landon from high school; they'd moved in different circles, but Landon was the best pianist he'd ever heard. How could Landon or the CD be connected to this mission, beyond the fact that his latest mission had entailed a hit on Landon's mom?

"I have seen your music testing scores, and your skills are passable. I want you to listen to those songs so many times that you can hum them in your sleep. If you are chosen, this step will make your enhanced skills easier to execute."

"Yes, Father, I will."

Father rose and gave him a nod. He strode toward the door, stopped, and turned back. "Just for the record, Gavin, whether you live or die means very little to me. The greater good is always my priority. Besides, I have several more sons, assassins just like you. If I lose one, what does it matter? I always have others to turn to."

PART 3

THE MALFUNCTIONER

30

J ust after ten thirty in my suite at the Hilton in downtown Houston, I eyed my laptop screen and monitored a program that told me more than I needed to know about Cynthia Lemke, the woman sleeping in the room next to mine.

Leaning back in my chair, I wrestled with my conscience, ill at ease with this forced form of voyeurism. Okay, I'd turned my back when she changed her clothes, but still the very idea of watching her every move through a variety of gadgets rankled my sensibilities.

In no way had *I* enjoyed being watched and controlled not so long ago. Giving her the same treatment the cop Ray Galotta had given me last fall must be nothing short of a twisted form of irony.

We'd met Stu, the tech guy, late in the afternoon before tonight's concert, and he'd given me tutorials and a gym bag full of gadgets: everything from hidden cameras and bugs to heat-seeking devices. Amazing. The program I watched now, using various cameras and listening devices covertly placed in Cynthia's room and stationed at various locations in the hotel, monitored her nighttime activity and alerted me if, for any reason, she got up in the night.

Right now Cynthia appeared to be asleep in bed. According to her file, she wasn't a sleepwalker, so if she rose in the night, beyond needing to use the restroom, she could be on a mission unless she had other reasons, as yet unknown.

Of course, if Amee had simply agreed to inform me when Cynthia would be sent on her next mission, I could have been prepared. But no. This was apparently my test, too. I knew nothing beyond my new role as the one assigned to watch her every move, thanks to a battery of high-tech surveillance devices.

Reality woke me shortly before midnight when a squealing alert from my laptop through earbuds made me lurch out of bed and hit the space bar to turn it off. In the live video feed, Cynthia pulled on a red jacket and headed toward the door.

Not knowing when or if I'd be needed, I'd slept in my jeans and now grabbed a black fleece and pulled it over my red T-shirt. I snagged a baseball cap and eased into the hallway.

Not a moment too soon.

In the same millisecond, a flash of red took a right at the hallway's end. The afternoon's crash course had provided know-how on shadowing someone without being detected, but with no previous experience, I couldn't shake the feeling of being an incompetent novice.

I reached the hotel's main lobby just as Cynthia pushed through the front glass doors and slipped into the night. She stuffed her hands into front jean pockets, her brown hair bouncing on her shoulders. Where could she be heading at this late hour?

Not until now had I given serious thought to how far my conscience would allow me to take this surveillance business. If the Justice Club controlled her steps, Cynthia likely had no idea where she was going, a fact both alarming and pathetic. My mission to educate her on how the Justice Club worked required that I track her and discern when she woke from her daydream state, if she woke at all. Amee had suggested Cynthia might be a malfunctioner like me, so perhaps I'd find my opportunity if I remained patient.

Then there came the inevitable question about her safety. If she found herself in danger, I'd been granted permission to step in. Even wake her from her implant-driven trance, if need be. But that was where my role ended. By no means could I interfere if she hurt or killed someone. After all, her mission could be a kill order, just as mine had been.

But if something went wrong for some reason, I had no weapon to defend her or myself. And if police showed up, we were supposed to run.

At the McDonald's across the street, I stayed hidden behind a shrub while she bought coffee and headed back outdoors, pausing to take off the lid and blow on the steaming brew. Without a glance my direction, she sauntered down the street toward tall, silent buildings, with so many windows alight against the blackness of night.

A question probed my instincts. Had she really been programmed to get coffee? Perhaps the coffee helped her blend in. Or maybe she could be tailing somebody who'd left McDonald's ahead of her. Nope, she appeared to be on her own with no trajectory of tailing anyone.

Perhaps she simply enjoyed nighttime strolls to clear her head. Getting a workout at a gym could be hard to come by while on tour.

Could she be on her way to meet a friend? Or lover? Who might she know in Houston?

The many questions batting around in my brain only revealed the stark reality that I knew very little about Cynthia Lemke. And for some reason, Amee had chosen to kept me mostly in the dark.

Remember, this is your test, too. Recall what Stu taught you. Find out what you can without tipping your hand.

Cynthia neared an empty intersection, yellow traffic lights blinking, and crossed without pausing. A block away she slowed at a bus stop, apparently intending to hitch a ride.

My first predicament.

If she grabbed a bus, I'd have no choice but to follow her. But what if she saw me? I'd blow my cover.

Didn't matter. By no means, I'd been told, could I lose her. Risks came with the territory.

Then don't let her see you.

At the opposite end of the bus stop, with my back facing her and her vague shape reflected in a building's window opposite, I waited for our ride. Surreptitious glances confirmed her fixation on the coffee; she never once glanced my direction. Perhaps the implant's directives were so single focused that she obeyed without awareness of anyone around her. The possibility made sense. Unless they were part of her mission, passersby could be only incidental to whatever the Justice Club had in mind.

The approaching rumble and squeaky brakes announced the bus's arrival. Cynthia and an old woman, who looked like she'd awoken from a park bench not so long ago, with gray hair matted on one side of her head, comprised the only passengers beyond me who initially occupied the bus. Cynthia chose a seat toward the back, so I slouched near the front, keeping my head down, glad I'd grabbed the hat. It gave at least some cover for my black crew cut and partially hid my face if I kept my head down.

The listless-eyed black driver closed the door and released the hissing brakes. We'd scarcely gone two blocks when he slowed to a stop. Three young men got on, one tall, thin black man and two short and stocky Hispanics. I overheard one of the Hispanic guys call the black guy Leonard. Their proximity suggested they must be traveling together. Their bling glittered, and their low voices droned in street talk peppered with Spanish and obscenities.

The unsavory aroma gusting me in their wake warmed my heart with gratitude that they'd chosen the middle of the bus to chortle and trade dirty jokes in Spanish. The driver's mirror, however, allowed me to keep an eye on them. Seemingly ensconced in her own world, Cynthia huddled in a window seat, gaze glued outdoors, as if mesmerized by the city sliding past the glass.

So far little activity justified my missing precious sleep. What if Cynthia's mission took all night, only to come to nothing? A fatigued Landon Jeffers wouldn't be so thrilled in the morning.

No, if she's on a mission, she's out here for a reason.

At the next stop, the threesome got off, with Cynthia tailing them.

Making my exit, I hung back in shadows and watched to see how this scenario might play itself out. Not so smart for her to be going after those homeboys. Nor logical, since she'd never seen them before. Could this move imply programming from the Justice Club? It seemed logical if Cynthia behaved out of character, but I didn't yet know her well enough to know that.

She matched their purposeful stride while lingering about forty feet back. After another forty-foot gap, I shadowed her, occasionally darting into doorways and behind telephone poles in case she might glance back. But she never did.

Could one of the guys be her mark? Her focused stride suggested as much. What if she made her move but something went wrong? Again, questions about her safety heightened my concern. If tables turned and the threesome went after Cynthia, I'd have no choice but to intervene.

A few blocks later, Cynthia took a quick right and strode toward ShortTrip, a small convenience store, with Leonard and his buddies nowhere to be seen. She slipped inside.

Had they gone inside ahead of her?

I lingered, undecided. If I went in after her, I risked tipping my hand. But if I stayed outside, waiting for her to come out, a rear exit could provide her means of vanishing into the night. I'd be in big trouble, maybe even lethal trouble, if Amee could be taken seriously.

No choice. I could pretend to be looking for the men's room. But if we bumped into each other, she still might recognize me.

So don't bump into her. If she's there, give her your back, keep your head down, and go down another aisle.

Bracing myself, I opened the glass door and entered, taking in my surroundings with one sweeping glance. No Cynthia anywhere.

The overly bright lights illumined narrow aisles crammed with everything from greeting cards and cold medicine to beef jerky and canned soups. Behind the counter, flanked by boxes of various types of cigarettes, a bored-looking Caucasian with round, Harry Potter-style glasses was glued to his smartphone, probably surfing the Net. He cast a disinterested glance in my direction before turning back to whatever intrigued him.

Maybe Cynthia had headed to the women's room, which a sign told me was near the back. Taking the nearest aisle, I froze. Leonard and his buddies were huddled around smutty magazines, their whispers punctuated by girlish giggles. Backtracking, I chose the next aisle, certain they hadn't spotted me. Surely they'd remember me from the bus; seeing me again so soon could trigger unwelcome attention.

Heading toward an aisle near the back of the store, I neared a stack of newspapers, and a cringe-worthy publicity photo of myself stared me down. The headline? JEFFERS PLAYS TRADEMARK FAVORITES DURING REUNION TOUR.

Priceless.

Pulling the hat lower to hide more of my face, I ambled past products for diarrhea and constipation, aware of the door to the women's restroom only six feet to my left.

Seconds later, the door squeaked open, and Cynthia swept by, only inches away, the aroma of her strong perfume chasing after her. Facing the products, I watched her retreating back out of the corner of my eye. She'd ditched the coffee cup.

My view over the aisles proved sufficient to track her movements. She wandered over to the hair products aisle and appeared to be choosing a new hair color while revealing a cute mannerism. Her index finger tapped her bottom lip while she considered the choices.

BAM!

The gun blast deafened me. My body jerked involuntarily.

Close.

It came from somewhere ahead to my right.

I flattened myself on the floor and shot a look toward the front of the store, the source of the sound. But the aisle ending confined my visual field.

Had somebody been shot?

Please, God, not Cynthia.

31

Monday, March 28

A male voice shouted. "What are you doing?"

The Harry Potter lookalike at the register.

On hands and knees, I crept toward the aisle opening. If Cynthia had any brains, she'd stay put.

Another voice.

"Look, we don't wanna hurt you, okay? Just give us your dough."

That was Leonard.

"What are you talking about, man? I'm not giving you anything."

Leonard: "C'mon, give me your money now. I'll hurt you if I have to."

Apparently, it had been a warning shot. But still no sign of Cynthia.

Near my aisle's end, I paused and questioned the wisdom of getting any closer. Though the cash register lay beyond sight, a round mirror in the corner near the ceiling provided a glimpse.

Sure enough. The threesome held the cashier at gunpoint.

One of the Hispanic guys stood by the store entrance, apparently to keep an eye out, while Leonard, the assumed leader, pointed a gun at the Harry Potter lookalike.

The second Hispanic guy had climbed over the counter and appeared to be trying without success to get the cash drawer open. The cashier pressed his back against the cigarette cartons, hands in the air, eyes wide and panicky.

What if Cynthia had used the distraction to make her exit? Too bad. I couldn't track her now unless I risked getting myself killed.

Voices rose in anger and alarm. In the mirror the cashier pulled out a hidden gun, and Leonard backed away with his Hispanic sidekicks, hands raised. While the Harry Potter lookalike cussed them out, the threesome sprang toward the doors and fled into the night.

But the cashier wasn't finished. Keeping his gun raised, he chased them and took the fight outdoors, profanity loud on his lips.

Seconds passed.

BAM! BAM!

The floor greeted my flattened frame again, my pulse tapping in my throat. The gunshots outdoors had been close.

Now what?

Silence.

Sucking in some air, I rose to my knees. Investigate or wait until I knew it was safe? But how would I know, and still I had no clue of Cynthia's whereabouts. Maybe the threesome had gunned down the cashier and would be back for—

A familiar red jacket flared across my aisle opening.

Rising, I edged forward and stole a peek.

Cynthia had somehow gotten the cash drawer open and stuffed wads of cash into her pockets. With a furtive glance around that missed me, she dashed toward the entrance and hustled outside. Nearby, the cry of sirens pierced the night.

THE HARRY POTTER lookalike lay on the bloody sidewalk only twenty feet from the store. Unseeing eyes fixed on the night sky, glasses positioned crookedly on his face, an ugly wound in his chest. People had started to gather. Cynthia knelt beside his body.

I glanced around. No sign of Leonard or his buddies.

Heart-chilling sirens wailed, perhaps only blocks away.

Cynthia's response to my appearance proved unpredictable, but I had no choice. The situation had deteriorated beyond caution and good sense. Where had the threesome gone? Most likely far from here, but if they'd seen Cynthia and thought she could ID them, the danger hadn't gone far.

Grabbing her arm, I helped her up, unsure whether she still operated in the Justice Club's daydream state. "We need to go," I said. "You can't stay here."

She blinked a few times and peered into my face. "Landon, wha—what are *you* doing here?"

"I—" I groped for words, realizing I hadn't preplanned my cover story. "I was concerned about you."

"You mean, you've been following me?"

What could I say?

She looked around as if in a daze. Clearly she'd just awoken from her mission, clueless about what she'd just done. Another malfunctioner like me. "Where am I? I was in bed just a few minutes ago. What's going on?"

"There's no time to explain now," I said. "We need to go."

I touched her arm, but she jerked away. "Why is this man lying here? Is he—"

"Yes, there's nothing we can do for him. C'mon."

"And flee a crime scene? I don't think so."

She wanted to be a Girl Scout at time like this?

Still gaping at the corpse, she shook her head. "What happened to him?"

Sirens, only a block away now, discouraged further delay. I grabbed her by the arm and pulled her from the scene. "We have to go. Now. You can't be found here."

Cynthia jerked from my hold and turned in a full circle, taking in the city around her. "How did I get downtown?"

"Cynthia, check your pockets."

Her hands dug in and came out loaded with cash. She gasped. "Where did all this money come from?"

"How are you going to explain that to the police? Are you coming with me now?"

She met my fast stride for several blocks before we paused in a dark alley to catch our breath. Then she demanded answers, and I told her everything she needed to know about the implant but wouldn't be happy to hear. Small featured and pretty, she had to be the last person anyone would suspect of robbing a convenience store. But rob it, she had.

When I finished detailing the implant and her now-stolen life, she leaned against a dumpster, shadowy in the streetlight. White-knuckled it with a curse. "You mean to tell me ... there's an implant in my head that's making me do these things?"

"I'm sorry."

A look of betrayal flashed in her eyes. "You're *sorry*? You mean, you're responsible?"

I lifted placating hands. "No, nothing like that. But I know what it's like. I've been there too."

"Of course. Your brain tumor. You mean, they've been controlling you too? They used the surgery to get to you, just like they did to me."

"Look, I know about the motorcycle accident and what happened to you and your fiancé. I'm sorry."

"There you go again—apologizing for something that isn't your fault." She pulled out the money, eyes bugging. "I can't believe I stole all this."

The sight of the cash surprised me too. Could the Justice Club have adjusted her mission in real time? No way could anyone have predicted the shootout or available cash. But maybe the Justice Club had computer algorithms that adjusted as events did.

No telling what technology could do these days in the wrong hands.

"You have no choice any more than I do," I said. "They control both of us now."

But even as I said the words, they rang false in my mind. Did I believe what I'd just told her? Had Jesus saved me from the Justice Club's evil control, or hadn't He? No time to wrestle with the answer now.

Her shaky fingers massaged her temples. Her voice quavered. "So let me get this straight. If I don't give in and let these—these lunatics—control my life, if I try to run, they'll kill my parents?"

My mom occupied the forefront of my thoughts. "Or hurt them really bad. Yeah."

"Okay." She nodded as if slowly taking things in, her gaze fixed on the cracked concrete.

Surprised, I studied her pretty face, expecting hysterics or something similar. Tears for sure. Definitely more than this. Could she be in shock? Only moments ago, she'd woken and found a dead man lying at her feet. Perhaps that trauma, coupled with this overwhelming news, had short-circuited something.

Part of me hungered to take her in my arms. When this impulse registered, I studied her with new eyes. Cynthia, after all, wasn't an unattractive woman, and we had more in common now.

She searched my face. "So how do I become free from this?"

Jesus's words from John 8 passed like a ticker tape across my mind. *Therefore if the Son makes you free, you shall be free indeed.*

Did I really believe those words?

"I can't talk about that," I said. "You run, and we're both dead."

"Great. So I'm sort of in your charge now, huh?"

"Something like that."

"They're listening to everything we say, aren't they?"

"And watching."

She cursed. "But there has to be a way out. This is ridiculous."

"I know how you feel, but don't even think about running. You try, and it won't end pretty."

"It sounds like you speak from experience."

"Let's just say I chose to run once. Innocent people died." I glanced at my watch. "C'mon. Let's get a taxi back to the hotel. I'll tell you all about it on the way."

"Wait." She looked down at the stolen money. "What do we do about all this? I shouldn't keep it."

A shadow separated from the dark building and congealed into a man. Leonard from the convenience store, minus his Hispanic buddies, pointed a gun at us. "I'll take care of that, lady. No problem."

"Please—please don't hurt us," Cynthia said.

"Look, I'm not gonna hurt anybody. I just want the money."

While Cynthia spilled the loot, I shook my head. Amazing that, after everything that had happened, this loser would still walk away with the cash.

"Thanks a lot. I appreciate it." He shoved the bills out of sight, gave us a toothy grin, and vanished in the night.

Cynthia buried her face in her hands, shoulders hiked. "Oh, this is nuts. I need to go home."

The urge to hug her nearly overwhelmed me. A hand on her shoulder sufficed. "C'mon, let's head back to the hotel and get some rest. You'll feel better in the morning."

She wiped her teary face. "No, I don't mean the hotel. I mean home —Indiana. It's too soon after Lee's death and my operation. And now this. I should have given everything more time. I see that now. I wasn't ready."

Unsure what to do, hating to see a woman cry, I put an arm around her. She didn't push me away. Rather, she leaned into me, the aroma of her heady perfume enveloping us. She wrapped her arms around me and pressed her head against my chest. My arms reciprocated in return without conscious thought.

Oh boy.

This didn't happen to me every day.

"Just give it more time, okay?" I said. "Really, everything will look a lot better in the morning. Besides, I haven't even heard you play your pipes yet. I've been looking forward to it."

Not even the tiniest smile could be had. Given the circumstances, I suppose my attempt at humor and encouragement sounded pretty lame. And inappropriate. Had I forgotten how I'd felt after learning the truth about my brain surgery and the implant?

And I'd been the bearer of the sad, pathetic truth. This new job stank, though holding a woman in my arms made it slightly less repulsive.

32

An almost indistinguishable cry roused Jade Hamilton from fragments of happy fantasies. The memory of her dreams, of her and Landon experiencing casual days, free from the Justice Club's clutches, fractured when her eyes flicked open.

She sat up in bed and rubbed her face, waiting for full awareness to descend. It took its sweet time in coming. A quick glance at her bedside clock confirmed it was well past two a.m.

Another sound creaked from somewhere in the house. She leaned forward and listened. Head cocked. Fingers tight on bedding.

Certainly couldn't be a prowler, not with her dad's fancy security system. Actually it was *her* system, since she'd paid for it.

So what could it be?

Swinging her legs to the floor, Jade slid her feet into plush slippers and crossed to her bedroom door. Eased it open. In the dark hallway, lit only by a yellowed beam cast by the bathroom night-light, she hesitated. The bedroom next to hers belonged to her dad. Nothing unusual emanated from his slightly open door.

She checked Henry's bedroom at the end of the hall and found him asleep, clutching a stuffed Buzz Lightyear. Smiling, she returned to the corridor.

From somewhere beyond the end of the hallway came a soft *thump*. Not of natural origin.

Could there be an intruder in the house?

Maggie had left for her hotel hours ago, anticipating a sleepless night while the FBI tracked the operative. If only she'd stayed …

To Jade's right stood the closed door to the guest bedroom, Sandra Jeffers's room. If the security system granted her a good night's rest, it had been worth every penny.

No need to wake Dad or Sandra. Time to check on whatever it is and get back to bed.

Jade halted when a new noise met her ears. The closing of a kitchen cupboard door.

Perhaps her dad, woken by nightmares fueled by Vietnam experiences, had decided to fix some warm milk. Sometimes insomnia came calling, but God had taught him long ago that no bottle offered the solution to his problem. But warm milk helped.

Jade crept closer to the kitchen, its lights casting shadows in odd geometric patterns across the hardwood floor. Rounding the corner, she faced the granite countertop, cherrywood cabinets, stainless-steel appliances.

And a stranger in a navy plaid shirt.

She stiffened.

A blond-haired man she'd never seen before turned and faced her, his handsome face registering no surprise by her presence. In fact, he didn't look at her. Face expressionless, the stranger had taken a sharp knife from the butcher block and held it before him, wide eyes fastened to it like he was mesmerized. He wore an odd headset with a tiny camera perched over his right ear.

Videotaping their house?

Did he even know she stood there?

She considered asking who he was, but an inner voice told her not to wake him from his apparent trance.

How had he gotten in without triggering the alarm? No time to figure that out now.

Sleepwalking mode, Maggie had said.

Could it be possible?

A Justice Club operative here? In their kitchen? On a mission? Right now?

A mission to do what?

Could it be the same guy Maggie had interviewed, who'd attacked Sandra?

A slight move to the left adjusted her field of vision. On the floor next to his feet, just beyond the island, lay Sandra Jeffers.

Eyes closed. Unmoving.

Jade's hand flew to her mouth to muffle her gasp. Had he stabbed her?

She involuntarily backed away, icy bands clamping so tightly around her chest that she could barely breathe. No visible signs of blood on the blade. But why didn't Sandra move? Had she passed out?

Maybe I interrupted him. But from what?

His eyes snapped to her face, jaw tightening.

Run, Jade. Get out of here.

The panic button in the living room—could she reach it in time? One way to find out.

She spun and fled.

Heavy footfalls thundered behind her in hot pursuit.

"Dad! Help me!" she screamed.

The moonlight-hazed dining room blurred past her. She sprinted down the hallway and rounded the corner, her slippered feet gripping the hardwood floor.

Grabbing the wall to keep her balance, she raced into the living room. His panting and grunting rang in her ears. The sharp knife close.

A sixth sense prodded her to lunge to the left. His hand slashed air, the blade barely missing her. The wind from his unsuccessful downward thrust caressed her.

Inertia sent his frame crashing into hers, and they both went down with grunts in a tangle of arms and legs. His free hand swung and met her face.

Stinging impact. Disorienting.

He rolled on top of her. Grabbed her left arm with a strong hand. Pinned it down.

The coppery flavor of blood from the corner of her mouth. Panic flamed. Gasps burst out of her.

A sliver of moonlight between the drapes silhouetted his face and silvered the steel. It swung down again—

—she somehow jerked away—

—and hit the carpeted floor.

"Dad! Dad!" she screamed.

The man pressed down on top of her again, so heavy. His gasps blasted her.

Panic writhed like a wild cat trapped under her skin, seeking a way out.

She kneed the intruder in the groin. He rolled off her in a whimper.

Springing to her feet, she raced to the bookshelf. Hit the panic button.

A deafening alarm. Help on the way.

Lights blazed from the hallway.

The operative rose with an evil smirk and lunged toward her again, knife raised.

She screamed.

Gunshots rang out. Once, twice.

With each blast, the man's body spasmed.

Hallway light silhouetted her father, gun at arms' length.

The intruder crumpled at her feet.

33

J ade clung to her dad in the dining room, waiting for his strong arms to cease her trembling. She avoided looking toward the living room, where the body of her would-be killer still lay. Unmoving.

Would someone please just take the body away?

The sobs made her chest ache, her eyes puffy from crying. She clutched a wad of sodden tissues and drew a shaky breath.

Thank God Henry was safe. Sandra had agreed to look after him and keep him from seeing the body.

Sirens wailing in the distance drew closer. Maybe a neighbor had heard the gunshots and called the police, since the security system had obviously been on the blink despite the alarm.

"Please don't let go of me," she said.

Gordon tightened his embrace. "Don't worry. I don't plan to."

"Did you kill him?"

"I'm afraid so."

"How do you know?"

"I know." The Vietnam vet who'd experienced atrocities he'd to this day never told her about could discern a living man from a dead one.

She sighed-sobbed. "I can't believe what just happened. They won't arrest you, will they?"

"I don't think so. I was just protecting you, and you were a witness. But let's hope Maggie shows up soon."

"You saved my life. If you hadn't shown up when you did—"

"Shhh. Try not to think about it."

"I can try all I want. Succeeding is another matter. I can still see his face, the evil in his eyes."

"Don't. You're safe. That's what matters."

"I just don't understand. Why Sandra? Why me?"

He hesitated. "I think you already know the answer."

Landon.

Somehow the attack must be connected to his being in the clutches of the Justice Club. They'd tried to kill Sandra and failed. It made perfect sense that they'd try again. And she'd apparently gotten in the way.

WHILE ONE COP led family members to Gordon's study to question them one by one, another cordoned off the crime scene. Later, Maggie arrived and spoke to the officers in hushed tones while Gordon, Jade, and Sandra sat across from each other at the dining room table and sipped herbal tea. Sandra cuddled Henry close, his wide-eyed, questioning glance darting from face to face.

Jade made eye contact with Sandra. "Are you doing okay?"

Sandra shook her head, arms wrapped around herself as if unable to get warm. "Not really. I don't understand what happened other than that I must have passed out. Why did that guy come after *me*? Merciful heavens, somebody tried to kill me just last week, and now this."

"Maggie will get all this sorted out," Gordon said.

"The important thing," Jade said, gripping Sandra's hand, "is that you're okay."

"I suppose so. But will I never have a moment's peace?" she said in a husky voice, eyes moist. "Getting stabbed once was bad enough. Now a second guy tried and failed. Won't somebody else come now that this guy failed? You know what they say. 'The third time's the charm.'"

"There won't be a third time if I have anything to say about it," Gordon said in an unflinching tone. "I'm putting a lock on your door, and you're keeping it locked at night from now on. And I'll sleep with a gun if I have to."

"It might be best if you go with the ambulance," Jade said to her, "and get everything checked out. After all, you were unconscious for a while."

"No, I'm okay. Really. But it's a good thing God brought you along when He did."

Maggie sauntered in, hair disheveled, eyes bloodshot like she'd already had a demanding day, and so far the night offered no reprieve. She filled a coffee cup to the brim and didn't even bother reaching for sweetener. "Wow, what a night!" she said, taking a seat across from Jade and sipping her joe.

"Is there anything you can tell us?" Jade said.

"You all gave the police a statement, right?" When everyone nodded, Maggie said, "We won't know much more until the cops finish up here. The police will take the body away after they're done processing the scene."

"Any idea who the intruder was?" Gordon asked.

Maggie shook her head, hands hugging her mug. "Not yet. He carried no ID, but there's a telling surgical scar on his head. For now that tells me all I need to know. There'll be a full investigation, of course—fingerprints, DNA, the whole nine yards—but don't worry. The sheriff and I have been working together, and this attack, I'm sorry to say, fits the general pattern. This attack again points to the Justice Club."

Glances passed around the table. Henry just stared at her.

"Now," Maggie said, "who wants to tell me what happened in your own words? I know you talked to the police, but I need to hear this for myself."

Jade went first, starting with the noise that woke her and described what everyone already knew. The others added their two cents, and Sandra told her side of the story.

"He obviously came for you, Sandra," Maggie said, "but I have no idea why, other than to perhaps finish the job when the other guy failed."

"Yeah, they want me dead all right," Sandra said in a shaky voice, "and they'll never stop." Jade gripped her hand.

Maggie said, "Did the guy say anything to you?"

"I don't remember. I must have passed out after he injected me."

Maggie stared. "What? I thought you just fainted."

"No. He must have snuck into my room and was bending over me. I woke up when I felt the pinprick in my arm. But then I drifted off after that. Couldn't keep my eyes open."

"We need to get you to the hospital," Maggie said, "and make sure you're okay. We don't know what he injected into you. We need to find out to make sure there are no long-term effects."

Sandra nodded, even more fear filling her eyes.

"What I want to know," Gordon said in an aggravated tone, "is how he even got in the house. I mean, why pay big bucks for a security system if it doesn't do what it's supposed to do?"

"I know the system was on before I went to bed," Jade said. "I checked."

"Were there any odd visitors to the house this week?" Maggie said, searching each face in turn. "Any strangers at the door? Maybe an unusual salesperson?"

"There was one guy I let in," Sandra said. "He said he was from the local power company and needed to check some wiring in the basement."

"That smells fishy to me," Gordon said, getting up. "I'll be right back."

He returned a few minutes later. "Our visitor—whoever he was—disarmed the component that notifies the police of any break-ins. So even if somebody forced a door or window open, none of the authorities would have been notified."

"But the panic button," Jade said.

He shook his head. "Just a lot of noise. Nobody was notified."

"But then how did the police know to come to the house?" Jade said.

"Neighbors heard gunshots and called them, the cops said." Maggie turned to Sandra. "Do you remember what this guy from the power company looked like?"

That finger worked at her upper lip again. "He was dark haired with a thick, black beard. Black eyes. I don't recall ever seeing him before."

Maggie jotted down the details. "Well, at least that's something. If you remember more details later, even if you don't think they're important, you will let me know, won't you?"

Sandra nodded, her chagrined gaze meeting Gordon's. "I'm sorry. It's all my fault. If I wasn't so gullible ..."

"Hey, no worries," Gordon said. "You had no reason to suspect anything other than what the guy said."

She gave him a grateful smile.

"So what do we do now?" Jade said.

"We consider ourselves very fortunate, especially the two of you." Maggie's gaze flicked between Jade and Sandra. "Things could have been much worse."

"How did your surveillance of the other operative go?" Jade asked Maggie.

"It didn't. The guy made up with his wife after their fight and went to bed. The last I heard, he hasn't left the house. I think the Justice Club realized we were onto him, and now they've backed off. But we'll keep an eye on him in case he moves."

Maggie leaned back and drained her cup. She gave Sandra an arm pat. "I'm so glad you're okay. I need to talk to Jade for a minute, but then I'm taking you to the hospital to get you checked out. Better safe than sorry."

After they all got up and put their dirty cups in a sink of sudsy water to soak, Maggie motioned Jade to Gordon's office and closed the door. That wedding band on Maggie's finger glinted in the half-light. Had her husband passed away?

Jade considered asking but instead said, eyebrows raised, "So what's up?"

Maggie sat on the edge of Gordon's massive desk. Patriotic buttons

and framed photos of renowned presidents and generals were everywhere. A die-hard patriot for sure.

"I'm not satisfied with Sandra's explanation," she said.

"What—you think she's lying?"

"Of course not. But things don't add up. So why was the intruder
here?"

Jade shrugged. "Like you and Sandra said, maybe he came to finish
the job."

"Okay, so let's assume we're right. Then why didn't he?"

"What do you mean?"

"Due to the hijacked security system, he could have quietly
killed Sandra in her bedroom and left without anybody knowing,
but that's not what he did. He carried her downstairs to the
kitchen. Then what did he do? He left her on the floor and lingered.
Why?"

Jade shrugged. "Yeah, it doesn't really make sense, does it?"

"It's what we in law enforcement call a 'high-risk crime.' The
longer he lingered in the house, the greater the likelihood that somebody would discover him. He purposely took his time and made so
much racket that you woke up and went to explore. By the time you
found him, Sandra lay unconscious on the floor, and he was playing
with a knife from the butcher block."

"I assumed he planned to use it on Sandra and that I must have
interrupted him."

"Maybe that's what he *wanted* you to think. It's almost like he was
waiting for you to show up."

Jade stared at her. "You don't think—"

"I think *you* may have been his target. And maybe Sandra was just
the bait."

The tightness in Jade's throat nearly strangled her reply. "What?
But why me?"

"I don't know. If things aren't going well for Landon, maybe they
want you for leverage. But the guy didn't seem interested in kidnapping you, did he?"

"No. He wanted me dead."

"Or maybe Landon is such putty in the Justice Club's hands now that you're no longer a needed pawn for persuasion." She paused. "But then why send someone after you at all?"

Jade shrugged. "I don't know. But I don't really get what's up with Landon these days. Maybe there's more to the story, and he's not saying. Or maybe he can't."

"Seems clear to me. The Justice Club must be in full control of him now. Otherwise he'd still be on the run."

"I wish we could know for sure."

"There may be a way, but first I have some breaking news you may find interesting. Please keep this between us."

"Of course. I'm all ears."

"On the same day Landon had a concert in a Dallas park, a woman, Leslie Neumann, jumped to her death from the fifty-third floor of the Waldorf Astoria Hotel across town."

"That's terrible. But what does it have to do with Landon?"

"I requested a copy of the police report. One detail caught my eye. Someone must have been at the scene at the same time or shortly after Leslie jumped. The unknown subject apparently lost his supper on the balcony. I know this is disgusting, but vomit is a valid source of DNA."

"I didn't know that. But again, what does any of this have to do with Landon?"

"It appeared to be a clear case of suicide, but on a hunch, I requested that the DNA be tested."

"Don't tell me. It's Landon's."

Maggie nodded. "Apparently that dead cop, Ray Galotta, had listed Landon's DNA in a national database."

Jade leveled her gaze at her. "Did you say the fifty-third floor? Landon has had a terrible fear of heights for years. That was certainly high enough to make him sick. But why would he be involved in somebody's suicide? Any idea what he was doing there?"

Maggie shook her head. "Several pieces are missing from the puzzle, but I've put a few together. After the outdoor concert, Landon was invited to a reception at the hotel. How he crossed paths with Leslie Neumann is anybody's guess."

"Surely there's video surveillance footage from the hotel and other public places."

"But that's what's odd. All video has been erased or oddly misplaced. It's like somebody has purposely scrubbed everything that might connect Landon to this woman's death."

"So you think the Justice Club is involved?"

"Uh-huh. We might be looking at more than a suicide."

"And Landon appears to be involved."

Maggie hesitated. "Has it occurred to you that Landon could be a willing participant with the Justice Club at this point? Maybe he even pushed her."

Jade folded her arms. "No way. That's ridiculous. If Landon *is* involved, it isn't because he wants to be. They probably have a large target painted on my back the minute he fails to comply."

"But see, maybe that's why somebody came after you tonight. Perhaps Landon blew an assignment, and they were dangling you as a threat. Maybe they decided to make good on it."

A sick feeling rippled through Jade's gut. "If only we could know for sure."

Maggie's eyes sparkled. "There's a way. Why not ask him?"

"Are you serious?"

"Absolutely. Look. We know exactly where he is, thanks to his concert schedule."

"I want to come too."

Maggie lifted a hand of refusal. "No way. That's absolutely out of the question. You're not an FBI agent, and it would be too dangerous."

"I guess you're right. I'd love to see him though."

"Maybe I could include you in a video conference call. But before I go, I need to do some prep work first. If he is working for the Justice Club, I want to give him an offer to walk away that is so sweet, he can't possibly refuse."

34

R oom service arrived on time, just as I'd requested, but my mind wandered elsewhere. I still gnawed on the topic of Cynthia and our nocturnal adventure, which had left me feeling well rested despite the sleep deprivation.

That feeling of my arm around her and her snuggling against me ...

But then thoughts of Jade stifled any romantic feelings I might have had for Cynthia Lemke.

Soon Amee would drop by, wanting a full rundown of what had transpired. Surely she already knew, so in many ways this debriefing comprised part of my training. How well I'd retained key details from the night before could factor into her evaluation.

While I puzzled over the contrasting images of diminutive Cynthia playing a flute onstage and stuffing her pockets with stolen cash, the attendant who'd delivered the meal on wheels waited patiently for his tip. I gave him a once-over to ensure I hadn't overlooked Monty in disguise.

Nope. Definitely not my friend from the resistance.

When had I last bumped into Monty anyhow? Two days ago? Some words of wisdom at this point might be helpful. He'd suggested that I had a role in something big coming down the pike, but playing babysitter to Cynthia hardly fit that picture.

"Oh sorry," I said to the attendant. Forgetting my wallet, I slid my hand into a front pocket and pulled out a large wad of cash.

My eyes rounded.

It was the money Cynthia had stolen from the convenience store, the same cash Leonard had later stolen from her—had to be. But how had it come into *my* possession?

My mouth watered. A subtle itch began at the back of my throat, the harbinger of a daymare. Trips to my past, once common, had been rare of late.

Oh no. Not now.

The attendant cleared his throat impatiently.

I stuffed the cash back into my pocket. Yanking out my wallet, I gave him a big tip and hurriedly sent him merrily on his way. The door had barely clicked shut behind him before the full-throttle daymare tackled me to the floor. Behind my closed eyelids, I …

… find myself heading down a dark alley, gun in hand. Hunting.

Leonard sees me and runs. I give chase and tackle him.

Knowing gunfire will attract too much attention, I put my gun away and wrap my hands around his neck. Start choking the guy. He begs me to stop, his words barely intelligible.

"Please, man! Take the money. I got little kids."

But I don't care about the money. This is for Cynthia …

Back in the hotel room, I crawled onto the bed. Staring at the ceiling, I hugged the life out of a pillow, my face and neck lathered in sweat. My heart pounded so fast and hard, my chest so tight, that I feared I might have a heart attack. Snatching several deep breaths, I waited for the ripple of nausea to pass. Tried to calm down.

How could I have hurt Leonard?

This wasn't supposed to happen.

The Justice Club must have sent me back downtown last night though I had no memory of them doing so. Once again that betrayed feeling of someone bypassing my free will stole over me.

Their using me for evil purposes while I slept had been the pattern last fall. Except hadn't God broken their stranglehold on my life?

In the blind corners of my eyes swelled a memory in full color, the image of a cop named Ray Galotta. Last October he'd commanded me to kill Jade, using my brain implant to literally point a gun at her head though I didn't want to. But I'd called on Jesus for help, trusting Him to save me—and not just because of the terrible deed Galotta wanted me to do.

And in that moment of transferred trust, the chains from Galotta and the puppet master had been broken. I had been set free, and I disobeyed his orders, saving both Jade and my mom.

My mother's words haunted me. *You don't have to do what these evil men want. You can say no.*

But if I was free, why had I last night behaved like an enslaved man?

If I possessed the money from Leonard, who'd stolen it from Cynthia, what had happened to him?

A knock on my door.

I sat up too quickly, and my head swam.

The familiar voice filtered through the door. "Maestro?"

When I opened the door, Amee breezed past me. Pausing, she turned as if seeing me for the first time and studied my face, then glanced at the untouched breakfast. "What? Not hungry this morning?"

I crossed to the bed and sat on the edge, deciding not to waste time. "I know what I did last night."

She leaned against the wall and nibbled on one of the snatched apple slices. "Of course, you do. That's why I'm here, to hear your side of how your adventure with Cynthia went."

"No, I mean later, after I brought her back to the hotel."

She stilled, the fruit poised an inch from her mouth. "Oh, you remember that, do you?"

"Your pals sent me back, didn't they?"

"So what do you recall?"

"I choking a man. Then I found this in my pocket this morning." I whipped out the cash and tossed it on the breakfast tray, glad to be rid of the blood money.

She lifted her eyes to mine. "Keep it. Consider it a perk for a job well done."

"I don't want the money. I just want to know what the Justice Club sent me to do and why."

Her mouth twisted to one side, half surprised, half irritated. "What do you think? None of this should come as any surprise to you. The man who held you up and took the money was a threat."

"A threat?"

"You're not thinking clearly, maestro. The guy held the two of you at gunpoint. Cynthia's life was threatened. That's a problem, remember? You were supposed to keep her safe. Then imagine if he recalled her face or yours. What sort of amazing stories could he share with the media or police about Landon Jeffers and the burglary of a convenience store? Now he won't be able to tell anyone."

An icicle traced a path down the middle of my back. "You mean—"

"You did what we programmed you to do. You terminated him, of course."

"What? But—" I sucked in a few breaths. Couldn't get enough oxygen. My head swam, and I sank to the edge of the bed, head in my hands.

She stepped closer with a taunting smile. "But what, Landon? Did you really think you'd somehow escaped our control? That was what you thought, wasn't it?"

Speech evaded me. My brain crept at the speed of sludge.

She waited for an answer I refused to give. "Wasn't it?"

I turned away from her and faced the wall.

Nevertheless, she inched closer, her exotic perfume tickling my nose, her voice only a decibel louder than a whisper. "You poor boy. You had some wild fantasy that finding Jesus would somehow make you immune from that implant still buried in your brain. Did you really think, just because we had you supervising Cynthia instead of doing missions in your sleep, that the Justice Club had somehow lost control of you? Maestro, I've got the slap of reality to deliver to you right now."

She drew closer until her hot breath made the back of my neck tingle. "You are just as much under the Justice Club's thumb as you ever were."

Lies. Had to be.

Or had I been terribly mistaken?

If so, death couldn't come any sooner.

Turning, I stared at her. Waited for this hellish speech to end. I could process the content later. If only she'd just go—

"As far as your role with Cynthia, you must have a poor memory of a policeman, a cop named Ray Galotta, who was in charge of overseeing you last fall. Remember what happened to a woman who tried to harm you?"

Sharon Bartholomew.

She'd thought I murdered her son, though Joey's fall long ago had been accidental. She didn't believe my declaration of innocence and rushed toward me with raised fists. But a bullet at the hands of Ray Galotta silenced her hollow allegations once and for all.

At the time I'd puzzled over Galotta's reason for eliminating Sharon. Now I understood. Her threat to my safety had provoked him.

Just as Ray Galotta had eliminated the threat to me, I'd eliminated the threat to Cynthia Lemke.

Of course.

But the realization that I'd actually killed a man this time and not just injured him nearly shoved me to my knees.

She must have confused my stunned silence with acquiescence. "Now that that part's settled," she said, "I want you to describe your little adventure last night in your own words. Those of us watching were most amused."

Yeah, I'm sure watching a man get gunned down outside a convenience store offered high entertainment.

But even as I described the event, the face of the man I'd murdered in cold blood burned in my brain.

35

The concert that night in New Orleans went off without a hitch. Despite the accusing voices shouting in my head—*Landon, you're a killer*—the band and I found our pace and seamlessly pulled everything together. The crowd got into the songs and several times rose to their feet in delight and appreciation, especially after I talked briefly about my cancer journey and the importance of having the right friends along for the ride. What I kept out, of course, was my strong urge to run for my life.

But even as I said the prepared words, I missed my mom and Jade, the loved ones I'd referred to indirectly. Where could they be? Had they really swallowed the deception about why I'd returned to the concert scene? I missed hearing their voices and their encouraging words—even just seeing their smiling faces from the other side of a kitchen table.

But how could I see them? I didn't want to place them in danger, and that was exactly where they'd be if I involved them in my problems again. Hopefully, they'd accepted my feeble excuses and would stay far away.

But the idea of running grew in its appeal. Every hour. Every minute.

How are you going to get out from under their thumb, Landon? What is the endgame? How will you know when you've found the information from the inside that Monty needs? What is the advanced program, and how are you supposed to know when you're in it?

Not a clue.

So we stick to the status quo. Until something happens to change it.

Monty's advice from the elevator slid back.

Consider the bigger picture. Think of the lives you'll be able to save because of your privileged position.

So if lives can be saved ...

How far are you willing to go? And what exactly is going too far?

Killing a man in my sleep?

During the concert, I suspected I might have glimpsed Monty somewhere in the crowd, a few rows back on house left, when I took my bow at the concert's end. But when I looked again, any hope of seeing him disintegrated. Must have been my imagination.

During the encore, Cynthia impressed the crowd with her penny-whistle solo of "Danny Boy." Earlier she'd played the flute effortlessly and then the uilleann pipes as if she'd grown up in Ireland.

Minutes after our final round of applause, the curtain came down, but the show was far from over. Two men in black suits and earpieces approached me backstage.

Secret service?

"You have a certain high-profile fan in the audience who would love to meet Cynthia Lemke," one said to me. "Is it possible for her to meet Cynthia in her dressing room? We'd need to escort her back, of course."

"Who exactly did you say you wanted to bring back here?" I said.

"Supreme Court Justice Maria Lamont."

Jaw dropping, I said, "Really?"

A patient smile. "We wouldn't be back here, speaking to you now, if we didn't mean it."

"Okay, well, sure. I guess it should be okay. I'll let Cynthia know. Then I can show you the way."

Within seconds the men in black left only their memory, and I kneaded my temples with two fingers, a dull ache throbbing above my eyebrows.

Amee materialized. "What's up?"

"Sorry. I guess I should have had them talk to you."

"Who?"

I told her what was up.

She beamed. "Maria Lamont wants to see Cynthia? Cool. Maria is quite talented on the woodwinds herself. Too bad she's a stinking conservative. We already have too many of her kind on the bench as it is."

"Wow, Amee. I never thought of you as political."

"Being your go-to girl never meant I didn't have a brain." She flashed me a grin and turned, giving me her back.

HOURS later my computer's alarm roused me from sleep, and I checked my video feed of Cynthia, still on assignment to watch her every move. I didn't look forward to more cloak-and-dagger missions at present, not with the latest revelation about my own nocturnal misadventures.

Stink.

An empty feed meant Cynthia had already fled. If I lost her, Amee would have my head.

Snatching my jacket, I grabbed my room key card and a flashlight, and barreled toward the hallway. I grabbed the elevator to the lobby and searched for my mark.

Not a trace of Cynthia anywhere.

If she'd already headed out on a mission and I'd lost her, how could I keep her safe?

I pushed through the front doors and searched the parking lot. In the distance Cynthia climbed into a taxi, which sped off seconds later. But I'd arrived too late.

Wait.

Earlier that day, after her sobering news that I'd murdered a black man named Leonard in cold blood, Amee had given me a new device, resembling a tiny cell phone, to aid me in my surveillance. Now the location of Cynthia's brain chip, represented by a blue dot on my screen, moved across a map of downtown New Orleans. As long as Cynthia didn't find a way to block the signal or achieve the herculean feat of finding someone to remove her implant, her signal would be detectable.

A few minutes later, my taxi headed away from the hotel, and Cynthia's blip on my screen dictated my driving directions. For all the driver knew, a friend was leading me on a scavenger hunt.

Eventually, the driver braked to a stop. "Buddy, is this really where you wanna be?" His accent, coupled with the deep voice, conjured visions of gumbo and southern fried chicken.

I'd been too glued to the screen to ensure I didn't lose Cynthia to take notice of our surroundings. A massive parking lot vanished in the darkness beyond his headlights.

"Where are we?" I said.

"Old abandoned Six Flags, the wrath of Hurricane Katrina. You sure this ain't some mistake?" The partially submerged amusement park had never recovered after the hurricane flooded New Orleans in 2005.

"No, this must be right." According to my gadget, Cynthia had to be somewhere straight ahead. I got out and paid him.

"I hear they still got security fellas keeping an eye on this place sometimes," he said with a warning look. "You be careful now."

"Thanks for the tip."

He grinned white teeth, flashing my cash. "No, thank *you*." I'd been generous.

Pulling away, he abandoned me to the night, which was humid and uncomfortably warm for a Midwesterner. Stripping off my jacket and tying it around my waist, I faced the dark and strode across the deserted parking lot. Ahead stood a high gate and the silhouettes of structures long forsaken.

An odd location to visit at the directive of the Justice Club. Or perhaps Cynthia had come here for another reason.

"Cynthia," I said under my breath, "what could a nice girl like you be doing in a strange place like this?"

36

I gripped the flashlight, tempted to turn it on, but reconsidered. If I used it, Cynthia might become wise to someone on her tail. Security personnel who roamed the acreage might see it too. On the other hand, the flashlight could be used as a weapon if the need arose, so I kept it handy but slid it into my pocket.

Moonlight offered sufficient ambient light to move around. Avoiding the front gate, I stuck to the barbwire fence encircling the massive place. One particular spot allowed easy entry without much fuss.

Inside the park, eyes glued to the tracker, I skirted a large building of unknown intent and adjusted my direction to keep myself centered on Cynthia's location. Debris crunched underfoot, and I winced.

Glancing around confirmed the reality and finality of the word *abandoned*. The fact that plenty of laughter and hot bodies had once crammed this place didn't seem possible. A first date, a first kiss, a first roller-coaster ride—they'd all happened here once. The surreal sensation of my haunting a place normally crammed with humanity but offering no more than two souls made the skin on the back of my neck pucker. I'd stepped onto the movie set for some apocalyptic flick.

What are you doing here, Cynthia?

Passing another dilapidated building, I approached an open area and stepped across asphalt littered with what resembled drywall and broken glass. Two feet away lay a busted fluorescent light fixture. Graffiti tattooed the side of the building across from me, its marquee announcing the home of Papa Russo's Pizza.

"Hide if you know what's good for you," someone had spray-painted on a wall along with a smattering of colorful expletives.

The message only enhanced the unsettling ambiance embracing this place.

The swinging flashlight beam ahead provoked my course correction. I darted toward the nearest building and hid behind a substantial column. Stole a glance.

Shining her flashlight on the cement before her, Cynthia sauntered down the middle of the street, as if oblivious of potential security guards monitoring this place.

Her stride slowed when she approached a large Ferris wheel called The Big Easy. Swiveling, she took in her derelict surroundings, including Jazz Burger Café, with its windows long smashed out. Her flashlight beam danced here and there, revealing only more depressing decay.

Did she know this place?

At the Ferris wheel, she stopped and pulled her shoulders back as if bracing herself. Empty passenger cars, still positioned around the wheel's circumference as if waiting for ghost riders, creaked in the wind.

I watched from behind an old trash dispenser, the gentle breeze picking up strength and carrying something unexpected in my direction. The sound of Cynthia's sobbing.

Certainly she didn't exist in daydream state. No feasible reason could explain the Justice Club's dragging her out of bed to visit this forsaken place.

Which meant she'd come for another reason. Could these depressing surroundings hold some personal significance for her?

Waves of regret washed over me that I'd been forced to pry,

through no fault of my own, into personal matters that didn't concern me. Now, how to get out of here? Following her had led me into the park, but no tracker blip pointed the way out. Then again, I shouldn't abandon her. What unknown dangers might lurk in the shadows?

I glanced at the tracker again and froze. A new blip, this one red, had entered the screen from the southeast and headed our way at a fast clip.

Another operative?

Perhaps red indicated no brain chip, a signal of another kind. Could be a security guard. And she had no idea he was coming.

Stay put? Or warn her?

Perhaps the Justice Club meant the security guard to accost her. Perhaps he was intended to be her mark. No way of telling.

I left my hiding place and strode toward Cynthia. She turned at the sound of my footsteps, her eyebrows shooting up.

She wiped her eyes. "Landon, wha—what are you doing here? Oh, yeah, I suppose you'll always be following me around now, right? Good grief. Can't a girl enjoy a private moment?"

"I'm sorry. I didn't mean to intrude, but I am supposed to make sure you don't come to harm."

She turned toward the Ferris wheel as if not hearing me. "Car number four is where Lee and I sat during our first date. Being in New Orleans, I had to see this place again, even if it is such a mess."

"I'm sorry, Cynthia, but I wanted to warn you. Somebody's coming."

She faced me, unsmiling, her less attractive front. "Look, I know you like playing my guardian angel, but I really am a big girl. Actually, I'm expecting someone, so you can go now. Please."

"Who?"

Annoyance sharpened her eyes. "This doesn't concern you, so you better leave. In fact, if you stay, you could get hurt. Goodbye." She turned the cold shoulder, her body language not open to interpretation.

Hadn't she heard what she just acknowledged? I'd always be watching, regardless of her appointments. But did staying here place my safety at risk?

Why would someone be a danger for me but not for her?

I backed away, accepting that I'd get nowhere by pressing the issue. But by no means could I simply walk away and not wait to see who her visitor might be.

37

Tuesday, March 29

Taking cover inside the doorway of one of the abandoned buildings, I waited, draped beneath a veil of shadows. Soon a man's voice rose on the gentle breeze. I stole a peek around the edge of the doorframe.

Cynthia turned toward a dark figure. Reflecting no apparent surprise, she shook the man's hand, and they spoke, though too far away for their words to be audible. The handshake communicated a formal relationship. Though no lovers' rendezvous, it proved to be a meeting nonetheless.

The man wore all black, but nothing covered his blond head. With Cynthia's flashlight directed toward the concrete, the glow was insufficient. His face evaded my scrutiny.

They strolled toward the moldering ruins of Jazz Burger Café and disappeared into its devastated shell. The interior glowed through busted-out windows; perhaps the man had brought a flashlight, too, its illumination joining forces with hers.

Curiosity piqued, I ventured closer, using nearby buildings for cover, avoiding debris that might crunch underfoot, and slinking closer to a window within earshot of their meeting. I pressed myself against the side of the building and strained to hear. Jagged glass fragments framed the window's opening.

Only murmurs and occasional random words drifted my way—something about "preparations" and "deadline." Their rising voices betrayed unmasked emotions. One spoken word left no doubt in my mind.

Lamont.

Maria Lamont, the Supreme Court justice, shared a love for woodwind instruments with Cynthia. Perhaps Cynthia had only told this man about her excitement in meeting Maria backstage. The name may have been uttered in a harmless context, but without hearing the full conversation, I had no way of knowing for sure.

Maybe Maria had something to do with a future mission of the Justice Club. Or had Cynthia shooed me away because of the independent nature of something else? Surely she understood that telling me to leave would only tempt me to stay and want to know more.

Taking a risk, I stole a peek through the broken window. Sure enough, Cynthia and the stranger sat cross-legged on the floor and faced each other, the upended flashlights between them. The light provided sufficient illumination to make out the man's face.

My pulse quickened.

No, it couldn't be.

Hadn't Chris Van Lanen, an old classmate, died years ago? Murdered, in fact?

If not Chris, this man must be the spitting image of him. Or perhaps a twin. Except I knew Chris's family; he didn't have a twin. In my eye screen flashed images from his memorial service, still stored in my brain for easy reference. Chris's mom, teary eyed from crying. His sister's harp solo of "Moon River," Chris's favorite song.

Could this be him after all these years?

But how could it be?

Lights shifted inside the building's shell, and I withdrew into shadows to wait unseen.

The two exited the building, the meeting apparently concluded. Cynthia waved and said something I couldn't hear; then they separated—her going one way and him going the opposite. She paused for one glance around, perhaps searching for me, before quickening her step, satisfied.

Watching her retreating back, I considered my options. I could follow her using the tracker and return to my bed, or …

A suspicion tempted me to follow the Chris lookalike and see where he might lead me. Amee had emphasized Cynthia's protection as one of my top priorities, but if Cynthia had become entangled in something beyond the Justice Club that could jeopardize future missions, surely Amee would want to know.

Technically, Cynthia's blip still appeared on my tracker, so she'd never truly be beyond my surveillance anyhow. I could always find her later.

Chris strode at a fast clip, and keeping up put me in panting mode. He neither paused nor glanced back to ensure no one shadowed him. After all, he had met Cynthia alone in an abandoned amusement park. Who else could be out here in the dead of night except ghosts, raccoons, and rare security guards?

Arriving at the parking lot, he vaulted over the forsaken entry barrier and strode toward a parked sedan. Something dark, expensive, and surely foreign.

Remembering something Stu, the surveillance expert, had taught me, I pulled off my shoes and dashed after Chris in my stocking feet, planning to hide behind a nearby light pole planter for a closer look. But just as he reached his car and before I could duck behind the planter, he swiveled and faced me.

A lightning-quick fist struck, and pain exploded in my nose. I fell to my knees, hands cradling my face. Another powerful strike descended on the back of my neck, and I face-planted the cement, mercifully avoiding more abuse to my smarting nose.

"Chris," I said, lifting my head, "what are you doing here? Does your mom even know you're alive?"

He glared down at me, perhaps intending more harm but reconsidering. "Stay out of my way, Landon. I mean it."

So he remembered me as well as I remembered him.

More importantly, his words had confirmed his identity.

I lowered my head and remained still, awaiting more abuse. Mercy gave me a nod instead.

A car door opened, and an engine started and revved. I looked up just in time to catch his license plate number, committing it to memory. The purr of his foreign ride faded in the distance, brake lights glowing like red eyes searching the dark.

Rising, I looked for my shoes, nose throbbing, a gentle breeze caressing my face. When I brushed a knuckle across my nose, it came away wet.

My shoes slipped back on, but before I could begin crossing the parking lot, a flashlight beam blinded me. I raised an arm, shielding my face.

"Put your hands on your head!" a man's no-nonsense voice said.

38

G *reat.*

Must be a cop or security guard.

Why not? Let's put a red bow on the ending of this most bizarre evening.

I complied without a word, all fight or flight gone. The man patted me down from behind, a low whistle on his lips, the playful tune a sharp contrast to my mood.

"Sir," he said, "you *are* aware that it's illegal to be trespassing here, right?"

Actually, that fact had escaped me in my mission to track Cynthia down. If posters prohibiting my entrance tattooed the buildings, the inky night had obscured them.

"Sorry, officer." I longed for my bed and wondered how long this fiasco might take. Surely he'd give me a warning or a ticket and send me on my way.

Didn't matter in the long run. Amee would just hide or delete anything that could be traced back to me. In fact, at this point she probably eyed my blip on her tracker and puzzled over why I lingered at the park entrance.

The uniformed cop stepped closer and faced me, his face shadowy in the flashlight's diffused beam. "Sorry isn't good enough, mister. I have a good mind to take matters into my own hands and execute you right here, right now."

"Excuse me?"

A familiar chuckle. "I'm just playing games with you, Landon."

That voice, minus the disguise. "Monty?"

He stepped in front of me and brought the flashlight to bear. I beheld my friend's grinning face, sporting a bushy, black beard.

Muscles tighter than taut rubber bands flexed. A knot formed in my throat, and it took all I could manage not to hug him. "I wondered when or if I might see you again."

"If? You know I'm always watching, buddy. I just can't always show my hand so overtly."

"Like you can now?"

"We've got a little time. And no worries—we're incognito."

He handed me a tissue and gestured to my nose. It still bled. I thanked him, the skin tender.

His mouth twisted as if he'd taken a bite of something nasty. "The Justice Club hates cops. Really, any law enforcement. Sort of ironic, huh, if they're supposedly all about meting out justice on those who deserve it? What are good cops about except justice?"

"Amazing what justice can mean in the wrong hands. You're a sight for sore eyes. I didn't realize how lonely I'd been in this job until now."

"Sorry. I know it can't be easy."

"Easy. Do you have any idea what I've gone through lately?"

"Of course. I just said I've been watching your every move."

I leaned my head toward my right shoulder, my neck cracking. Some muscle tension eased. "Then you already know the worst, that they made me kill somebody this time."

He cocked his head. "Not so fast. First, they can't *make* you do anything anymore. You need to change your thinking. Second, you beat Leonard up pretty bad—but no, you didn't kill him."

I gasped. "But Amee said—"

"Amee lied. But why should that surprise you? She's a psychopath."

"But why lie about something like that?"

"Remember her goal. She wants to wear you down and persuade you to get with the program. The sooner you give up hope, accept that you're a killer, and assent to doing whatever they want, the sooner you'll be putty in their hands."

"She said I'm just as much in the Justice Club's control as I've ever been."

He jabbed a finger in my chest. "Don't you believe a word of it. You've got somebody living inside you now who's calling the shots. Don't you ever forget that."

"But they still tempted me to beat Leonard up, and of course in my sleep when I couldn't do anything about it." A pause. "Monty, I don't understand what's going on here. I thought God had broken their control over my life. I just want to know the truth. Did Jesus save me, or didn't He?"

Monty grinned. "Oh, He saved you all right—and for all time. Don't you ever doubt that. Not even the evil that happens in this world is beyond His control. But let me remind you of something your youth pastor told you long ago."

"What's that?"

"Jesus broke the power of sin, but that doesn't mean you will never be tempted to do bad things. The problem with ninety-nine percent of the church today is that we don't live like the redeemed people we are. We're still like the dog going back to its vomit, even though we have steak to feast on."

"I want to do what's right."

"Of course you do, but just like the apostle Paul, you're divided. Part of you wants to do what's right, but the other part still wants to do evil. Join the club. Landon, you *can* say no, but that doesn't mean you always will. Sometimes you make poor choices, not so much because sin is in control but because you forget it isn't. You keep living like an enslaved man. And I realize it's not easy not to. You've been enslaved most of your life."

"So how do I stop?"

"Choose God's way over your own every minute of every day. Remember, God's Spirit lives inside you now. Ask Him for help, and He'll guide you. The path isn't easy, but it's right."

"And if evil calls to me again in the night?"

"Resist it. Keep a Bible by your bed, Landon. I'll plant one in your hotel room with certain verses highlighted. Go over them several times right before bed. Repeat them in your mind. They'll help you stay true."

"I can't stand the thought of me hurting anyone else without realizing it."

"But Landon, though you may not remember what you do at the moment you do it, you always have a choice. Always. The Justice Club doesn't control you, but it tempts that evil part of you that wants to give in."

"On the day I met you, they turned off my sight and hearing through the implant."

"You forgot you could deny them, so you didn't."

"But what about Leonard? I *chose* to hurt him?"

"He threatened Cynthia, didn't he? Your masculine pride wanted to protect her, to avenge her. So you yielded to temptation and acted on impulse."

A sudden thought overwhelmed me. *I should report myself to the police. Then they'll lock me away. I may be safer in a jail cell than I am right now.*

But then I'd thwart the mission of the resistance, and they still had plans for me.

A gentle breeze tousled our hair.

"Let me check that nose," he said, his fingers probing tender skin. I winced.

"Nope," he said, "he didn't break it. You'll be fine."

"That guy who hit me—I know him from high school. I thought he was dead."

"Chris Van Lanen, a.k.a. Gavin Dane Morrison. We know all about him. He's a ruthless killer. You're fortunate all he did was almost break your nose."

"I have his license plate number if you want it."

A head shake. "Don't bother. He's too smart not to cover his tracks."

"So Chris is somehow involved? How?"

"A big event is on the horizon, all right, and you, Chris, and Cynthia—you're all smack-dab in the middle of it."

"Cynthia, too?"

"Of course."

"I don't understand. What was this meeting between Cynthia and Chris tonight all about? Why can't you just tell me what's going on?"

"Because knowing everything now will make you vulnerable in ways you can't possibly imagine. Ever heard of plausible deniability? It's best that you act clueless because you are. If you know too much, it will be hard to conceal, and you could show your hand without even meaning to. We can't risk that. When the time comes, you'll understand."

I sighed, my emotions riding a wave of frustration. "Riddles as usual. Why should I expect anything less? Can't you tell me anything?"

We stood side by side and took in the night, our backs to an abandoned amusement park that moldered under another night sky and promised no return of happy children in the morning.

"Soon Amee will take you target shooting," he said, "so you can get experience using some fancy guns."

"Why?"

"Like I said, there's a big event on the horizon, and you're part of it."

"I don't understand. They made me a handler for Cynthia. And now this?"

"The element of surprise, Landon. They may still doubt which side you're on. You've denied them in the past, remember? There's one way to remove all doubt."

"Why not just make me do what they want in my sleep?"

"It's not that simple. You're a malfunctioner, remember. And they can only tempt you and hope you give in. They don't like what's unpredictable."

"Then why me?"

"We talked about this before. Don't forget your gifts and what they could mean in the wrong hands."

Hysterical strength, an ability I had no idea how to use. Could that be part of all this?

"They've been trying to give you the impression that you're nothing more than a babysitter for Cynthia. But things are about to change in a big way."

"So the target practice—does that mean I'm going to be the shooter? Something on the scale of Las Vegas?"

"I can't say any more. Just go with the flow for now. You'll know what to do when more information is provided."

"What about Justice Lamont? Do they plan to harm her?"

"Just keep your eyes on the One who knows best. Your path will become clear." He glanced at his watch. "Sorry, Landon, I should be going, and you should leave, too."

"Not so fast. I have a few questions."

"Okay, but make them fast. We've stood here too long."

"Why are you willing to take so many risks to stop the Justice Club?"

A pause. "They killed my wife and daughter. Long story."

"I'm sorry."

"If I can help stop them from hurting anyone else the way they hurt me, then I figure any sacrifice is worth it."

"What's this advanced program you told me about? How will I know when I've qualified for it?"

"You're already in it. You were the second the Justice Club thought you pushed Leslie off that balcony. More doors will open for you. Keep walking through them."

"You mentioned my helping you from the inside, but Amee is pretty tight lipped around me. How can I be useful from the inside if I don't hear anything of value I can share?"

"You're valuable just by staying where you are—and like I said, a big event is coming. You'll soon show your value. So if you think for one minute you're not in a position to do something important to stop the Justice Club, kick that thought to the curb. You are in a pivotal position, Landon. Just wait and see."

A quarter mile away, two separate flashlight beams swiveled and danced across the parking lot, heading our way.

"Time's up, Landon. Here come some security guards. You need to go."

"When will I see you again?"

"When the time's right, I'll find you, and you'll behold my handsome, smiling face."

I shook my head. "Won't everyone be envious?"

"I love you too, bro."

39

22 hours left ...

In a restaurant after our first concert in Los Angeles, serenaded by country-western music while members of my band gossiped, I longed for my hotel room bed and ached for solitude. The ice melted in my cup of ginger ale, a slow transformation from solid to liquid. A reminder of how easily one could be manipulated while in the grip of the Justice Club.

A smiling, warm-hearted person one minute. A cold-blooded creature the next. Just like Cynthia.

Who would have thought the petite beauty could beat up someone as easily as she had last night? I'd been following her after the trip to Six Flags, but I'd been directed not to prevent her.

Monty had told me to hang in there, but how much more of this sitting on the sidelines could I take? When would the time come to act?

"Maestro! Maestro?"

Amee poked me in the arm. More like a jab.

"Ouch!" My thoughts scattered, and I couldn't help the glare.

"Sorry," she said, "but I needed to get your attention. They are ordering dessert, but you appear to be in another world tonight."

A world free of violence. A world lacking nags like you.

"I don't want any."

"Seriously? It's fudge with pistachios, and I know how much you like those nuts. I just figured—"

"I'll pass, but thanks for letting me know."

"What's eating you? You don't seem like yourself tonight. I thought the concert went great."

It's not about the concert. It's about people getting hurt right in front of my eyes and my inability to do anything about it. And if you don't realize by now why that bothers me, Amee, then you've never known me to begin with.

"I don't want to talk about it." I got up, unsure of what to do next.

She arched an eyebrow. "Going someplace?"

"Just to the men's room. That's okay, right?"

"I don't think you need permission to do that."

"Thanks for the clarification."

I cast my napkin down and headed away, hanging a left past several servers, who balanced entrees as if by magic. A heavy footfall behind me registered at the same moment something hard pressed against my lower back.

"I've got a gun pointed at you," said a woman with a mild southern accent. "Don't cry out. Just keep walking."

Say what? If this had nothing to do with the Justice Club, it could only mean—

The barrel poked me hard enough to make me wince. "The men's room. Move."

I did. "But you can't go in there."

She ignored me. Maybe I was meeting someone else there, but how brazen to force a meeting here with Amee only a room away. Must be important.

Despite the door sign that said, "Out of Order," I entered, the armed woman right behind me.

"Landon!" Jade wore blue slacks and a pink blouse, her favorite color. Around her neck glinted a shiny gold necklace and a locket, *the* locket I'd given her on her twelfth birthday. Even after all these years, she still wore it.

We embraced, my galloping heart overflowing with exhilaration and delight, overwhelmed by this sudden pang-filled visitation of home. How I longed to tell her how much I loved her. How would she react if I spoke those thoughts aloud?

We parted, and I turned toward a stern-faced woman with Hispanic features, who lowered the gun. The woman fiddled with the door, apparently jimmy-rigging it to prevent anyone from entering.

"Don't you need to use a wireless jammer?" I said. "Won't they hear or see us?"

The woman shook her head. "If we use a jammer, they'll come running to see why your GPS is blocked. I checked the room for any devices. We're clean." She moved to stand beside Jade.

Jade gave quick introductions. So this was Maggie Songbird, the FBI agent who'd been on my scent. As much as seeing Jade thrilled me, Monty's absence deflated me.

"Are you out of your mind?" I said to Jade. "You shouldn't be here. It's too dangerous."

"That's what I told her, but you've got one stubborn friend here," Maggie said with a displeased head shake. "Jade here was *supposed* to stay home and talk to you via video, but no. She followed me all the way to California and nearly blew my cover."

"I had to see you," Jade said, eyes brimming with emotion.

I shook my head. "I don't understand. What's this all about? Is my mom okay?"

"She's fine," Maggie said.

"Then what's up?"

"We're here to rescue you," Jade said.

"*Rescue* me." At one time I would have longed to hear those words, but so much had happened since. "Why did you think I wanted rescuing?"

As if not hearing me, Jade pushed a familiar-looking men's golden wristwatch into my hand. "I brought one of the jammers, but my cousin Wade enhanced it. It blocks the wireless signal within twenty feet of whoever wears it. Pretty cool, huh?"

I accepted it, unsure what to say.

"Okay, so maybe now isn't the right time for your exit," Jade said. "But later, after we're gone, when you need it, use it."

Maggie said, "Several FBI agents are in the city, keeping you under constant surveillance. The minute you walk away, they've got your back."

Protection. And a way out.

All rolled into one.

Pocketing the watch, I swallowed hard—tired, weary, and wanting so much to go home. Only a fool would walk away from what she offered.

"It's time for your extraction, Landon," Maggie said. "I have no idea what they are hanging over your head to keep you in line, but you can be on a plane and out of here within a half hour. Not only that, but whenever you're ready, we have a brain specialist on standby at a secret location to do surgery and remove your implant."

I stared. Could she really make such a promise?

"By tomorrow you and your mom could be in the witness protection program and on your way to a secret location of your choosing. I give you my word that the Justice Club will never be able to track you down."

Didn't she understand who these people were? *Escape* didn't exist in their vocabulary. What had Amee said? Either I'm all in, or I'm dead.

"I'm sorry," I said, "but I can't go. Not right now."

Disappointment couldn't have been more evident on their faces. No doubt Maggie had gone to a lot of trouble to arrange this impressive intervention.

"Don't you want to be free of these evil people?" Jade said.

"Of course, but you don't understand."

After a glance at my watch—how many minutes had passed?—I brought them up to speed. I included meeting Monty in Georgia and my decision to help the resistance from the inside. "Sure, my walking away will help me, but it won't fix anything. The Justice Club will just continue doing its evil work and killing people. But by staying, I can perhaps help stop them from the inside."

Maggie folded her arms, her mouth a displeased seam. "I just want to be sure you understand what we're offering and the danger you've put yourself in by saying no."

"I understand."

The agent shrugged. "I think you're crazy, but it's your choice. I have a few questions before you go. A woman named Leslie Neumann jumped from her balcony at the Waldorf Astoria in Dallas. We traced your DNA to her balcony. What's your connection?"

I shoved the more unsettling memories aside and provided a summary.

Tears glistened in Jade's eyes. "Oh, Landon, what else have they tried to make you do?"

The memory of Leonard, my hands tight around his throat, leaped to recall, but I remained silent. If I told her everything, I'd risk losing her respect.

"We can talk about that another time," Maggie said. "We're offering you a way out. Do you want it or not?"

"I can't right now. I'm sorry. You've got to give me more time."

Maggie's fingertips kneaded her temples. "Time for what?"

"Something big is about to happen, and I'm a key player in it, Monty says. If I play my cards right, I just might be able to prevent it."

"How do you know this Monty can be trusted?" Maggie said.

Surely no imposter could have spoken so convincingly about God's pull on my heart. "I just know. Look, they took me target shooting with automatic weapons I've never handled before. Another test of my allegiance perhaps."

Jade shook her head. "But don't you see? You think you can stop them by working with them. Stooping to their level doesn't enable you to defeat them. It just makes you stink as bad as they do."

How could she oppose my plan too? "Jade, you don't understand."

"They'll make you do things you'll later regret," she said. "Are you willing to sell your soul just so you might have a chance to stop them?"

"I'm sorry, but I have to do this." A glance at my watch. "They'll be looking for me. I have to go. You're both in danger just by being here. You need to go. Now."

Jade reached for my hand and squeezed it, her face more beautiful than I remembered, those toggling pupils frenetic. "Please, Landon, come with us now. It's just too dangerous."

"If you walk away from us now," Maggie said, "I can't protect you."

"No offense, but I've been on my own with only Monty's assistance so far. He hasn't led me wrong. I plan to see this through."

"You may survive," Jade said, "but what about your conscience if you continue to cooperate with them? You'll never be you again."

Air whooshed between my lips. "I'm sorry, but there's more than me at stake here. There are others under the control of the Justice Club, and I feel like maybe I can help them break free, too. I don't exactly know how yet, but I have to try. If you want to help me, listen up. Whatever is coming might involve Supreme Court Justice Maria Lamont. I don't know for sure, but I think she might be a target."

Maggie's eyes widened. "Where? When?"

"I don't know specifics, but maybe you can tell whoever protects her to keep an eye out. Another thing. Amee Presley, my agent and manager, likes to use needles a little too much. See what you can dig up from her past. You might find something useful for leverage."

Jade's determined nod. "Okay. What else?"

"I mentioned this to my mom, but she may have forgotten to tell you. A priest has been visiting my father at the psych ward. My father isn't Catholic. Find out who this man is. He could be important."

Maggie handed me a sheet of paper. "We already looked into him. No one, including your mom, knows how this man got on your dad's visitors' log. Do you know who he is?"

Despite the graininess of the photo, the profile captured from a surveillance camera pushed air out of my lungs. "It's Monty. I can't believe it. He implied that my dad has some sort of role to play in this business with the Justice Club, but I didn't know for sure what he meant."

Monty had known the importance of the name Sonora. But instead of whispering the name in my father's ear, he'd needed *me* to do it. Why?

Monty and my dad had been train buffs for years, but why regular visits to my dad in the psych ward? And why not tell me?

Plausible deniability?

No time to puzzle this mystery out now. "Oh, one more thing. Jade, you remember Chris Van Lanen from high school?"

"Sure. He died a long time ago."

"No, he's alive. He's working for the Justice Club."

Jade shook her head. "No, that's not possible. Remember, we were both at his funeral."

I met Maggie's eyes. "He spoke to me. It's him. I don't know who's buried in his grave, but it can't possibly be Chris. Exhume his body, and you'll see that I'm right. He's somehow mixed up in what's about to happen."

"What *is* about to happen, Landon?" Maggie said.

"I wish I knew. A mass shooting maybe? I don't know."

Jade raised her eyebrows. "And they've been training you to be the trigger guy."

"I don't know that for sure."

"But what if they somehow make you?" Jade said. "Landon, you aren't a killer. How are you going to get out of this?"

"I guess the same way I didn't kill you or my mom last fall when Ray Galotta tried to make me. That was when I trusted Christ, Jade. God broke the power of evil in my life. I have to believe I *can* say no to their evil purposes."

Jade's eyes sparkled. "Oh, Landon, I'm so glad."

"There's no time for that right now," Maggie said. "What if they threaten someone's life to pressure you? What if for some reason you can't resist?"

"I don't know, but I may be able to help Maria Lamont if she needs it."

"Why do you believe Lamont may be a target?" Maggie said.

I described the overheard words at the amusement park and shared Cynthia's connection to Lamont through their shared interest in woodwinds. "Investigate Cynthia Lemke, a new flute player on our band," I said. "She got a brain implant about three months ago after a motorcycle accident. I've been assigned to be her handler of sorts. Find out as much about her as you can. She may be a key player in what's about to go down."

Any minute Amee would come knocking on the door and wonder if I was okay. If she found Jade and Maggie here …

Another glance at Jade made me pause, something different about her face. I reached toward her; before she could jerk away, I smoothed away makeup hiding a wound at the corner of her mouth. "What happened to you?"

"A second operative came after your mom, Landon, in our house. When I interfered, he came after me with a knife. He nearly killed me, but my dad stopped him."

I met her gaze, processing her words. "Wow. I'm so glad you're both okay."

"We thought maybe he came to eliminate Jade because you failed a mission," Maggie said.

A head shake. "But nothing like that has happened. If anything, I've succeeded in their eyes. I can't explain it." I turned toward the door. "I'm sorry, but I have to go."

"Landon."

Turning back, I almost lost my balance due to the crushing momentum of Jade's hug. "I'm praying for you," she said before pulling away.

"Thanks. I'm going to need it." I gave her one last glance, telegraphing that I didn't want to go but had no choice. Would Jade and I ever find an opportunity to spend time together in safety?

"Jade, I haven't had much time to grow in my faith. But if I can trust God to save my soul, I can trust Him to help me do some good and get me out of this mess."

She nodded, eyes bright. "Just keep trusting Him then."

40

21 hours left …

Safe in my hotel room alone, I rehashed everything Maggie and Jade had said, a dull ache throbbing behind my eyes. They'd made their exit from the restaurant without event, and I'd returned to my table, complaining of feeling sick, which wasn't a fib. My stomach was definitely out of sorts.

Amee had expressed only minor interest, then later escorted me to my hotel room. Again, as if I were a child who needed tucking in. But no needle this time.

Everything had been too easy. No questions about my taking so long in the bathroom.

Could she be getting careless? Trusting me too much? Or could her lack of curiosity be a ruse? Perhaps she had known the truth about my shenanigans all along and had simply humored me.

But how could that be? According to Maggie, the bathroom had been clean of any Justice Club surveillance. How could they have known in advance I'd be in there?

While I was getting ready for bed, I spotted it. A navy MP3 player perched on top of the TV, wrapped in black earbuds.

Not mine. So who did the player belong to?

The cleaning lady?

Had Monty left it for me? What other explanation could there be?

In bed, I placed the earbuds to listen to an audiobook and found a single sound file on the player. I selected "play." Monty spoke.

Greetings, Landon. I told you something big was coming. Well, this is it. Tomorrow night your second concert in Los Angeles is D-Day. I should be there at some point to help out, but if you don't see me, then something went wrong. No matter. Carry on as if you don't need me, because you won't. You're ready to do this.

Listen very carefully to this audio file twice to make sure you understand the details. It's imperative that you listen closely, because after the second play, the file will self-delete.

You've complained about my use of riddles, so I'm going to make these directions very clear. Tomorrow afternoon before your next big concert, Amee will recommend that you take a nap. You will assent. She will think your response reveals a certain level of suggestibility, which will work in your favor later. Just play along.

While you're sleeping, the Justice Club plans to trigger daydream state and try to take control of your actions through the operation tomorrow evening. Yes, they successfully used you to go after Leonard, at least to beat him up, but this time they will fail because we have plans too.

Yes, the Justice Club can still tempt you. You may feel like you are able to resist their evil plans, but to avoid any question, since they tend to engage you while you sleep, we are eliminating any guesswork. We are removing your choice.

Under your pillow is a capsule you need to swallow during breakfast tomorrow. Once you take it, you will not be able to sleep for twenty-four hours. Because you will not be able to sleep, the Justice Club will not even be able to tempt you and will be forced to go with plan B, which our sources have not revealed.

Be vigilant because something big is about to happen. What exactly that is, we don't know. Tomorrow, my friend, we will find out.

41

21 hours left …

In Maggie's hotel room, Jade sat on the edge of the second bed, head down, while the agent paced.

"I told you it was too dangerous for you to come," Maggie said. "What were you thinking, tracking me down and following me to Landon's restaurant?"

"I was worried about him. I needed to make sure he was okay."

Maggie stopped and faced her. "I know you care for him, but you aren't even supposed to be here."

"Now that I'm here, please don't send me home. There's gotta be something I can do."

Maggie put her hands on her hips. "Do? Yeah, you can stay in this room and not go anywhere or talk to anyone unless I tell you otherwise."

Jade dropped her head.

Maggie sighed. "Sorry, I don't mean to be harsh, but if you got hurt or killed due to your connection to me and this investigation, I'd never forgive myself. We're not playing games here, Jade."

Jade looked up. Met her eyes. "I realize that. I'm sorry. I knew you'd be seeing him, so it only seemed logical ..." She shook her head. "I didn't mean to put you in a difficult spot. But based on Landon's reaction, it doesn't seem like there's much you can do anyhow."

Maggie spanned the room to the window and parted the drapes. Peered out. "I can't believe he wouldn't accept our offer. And to think of all the work the FBI did to set it up."

"Oh, he wanted to accept it, all right. But you heard him—he thinks he can make a difference where he is."

Maggie turned and folded her arms. "While I sit around and watch? He's delusional."

"Please don't say that. I have to hope he can truly make a difference. I don't want to consider the alternative."

Maggie gave her an apologetic glance. "Sorry, you're right. I need to be more optimistic. I just have a hard time swallowing that he can somehow thwart their plans, whatever they may be."

She crossed to her bed and sat on the edge, arms braced against her knees. "I was assigned to Landon's case, and I didn't come all this way just to turn around and go back home with my tail tucked between my legs."

"Then we should do something to help him."

Maggie shot her a look. "We?"

"Look, I can bring you coffee and even iron your clothes. Surely there's something I could do to be useful without putting myself in danger or interfering in your investigation."

Maggie blew air between her lips. Gave a grudging nod. "I'm not going to send you home, Jade, but it may be smarter for you to have your own room down the hall."

"Whatever you think is best."

Another nod. "I called Brad McCarthy, my partner, to check into Maria Lamont's safety through the US Marshals service. Those are the guys who protect justices of the Supreme Court when they travel outside Washington, DC. He's supposed to get back to me. He's also going to run a background check on Amee Presley. Maybe Landon's right. Perhaps there's something useful buried in her past."

"What about Chris Van Lanen?"

Maggie gave her a measured look. "You know Landon better than I do. Do you think there's anything to what he said?"

"Landon is pretty good at recognizing familiar faces, but it's a bizarre story if what he suggests is true. Why would someone pretend to be dead years ago and then suddenly turn up, working for the Justice Club?"

"If everybody thought you were dead, you could do all sorts of illegal things and essentially be anonymous." A pause. "Maybe Landon just met somebody who resembles Chris. Could he have been mistaken?"

"I don't think so. If Landon says Chris spoke to him, then Chris did."

"I have a connection at the Bureau who specializes in age-progression portraits of missing children. I'm eager to see what he comes up with for Chris based on his photo on file. That might help us ID him."

"So are you going to have Chris's grave exhumed?"

Maggie chewed her bottom lip. "I'd have a hard time making my case based on only one person's sighting and strong hunch. Ordering an exhumation is a big deal, and we'd have to work with local authorities and even get approval from family members. It's a time-consuming process, and I'd need strong evidence. I'll talk to Brad about it, but I think he'll say the same thing I'm thinking.

"Which is?"

"We need more, like a recent photo of the guy. DNA evidence would be prime."

"I figured it was a long shot," Jade said, shaking her head. "How much time do you think before we get some answers on Amee's background?"

"Probably not before tomorrow night's concert, I'm afraid."

"So you're still planning to go?"

"Of course," Maggie said, eyeing her. "Next thing I know, you'll want to go too."

"I did bring a ticket. Just in case."

The FBI agent sighed. "Jade, you're putting me in an awkward position here."

Jade folded her hands as if pleading for mercy. "Okay, okay. I'll stay here tomorrow night all by my lonesome and do whatever you say. What can I do right now to be useful?"

"I need to make a few more phone calls. Two heads are better than one, so sure, you can be useful. I just don't want you in danger."

"I understand."

"Let's give our brains time to work on these various issues, okay? Maybe there's still time for a breakthrough of some kind." She hesitated with a small smile. "If you really want to be useful, do you mind bringing me some coffee and a couple of cookies from the lobby?"

Jade leaped up. "Sure. I'll be back in five."

Maggie thanked her and reached for her phone.

Five minutes later, Jade returned and set the food on the desk. Still on the phone, the agent gave her an appreciative smile. Munching on her own warm, gooey cookies and not knowing what else to do, Jade gave Henry a quick call to check in on him. Sounded like he was having a blast with Grandpa. After saying goodbye and clicking off, she slouched on the bed and googled the Amberson Theater, the location of Landon's next concert, on her laptop.

Maggie ended her call, a puzzled look on her face.

"You okay?" Jade said. "Is something wrong?"

"I can't go into all of it. It's just that there are a number of questions I've had about this implant investigation, even questions about your Uncle Jed's death, but every time I feel like I'm hitting a brick wall. It's like somebody is hiding something."

"You mean, within the FBI?"

"I'm afraid so." She sighed, shaking her head. "On another matter, there's still no word on the man who attacked you at your house. His DNA doesn't show up in any of our databases."

"For some reason, that doesn't surprise me."

"I just spoke to somebody in charge of the US Marshals. There's not much they can do about Maria Lamont without a specific, known threat, but they said they'd be especially vigilant of her safety over the next few days. I doubt we can do much more than that. Have you found anything interesting?"

"Yeah. Listen to this. The capacity at Amberson Theater is eight thousand, and if you go to the website, it says tickets are sold out. That's a lot of people in one place."

"Just imagine what could happen if the right person had the right gun or a biological weapon in a place like that. That's another reason why you're staying here."

Jade winced. "You do realize that if somebody starts shooting, you could end up in the crossfire."

"Remember, I'm trained to handle this sort of stuff. Who knows? By being there, maybe I could help bring the guy down."

That could be Landon.

"Let's just pray it doesn't come to that," Jade said.

"Can you think of any other way to help Landon? Other than to somehow get his concert canceled, which isn't likely at this point?"

Jade shook her head.

"Being there is the only way to help him on the inside. Who knows? Maybe I can find a way backstage and snoop around."

"And do what exactly?"

"I'm thinking, I'm thinking." Maggie got up and paced back and forth, hands perched on her head. Either battling a terrible headache or applying her brain to the problem. She stopped and faced Jade. "You want to help? I need to find as much information about that flute player, Cynthia Lemke, as possible—and fast. Any idea what she looks like? That would be a good place to start."

Not long ago, Jade had found a Facebook photo of her and Landon at a recent concert, his arm around her, his flirtatious gaze meeting hers as if they were close. She shook off the jealous thoughts. "Yeah. I just saw a photo of her. Hold on." Jade hunted down the photo and turned her laptop so Maggie could see. "There she is. That's Cynthia."

Maggie pressed a hand to her mouth. "No way. That's *her*."

"That's who? What are you talking about?"

"Oh wow. Remember the DNA we traced from Sandra's attack? It led us to John Smith, that guy with the implant I interviewed who didn't have a clue."

"Yeah. So?"

"I couldn't figure out how John Smith had an implant when he'd never had brain surgery. A colleague of mine did some research and discovered something surprising. It's all pretty advanced stuff, but now there's a device that can insert a brain chip on the surface of the brain without surgery as invasive as Landon's. In the hands of a trained nurse, the implant could be inserted without too much fuss."

"Okay, but what does that have to do with Cynthia?"

"Oh sorry. I found the hospital where John Smith was treated for that head injury due to a biking accident. That's when we believe the implant was inserted. Through a subpoena, I tracked down the nurse logs of those working in the ER when he was there. This morning the hospital released photos of the nurses on duty. One particular nurse, Tammi Sue Hudson, took care of John Smith during his overnight stay. They even have video of her doing suspicious activity with her back turned to the camera. Here she is."

Maggie showed Jade her smartphone. The photo of Tammi Sue filled the screen: brown hair and eyes, sparkling smile. "Do you think that's Cynthia Lemke, or do Cynthia and this woman just have a close resemblance?"

Jade compared the two women, her face close to the screen, and whistled. "I'd bet a hundred dollars this nurse and Cynthia Lemke are the same person."

"Let's assume we're right. So Cynthia places a brain implant in John Smith. Later the Justice Club directs him to attack Landon's mom. And just recently Cynthia joins Landon's band. See the connection?"

"Wow, that's creepy. It's like Cynthia is out to get Landon and his mom."

"Landon thinks he's assigned to keep an eye on Cynthia, but maybe it's the other way around."

"That's even creepier. Hey, mind if I see that photo on your phone again?"

"Hold on. I'll e-mail it to you."

Seconds later, Jade pulled up her e-mail account and enlarged the photo on her screen so the pictures of the two women were displayed side by side. "Both photos are Cynthia all right. I'm positive." She paused and leaned back. Nibbled on a fingernail. "Hey, wait a minute."

"What is it?" Maggie said.

"When did this nurse allegedly give John Smith the implant?"

"About six months ago. Why?"

"Either Cynthia has a twin and doesn't know it, or the timeline doesn't work."

"What timeline?"

"Cynthia's timeline with the Justice Club. According to Landon, Cynthia got her implant about three months ago after a motorcycle accident. But if she gave John Smith his implant, she was *already* working for the Justice Club six months ago."

"They've been lying to Landon," Maggie said with wide eyes. "Cynthia isn't who Landon thinks she is."

"You mean—"

"I bet the Justice Club has been working on this conspiracy for some time, but Landon thinks Cynthia is just another victim getting started and that he's merely her handler. He has underestimated her."

"We need to let him know." Jade paused. "But really, it's all circumstantial. We don't know for sure the nurse is Cynthia."

"Let's find out. I have a friend who could run these photos through the FBI's facial recognition software. I could make the request high priority."

"That would be great. In the meantime, we need to let Landon know what we suspect. But how?"

Maggie shrugged. "I'm not sure. If we send him a message, the Justice Club could find out." She hesitated. "And there's something else."

"What?"

"I'm concerned that Landon is in way over his head, regardless of who is helping him on the inside."

"That's just one more reason for you to be at that concert tomorrow night," Jade said. "He needs you."

42

Wednesday, March 30
11.5 hours left …

Morning light seeped past the curtains, blinding me.
I slid one hand under the pillow until my fingertips came into contact with the all-important capsule. Beside it lay the wireless jammer/watch Jade had given me. I'd kept it hidden in my shoe until bedtime, puzzling over the best time to use it. The moment I turned it on, the Justice Club would know.

Getting up, I reached for the new Gideon Bible, stunned that Monty had already highlighted several verses for me to read. One verse, in particular, Isaiah 41:10, transfixed me.

Fear not, for I am with you;
Be not dismayed, for I am your God.
I will strengthen you,
Yes, I will help you,
I will uphold you with My righteous right hand.

No matter what happens this day, God, You are with me and will strengthen me for it.

Later, on my way to the breakfast room, I slid the pill into my shirt pocket, planning to simply slip it in when I drank my coffee. What could be more natural? If anyone in the band noticed, it would be no big deal.

One capsule resembled any other.

Simple.

Flashing a flirtatious smile, Cynthia had saved a spot for me at the crowded table. I'd expected an annoyed reception after I had crashed her meeting at the amusement park. Why so warm this morning?

I asked the waiter to bring my typical breakfast of an omelet, grapefruit, and toast, though I added a small bowl of oatmeal for good measure. It would be an especially taxing day.

Across the table, Amee eyed me. "Maestro, you look tired. You didn't sleep well?"

I shrugged. "Not really. I should be used to hotels by now, but … well …"

"Later, after the sound check and lunch, you should take a nap. You need to be fresh for the concert tonight."

And why would I especially need to be fresh tonight, Amee?

I gave her a perfunctory nod—Monty had been right yet again—and sipped my coffee, the capsule on my mind. But just as my fingers slid into my pocket, Cynthia leaped up and clutched a naked earlobe. "Oh no! I've lost my earring. Would you all help me find it?"

"Of course," Amee said.

"Sure," Carrie, the makeup lady, added. "What does it look like?"

"It's a diamond stud surrounded by sapphires, like this." She turned her head, displaying the matching earring in her earlobe. "They were a special gift from my godmother at my high school graduation. Oh no, I hope I can find it."

On hands and knees, we crawled around on the burgundy carpet and searched under the table and below chairs. Cynthia gave a triumphant cry and held up the missing item. "Oh, yay! I found it! Thanks so much for your help."

By then my grapefruit, oatmeal, and toast had arrived. I was told the omelet would arrive shortly.

Amee sauntered off, cell phone pressed to her ear, not paying attention. Perfect timing.

Eyeing my coffee, I reached into my shirt pocket for the capsule, but my fingertips met only empty space. A hot flash crept up my neck.

Gone?

Could the pill have fallen out of my pocket while I'd been looking for Cynthia's earring?

Back on the floor, I searched for the pill until somebody chuckled and wondered aloud what I was doing. Cynthia mussed my hair. "Silly Landon. Didn't you hear? I found my earring a few minutes ago. You can stop looking for it now."

How to explain?

I returned to my seat, not as hungry as I'd been earlier. "I had a pill in my pocket. It must have fallen out when we were looking for the earring. Did anybody happen to see it?"

Nobody spoke up, though several offered other pain relievers if I wanted one. I declined.

The oatmeal stuck in my throat. The pill must have been lost when I was on my hands and knees, but the dark carpeting hadn't revealed it anywhere.

Could the missing earring have been contrived just so I'd lose the capsule on the floor and someone could grab it? Maybe Amee had somehow discovered Monty's plan and desired to thwart it.

Or maybe you have an overactive imagination, and you simply lost it. End of story. Maybe God wants you to trust Him in this situation instead of putting your trust in a pill.

My brain strained at my options. I needed to get a message to Monty that his plan had been compromised. But how? I had no way of reaching him.

Great.

The Justice Club would try to take control during my nap. I could always force myself to stay awake, but something told me the solution wouldn't be that simple.

SOUND CHECK COULD HAVE GONE BETTER. I played through a few songs like an automaton; I'd pour on the emotion tonight. Right now only one word dominated my mind.

Trapped.

If only I'd taken Maggie and Jade's advice and gotten out of the Justice Club when I could. The feeling of walls closing in around me made me sweat and dread the upcoming concert.

After lunch Amee predictably pulled me aside. "Are you feeling okay? You don't look so good."

"Just nerves, I guess."

She cocked her head. "Nerves? Surely you're over those by now. A nap will do you a world of good. No, don't give me that look. I mean it."

Yes, Mother.

She grabbed me by the arm and led me toward the elevator. "Landon, I won't take no for an answer." She lingered like glue, even as I stepped off the elevator and approached my door.

I intended to say I'd see her in a few hours, but her massive hug coming out of nowhere stunned me. Something else registered—the needle-sharp prick of something penetrating the skin near my right elbow.

I pulled away. "Ouch. What did you do?"

Ignoring me, she sauntered away and turned with a small smile. "Have a nice nap."

In my room, I locked the door, then bolted into the bathroom. I shed my shirt and searched my arm for the source of the agony. A tiny needle, broken from a syringe, jutted from my arm. A disturbing souvenir from the Needle Queen.

If she'd drugged me, how could I possibly force myself to stay awake? What about Monty's plan?

God, please keep me awake. Don't let them tempt me during my dreams.

Within seconds the room tilted. My head swam. I barely reached my bed before the lights went out.

I JOLTED AWAKE, head woozy, and found myself standing a mere foot from my hotel room door, hand extended as if reaching for the doorknob.

The blaring alarm from my laptop across the room sent realization coursing through my veins. I crossed the room and hit the space bar, silencing the alarm.

My head swiveled toward the alarm clock. 3:37.

That morning, more on a whim than anything, I'd programmed my laptop to surveil *myself* in the afternoon instead of Cynthia, just in case something in Monty's plan went wrong. But then I'd had no way of knowing about the lost pill or Amee's injection.

Breathing hard in the stillness, perched on the edge of my bed, I concluded with relief that the alarm had successfully shattered the spell of daydream state. But on what errand had the Justice Club intended to send me? God had intervened and thwarted their plans for me.

Still, the show must go on, but at least I wouldn't be their errand boy.

Wait.

On the bedside table lay an envelope with my name scrawled on top. Amee's handwriting. Inside I found several photos of Jade Hamilton from the perspective of someone pursuing her. I swallowed hard, barely able to breathe.

In one shot Jade was running away from the point of view, back turned. The person in pursuit clutched a knife, the blade, pointing down, occupying the right foreground. In several others the pursuer must have been peering at Jade while he pinned her down, a knife again in the right foreground, ready to plunge into her, her eyes large and terror filled.

My fingers pulled into fists.

These were from the attack at Jade's house. The operative must have been wearing a camera.

At the bottom of the photos lay a piece of paper with a handwritten note from Amee.

He almost killed her. Mess with our plans, and next time she'll be six feet under.

Chilled to the bone, I considered this new wrinkle.

The disturbing pictures revealed an unmistakable truth. The Justice Club must doubt they could control me, so they had chosen an old-fashioned method: threatening those I loved.

But could they get to Jade a second time if I continued with the resistance's plans? Gordon would never let an attack like this happen again.

Hunting for my cell phone, I tried calling her, doubting the Justice Club would let the call go through. My fears were confirmed, and I set the phone down. Even if I jumped on a plane this second, could I even reach her in time?

And I had a small event tonight called a concert.

I could only trust God to protect her no matter what happened next.

PART 4

GREATER IS HE

43

27 minutes left …

Beyond the edge of light where darkness reigned, thousands watched, clapped, and occasionally hooted or whistled. The mini orchestra pulsed, and violins rose and peaked with the melody while I approached the ending of the opener, my newest composition, "A Parting Glance."

Despite the unknowns lying before me, my fingers glided across the keys with an ease that made me smile. I couldn't help it. There was something truly magical about performing onstage again, despite the threat and tension lingering beneath the surface.

Every performer does it. Smiles. Glistens. Puts on a show. After all, it's what fans pay for—even on this night of nights when everything could go so terribly wrong. Would I later regret not taking Maggie's one-way ticket out of this scene of impending doom?

Perhaps what I sensed now embodied the same atmosphere someone on his deathbed experienced, the certainty that the grim reaper waited just around the corner with his scythe. Ready to mow someone down.

But would I, instead of the grim reaper, be the mower?

The song ended, and I took my bow. I gestured to acknowledge my band, all stunning and dressed to the nines, not a hair out of place, whitened teeth glimmering.

Out of the corner of my eye, Amee stood just off stage right in the wings, her eyes glued to me, studying my every move. I had choices on this night of nights, and Amee of all people knew that. Which explained her probing eye.

What would happen on this night?

While the crowd rose and rained down their worship on us, my gaze skimmed the myriad faces before me, seeking Monty somewhere among them. No sight of him.

If he didn't show, I'd have no choice but to face the evil alone, unprepared and insufficient.

But just as this thought registered, an inaudible voice, as gentle as a summer breeze, as voiceless as a hummingbird's blurring wing, revealed the lie I'd already accepted without thinking.

How could I ever think I'd be alone?

God wouldn't abandon me on this night of nights.

And with the acknowledgment of this truth, the lies shattered and skittered away.

44

23 minutes left …

"Sure it's tonight?" Thad, an FBI agent from the California field office, said into Maggie's earpiece from the thirtieth row.

"Oh yeah, I'm sure," Maggie said into the tiny microphone on her wrist.

From the tenth row back in house left, with an exit mere feet away, she sampled the ambiance around her as the crowd, like one massive living and breathing thing, listened intently to another song. An expectant *something* held the atmosphere around her in a tight grip, unwilling to let go until …

Something happened.

Something unexpected.

"Thanks for being my eyes and ears at such short notice," Maggie said.

"Hey, no problem. I've been wanting to hear this guy anyhow. Very thoughtful of the Bureau to give me a ticket."

Maggie rolled her eyes. This deal wasn't about seeing a Landon Jeffers concert. "We may be able to save lives if we can figure out what's going to happen and help prevent it. Let me know if you see anything unusual."

"Shh." This came from the woman sitting in front of Maggie, whose face had swiveled toward her with a glare.

"Sorry," Maggie whispered, hoping the woman hadn't overheard anything she said. The last thing she needed to stoke was mass panic.

IN THE HOTEL room two blocks away, cozy with a bag of potato chips and her laptop, Jade accepted the fact that this was as close to Landon as she was going to get. At least Maggie had provided access to a live video feed of the concert. Every thirty seconds, the visual looped through various vantage points in both the auditorium and lobby.

Be my eyes and ears, Jade, Maggie had told her. *Even from a hotel room, you might see something suspicious. If you do, call me.*

Some camera angles of the crammed auditorium were from too far away to be helpful. She could barely distinguish individuals, never mind weapons. But other shots captured a section of maybe a dozen people at a time.

God, please give me eyes to see.

45

21 minutes left …

K im Ono, my cellist, took a bow after our new arrangement of "Somewhere over the Rainbow," which the crowd adored. I rose from the piano and reached for her hand, and we took a bow together. The masses roared, and I faked a smile, muscles tense.

When the clapping and hooting faded, I talked a bit about my cancer journey—of course, staying away from the true reason for the event—and concluded with "As Long as I Have Breath," a new song I'd written and dedicated to those struggling with terminal illnesses. Oh, the power of music. Few listened to the piece's conclusion with dry eyes.

After the song's climax, the arrangement naturally led into "Amazing Grace," and right on cue, Cynthia appeared on my right with her pennywhistle and a smile. She looked stunning in her emerald-green sequined dress, her brown hair swept back and slung over one shoulder in a short single braid.

She took the lead, and I accompanied, her presence alone making me wary of what she might do next. If there would even *be* a next.

Could a certain high note on her instrument audibly trigger a bomb? If so, I couldn't think of a better song in which to make my exit.

The song concluded, and Cynthia took a bow, then grabbed a nearby microphone. "Wow, thank you. You are all too kind. You know, we really do have a schedule to keep tonight, but sometimes rules are meant to be broken."

I just nodded and smiled, rolling with it but having no idea what she meant. No departures from the song lineup had been run by me, and right now anything unexpected set my teeth on edge.

She turned to me apologetically. "You don't mind, do you, Landon?"

And my response should have been—what? Outrage? I smiled along and shrugged, while my palms moistened.

"You may think we're talented here onstage," Cynthia said, "but sometimes talent lies in the very people sitting next to you, but you have no idea. Just recently I met a very special lady who can play the flute better than I can—and I really mean that.

"When she's not practicing her music and spoiling her eight grandchildren, she spends her time doing nothing very important, just helping to decide some of the most important and sometimes-controversial court cases of our land. Please put your hands together and welcome one of our very talented justices of the United States Supreme Court, the Honorable Maria Lamont. We're going to play a duet together."

46

17 minutes left …

Maria Lamont?

"Thad, you there?" Maggie said into her wrist mic.

"Yeah."

"We were warned that Lamont might be a target. And now this. Take the exit and meet me in the lobby."

Once they met, Maggie unpocketed her cell phone without breaking her stride. "This could be turning into something big, all right. We need reinforcements here now." She hunted for the number of Ted Olinger, her contact at the California field office.

Thad, overweight and brown haired with a roly-poly face shielded by black-framed glasses, watched with an annoyed look, apparently peeved that he had to miss part of the concert. "So you had a warning about this?"

Phone pressed to her ear, waiting, Maggie nodded. "Yeah, but we didn't have any specifics. The guy didn't even know whether anything would happen. It looks like it may be tonight."

"Lamont has her own security team. Won't they be enough?"

"Let's hope so. If anything happens before a team can get here, they'll have no choice but to handle things on their own." Her party picked up, and she spoke to Ted in hurried and excited tones. Then hung up.

A split second later, Maggie's phone rang. Jade.

"Are you seeing what I'm seeing, Maggie?" Jade said. "It's exactly as Landon feared."

"I know, Jade. I've got some agents on the way. If there's a credible threat of firearms, the ATF may be notified too."

"Of course the threat's credible," Jade said. "What more do they need?"

"No. We have nothing to go on but what Landon said, which was hardly abundant in specifics. Lamont and Cynthia are musical friends. There may not be anything unusual about her appearance."

"We're talking about a justice of the Supreme Court here," Jade said.

"It's up to my contacts at the FBI field office. My hands are tied. But one thing I do know. As we suspected, Jade, I received confirmation that Cynthia and that nurse are the same person. Not only that, but my colleague connected Cynthia's facial profile to several unsolved crimes across the country over the last few months. She's bad news."

"Then why not arrest her?"

"Interrupt the concert with eight thousand people looking on? I don't think so. Nobody wants to create mass hysteria. We'll have to wait for the right moment to confront her."

"But what if waiting for that moment means you're too late to stop whatever's about to happen?"

"I know, Jade. It's not an easy scenario. Thanks for calling. Talk to you later."

End call.

A scan of the lobby revealed security personnel stationed at various closed doors. "So what do we do while we wait?" Thad said.

"Follow me." Approaching the closest official, Maggie reached into her purse for her ID.

47

13 minutes left …

The duet of "Danny Boy" by Maria Lamont on the flute and Cynthia Lemke on the pennywhistle proved flawless and moving. I provided simple, light accompaniment while fixing my gaze on Cynthia's every move.

The image of her and Chris Van Lanen huddled over two upended flashlights in an abandoned amusement park flared in my mind screen.

If Chris showed up, what could they be planning? To kill the justice while eight thousand people looked on?

I glanced at the wireless-jamming watch, glad to have it with me but unsure when or if to trigger it.

Two of Justice Lamont's security guards had taken positions offstage to the right and left, their eyes pinned to the justice with frequent, searching glances sweeping the first few rows of spectators. One false move, and they'd usher her out of there pronto.

So far nothing had happened to arouse alarm.

The audience loved the duet and gave Cynthia and Maria—a short, husky woman with shoulder-length auburn hair—a standing ovation.

The women slapped each other on the backs like pals and took their bows. The crowd chanted, "La-mont, La-mont, La-mont!"

Guess they wanted an encore.

Thankfully, the women had practiced their version of "Shenandoah" and impressed while I watched, hands away from the keys this time.

The roar of applause jerked me back to the women, who took another bow before slipping off to the wings of stage right, where they lingered and watched just beyond the audience's view. Why didn't security take Maria back to her VIP seat, where she'd be protected and safe? Had Cynthia invited her to watch the show from there?

I didn't have long to dwell on this new concern because the next part of the concert, a fan favorite wherever I went, entailed asking the audience for a volunteer to play the piano with me on stage. Typically, the stage manager had already vetted a few entries and made an educated choice based on aptitude. A lot of folks at house right gave attention to a certain guy by chanting, "Ga-vin, Ga-vin, Ga-vin!"

Putting a hand to my forehead to block the lights, I struggled to make him out. "All right, Gavin, I guess you're the lucky guy. You wanna join me up here at a piano? You can play more than chopsticks, right?"

A smattering of chuckles.

Several people patted the guy on the back as he made his way to the stage like a game show contestant. He arrived at the steps near the pianos and ascended them, his face coming into view.

Chris Van Lanen flashed a dazzling smile.

48

9 minutes left ...

After seeing Maggie's creds, the security manager, an overweight bald guy, led her and Thad to the main office. Computers occupied various workstations. On the monitors strung along the wall appeared live video feeds of various locations: several shots of the parking lots, multiple views of the lobby, and many angles of the auditorium.

While Maggie talked a mile a minute, the manager sank into the chair at his desk and motioned to two chairs across from him. "Please, just slow down. You're saying *what's* going to happen tonight?"

Poised on her chair's edge, Maggie fumed, hands knotted. "Maria Lamont, a justice of the Supreme Court—she's here tonight. In fact, she was just onstage. We have reason to believe her life may be in danger."

The guy nodded. "Yeah, we know all about her appearance. Her security people are here, too. She should be in good hands."

"Good hands!" Maggie said. "You have no idea what you're dealing with here. I have intel that suggests there may be some sort of attempt on her life tonight."

His eyebrows shot up. "Attempt by whom? When?"

"We don't know exactly," Maggie said.

He cast a doubtful look at her. Folded his arms. Shot a look at Thad as if wishing he'd calm her down. "So what do you expect me to do? Stop the concert?"

"No, not at all. I would just like to speak to Maria or to the guy in charge of her security team."

He checked his watch, taking only seconds to process. Studying his computer monitor, he typed in something. Looked at Maggie. "Um, all right. Just stay here. Let me see what I can find out."

He pushed out of his chair and disappeared down a hallway. No sense of urgency in his step.

Maggie leaned forward, forking her fingers through her hair. "Unbelievable. We don't have time for this."

Her phone rang. Jade.

"Are you seeing this?" Jade said. "Guess who is joining Landon at one of the pianos?"

On the largest monitor played a live feed of the stage.

"No way." Maggie rose, cursing under her breath. "I was e-mailed an age-progression portrait of Chris Van Lanen. That's him all right, risen from the dead. Landon was right."

"Then Landon's in danger," Jade said. "I'm on my way."

"Jade, don't—"

"Sorry, Maggie, but I'm not sitting in this hotel room a second longer. Text me on the way so I know where and how to find you."

"Will do. I'll have someone at the main entrance lead you here."

49

6 minutes left ...

Two black grand pianos had been stationed side by side so the pianists could face each other, profiles to the audience. My piano was closest to the audience. Chris Van Lanen took a seat at the piano across from mine, just to my right.

I leaned toward the mic. "So, Chris—I mean, Gavin—welcome to my stage." My slipup didn't faze him. Or if it did, he chose not to show it. Speaking coherently would now require a good bit of my concentration.

Monty had said Chris was part of something big, but Chris hadn't appeared in a trench coat with machine guns hidden at his sides. No visible weapons. Just blue jeans and a red-and-black checkered shirt.

If I hadn't known his true identity, I never would have thought twice. He grinned, playing the part of starstruck fan who couldn't believe he'd gotten on stage with Landon Jeffers. Convincing performance.

"Wow. I can't believe I'm here," Chris said.

Molly Leonard, a stage assistant, appeared and moved his microphone closer to his mouth.

"You'll need to talk into the mic, Gavin," I said, "so people can hear you."

"Oh, sure. No problem." He grabbed the mic and thrust it toward his face, barely an inch away. "Is that better?"

A high-pitched squeal filled the expansive space before abating. My gritted teeth let up, aching jaw releasing.

"Oh, sorry about that." He chuckled nervously, gaze shifting to the audience. Then, as if realizing the sight made him only more nervous, he faced forward and kept his eyes on me.

I gave him a comforting smile. "It's okay, Gavin. Don't be nervous. You aren't nervous, are you?"

"Uh-huh."

"Why? There are only eight thousand people or so out there. Nobody's watching you."

Everybody laughed, and I joined in. "But you know what? They love you."

Instant applause followed. Somebody shouted his name.

"Gavin!" a woman cried in an emotional voice. "We love you!"

He blushed.

So what's up your sleeve, Chris?

I followed the script despite taut muscles screaming throughout my body. "Do you want to say hi to your mom?"

"Sure." To the mic he said, "Hi, Mom."

How ironic. His mom still thought him dead after all these years. If video clips of the concert hit the Internet, wouldn't his family recognize him? Why expose himself?

That part didn't make sense. Or maybe it did.

Maybe because of what he has planned tonight, being recognized won't matter.

"That wasn't so bad, was it?" I said. "You did a great job. See, you're a star." More applause. No need to drag this out. "Okay, Gavin, what do you wanna play with me tonight?"

"'The Parting.'"

Hoots and whistles. The song had made my greatest hits collection for good reason.

I nodded. "Nice choice. You have my sheet music, right? You've

246

practiced this song?"

He rolled his eyes. "You think I'd come up here and wanna play a song I haven't practiced?"

"Excellent. You're impressing me more and more. Now, Gavin, do you know the story behind this song?"

"Actually, I don't."

"That's okay." I turned to the crowd, their faces shadowy and subdued due to the bright stage lights. "I wrote this song and dedicated it to the first love of my life. When I wrote it, I didn't say who I meant. She may be watching this from the audience tonight or later see a video clip, and I don't want to embarrass her, so I won't say her name. You never want to embarrass a lady, now do you, Gavin?"

"Whatever you say, Landon."

Laughter erupted.

"Surely you know what I mean. Do you have a girlfriend? No? There's *nobody* on your mind?"

"Well, maybe there is, but I'm not saying her name either."

"Aww," came from the crowd, followed by more laughter and scattered applause.

"We were high school sweethearts," I said, "but due to circumstances neither of us could have anticipated, I had to move away and leave my love behind. True story. I know, it's hard to understand why two people who really loved each other would ever have to be parted like that, but it really happened, and that's the story behind the song."

I turned to him. "Have you ever had to leave someone you loved behind and tried to go on without them?"

Certainly he couldn't miss the irony, because that was exactly what he'd done to his family, pretending to be dead all these years. But he wagged his head no.

Little liar.

"Well, consider yourself fortunate." I rubbed my hands together. "Okay, Gavin, are you ready to play? My band will give us a little introduction. If you know the song like I suspect you do, you'll know exactly when to start."

The band did an intro, and Chris began playing the song flawlessly while I added flourishes and scrutinized his hairline, seeking signs of an implant but finding none. Perhaps he'd had surgery too long ago for it to leave any traces.

Maybe the Justice Club had wiped his memory clean of his family, deleting any connecting memories to them. If so, then he deserved my pity, not my anger. Could he possibly have no idea what he was doing? Or who he once had been?

How much of this guy was really Chris Van Lanen? Or a product of the Justice Club's clever manipulation?

The Chris I knew had never so much as touched a piano key. The conviction that he couldn't possibly play this well without help sent a shiver down my spine.

Oh yes, the Justice Club is here. Right now. Controlling Chris.

My focus swept the crowd, shadowy and indistinct, mostly hidden in shadow. In the wings stood my producer and stage crew members. Cynthia and Maria Lamont looked on from off stage right. Security from the US Marshals service were stationed near Maria and no doubt scattered throughout the auditorium.

If only Maria had taken her seat. Cynthia had placed her in a position of great vulnerability.

Coincidence?

When Chris finished, the crowd went crazy. I laughed, saying into my mic, "Boy, I guess I'm out of a job now that Gavin is in town. Wow, am I impressed! You nailed it."

I rose and crossed to him with a smile, then shook his hand and patted his back. He rose, and together we turned as one and faced the audience. Took a bow.

More thunderous applause, whistles, and hoots. Then a growing chant: "Gav-in! Gav-in! Gav-in!"

"Go ahead," I said to him. "Take your own bow. You deserve it."

He stood tall and swept down as if he'd rehearsed the move. Then he fell to one knee like he'd dropped something or merely tripped on a microphone cord. Without thinking, I crouched beside him to see what was wrong or to help retrieve whatever he'd lost.

In that split second, he shot a look under my grand piano. I followed his line of sight, my scalp tightening.

Someone had duct-taped an AR-15 to the piano's underside.

50

66 seconds left …

Time decelerated to a crawl. My temples pounded.

The hand of evil reached into my mind and pushed a metaphorical button. My gaze locked on the weapon, the same rifle Amee had introduced me to during shooting practice.

The back of my throat itched. My mouth watered.

Harbingers of a daymare.

In a snapshot of recent memory, a voice sliced through my thoughts —Amee's voice talking to me during my drug-induced nap. She'd apparently found a way back into my room and used the drugs to program a susceptible mind for my role in events yet to come.

You will take the gun, Landon. You will point it at the audience and pull the trigger again and again. It doesn't matter who you hit. Just shoot as many people as you can. Gavin will be there to direct you to the weapon. At first you won't know why he's there, but when you see the gun, you will remember what I'm telling you now. You will know what you need to do.

Dragged back to the present, seconds crawling in slo-mo, I knew my orders. Without thinking, I reached for the weapon at the same instant something inside me whispered, *You have been bought with a price, Landon. You are not your own. You don't need to do what these wicked people want. You* can *say no.*

But an evil voice countered. *Look at them—those fickle fans. Remember how hard you worked on those first few recordings and how little they gave in return? They were your best work, but the public was so slow in responding. In recognizing your talent.*

Look at them on the front row: arms folded, faces sullen, so judgmental, so hard to please. They grudgingly plunk down their cash, but they're empty shells. Aren't you sick and tired of trying to please them, especially those who write negative reviews after you work so hard?

Don't they deserve to be put away for good?

Eliminated?

You have the power and the means. Accept the weapon and take out that frustration that has been tucked away for so long. Those hard-to-please fans deserve to die.

Right now.

Do it!

I blinked. Shook my head as if casting off these bizarre thoughts. Hands fisted.

No, Landon, you don't have to do this. You won't.

They have no control over you.

Greater is He who is in you than he who is in the world.

Could the Justice Club really be so stupid? They had to know by now that I couldn't be controlled unless I yielded to temptation and chose to go along with their plans.

In that split second of sorting truth from lies, Chris's gaze met mine. He discerned my resistance. Knew I'd never give in.

And here I'd forgotten to turn on the wireless jammer. God had intervened instead.

Eyes glazing over, he reached for the AR-15; it had a bump stock in place, making his semiautomatic rifle operate like a fully automatic weapon. His movement was robot like, like someone somewhere had pressed a button, setting plan B into motion.

Chris stripped away the duct tape and grabbed the rifle. I rose to my feet and reached for the gun. Too slow.

He shoved me, and I tripped on a microphone cord. Went down with a painful impact on my knees.

Rising, he swiveled toward the audience. Fired the weapon. And sprayed bullets into the crowd.

51

Through a phone call, with Maggie directing Jade to the right door and the right usher, Jade joined her. Just in time.

At the boom of gunfire, Maggie lurched to her feet. Thad ran from the room.

In two paces, Jade looked at the monitor, voice shaking. "Chris has a gun. He's—oh no!" Nausea seared the back of her throat.

"We can't wait any longer," Maggie said. "C'mon!"

"But those poor people. And Landon."

"Let someone there deal with them. And Landon can take care of himself. We gotta find Justice Lamont. *Now.*"

"She was onstage just a few minutes ago."

Maggie grabbed her hand. Yanked her toward the door. "Let's go. Now that we're backstage, let's see if we can help. Stay close to me, Jade."

Jade yielded. Down wood-paneled corridors, they jogged. People shrieked and ran in every direction without any semblance of order.

More nearby gunfire pounded. Women screamed.

Maggie took a right at a sign pointing toward the stage. Jade did her best to keep up despite a pinch in her side. She gave the hallway a quick head check. No sign of security personnel or Maria Lamont's security detail anywhere. They were probably in the auditorium, rushing the stage.

They ascended a few steps and came to a small room leading to a closed, windowed door. Several people, women and men in dark suits, lay on the floor in pools of blood. Some didn't move. Others groaned.

A woman matching the description of Cynthia Lemke huddled over a dark-haired woman lying beside the stage door. Jade and Maggie exchanged glances, and Maggie pulled out her gun to cover for Jade. Recognizing Maria Lamont, Jade brushed past Cynthia and knelt beside the injured woman. Reached for her wrist.

"Hey, who are you?" Cynthia said.

"I'm a nurse," Jade said.

The pulse was sluggish. Maria Lamont's eyes were closed as if asleep. Shallow breaths issued between parted lips.

Perhaps at the sound of gunfire, her security guys had rushed her to this place and stormed through the door, going after Chris. No, that couldn't be; certainly they wouldn't have left Maria unprotected. Somebody must have stayed behind to guard her. Yet where were they? Among the wounded and dying?

Didn't matter. Either way, Maria was hurt.

Jade drew in a shuddering breath while searching the justice's body.

No obvious wounds from gunfire. So what could be wrong with her?

52

———

Surreal. What can happen in mere seconds.

Life pulled back to slo-mo.

Rat-a-tat-tat-tat-tat-tat.

Chris's torso and arms jerked with the reverberations of gunfire. His jaw clenched.

People in the closest rows either dove for cover or toppled like dominoes in the fusillade of bullets.

Screams and shrieks rose from those cramming the aisles and running or diving toward the exits. Groans and wails rose from those already crumpled on the floor, wounded or dying.

All this happened in mere seconds before my stunned mind accepted the reality unfolding in real time before my eyes. The unimaginable reality I couldn't allow to continue.

Only three paces away, I got up and charged Chris. Tackled him from the side.

We both went down, his remaining shots going wild above our heads. On top of him, I reached for the rifle, but he held it tight. Wrenched it beyond my reach, malice pouring from his face.

He head-butted me. My head snapped back, fire blazing in my

skull while teeth clamped down on my tongue. The coppery taste of blood registered.

In my peripheral vision blurred a rush of movement. Had some bystanders come to tackle Chris before he could get back on his feet?

I couldn't wait for them. Ignoring the agony, I reached for the rifle again.

We wrestled for it. He swung the butt toward my temple.

Lights exploded behind my eyes. Searing pain pushed a moan from my lips.

I toppled, and Chris swiveled away. On his knees, he brought the AR-15 to bear.

More percussive explosions jerked my chest.

Bullets riddled the closest would-be saviors, perhaps US Marshals rushing toward Chris on Maria's behalf. They fell like bowling pins.

Get up, Landon. Move!

Rising on one elbow, I stared at the carnage, unable to process. Lost in a stupor.

So cold. My teeth chattered. My head pulsed fire where Chris had nailed it.

Chris ran out of ammo and scampered back to the piano. Someone had duct-taped several thirty-round magazines to the bottom.

Who could have done this?

People shrieked and ran, stampeding the aisles in that precious lull before certain death came calling again.

Chris turned his back to me while inserting a clip into the magazine well. Before the rifle could fire, he'd need to chamber a round first.

Seeing my chance, I got up and rushed him from behind. Tackled him. He collapsed facedown under my weight with a grunt, the rifle somewhere beneath us.

Reaching for the rifle with a grunt, I clamped a hand around the stock. But so did he. With his other hand, he slapped the bolt release. He could kill anyone now, including me—that was, if he controlled the rifle.

Gasps exploded out of me. "Drop it, Chris. This ends now!"

"You and who else are going to make me?" Raising his torso beneath my weight, he swung his head back, as if to head-butt my nose. But I angled away just in time. Slinking an arm under his chin, I put him in a headlock, applying pressure to his throat.

"Drop it!" I yelled.

His right elbow rammed my side.

My gasp, wedded with sheer agony, exploded out of me. Reflexes forced me to let go.

Roles reversed in a split second. He rolled on top of me. Aimed the rifle at my face. "Now you're a dead man, Landon Jeffers."

53

"What's wrong with her?" Jade said, gaze cutting to Cynthia.

"I don't know," Cynthia said. "We were running away, and she just went down."

There had to be an explanation for her condition. Frantically, Jade checked her pulse again. Scanned her body. No blood. No entry or exit wounds.

She gave Maggie a nod. "She appears to be okay. Just unconscious for some reason."

Cynthia glared at both of them. "Who *are* you?"

Maggie flashed her FBI creds. "And who exactly are *you*?"

Cynthia introduced herself.

"What's wrong with Justice Lamont?" Maggie said in an accusatory tone.

Cynthia shrugged. "I guess she fainted. Some folks just can't handle seeing stuff like that." She gestured with her head toward the stage.

"Where's her security detail?" Maggie said.

Cynthia gestured toward the nearby bodies. "Are you blind? Some are lying here. Others went out this door, but they never came back."

More gunfire. Close. Louder this time.

With each thunderous percussion, Jade's body jerked. "So what should we do?"

Maggie eyed the stage door. "Protect Justice Lamont at all costs."

Jade shared her uneasiness. "But we don't know where the gunman is. What if he tries to exit the stage this way?"

"He won't now." Maggie found a nearby chair and wedged it under the doorknob. She peered out the small window onto the stage. Swallowed hard.

"What do you see?" Jade said.

"Chaos. No telling where the shooter is."

Through the door seeped more sounds of confusion and panic. More automatic gunfire.

Jade bit her lip.

God, please keep Landon safe. Somebody, please take Chris down.

Jade studied Maria. "We need to get her out of here. She's not safe."

Maggie nodded. "The gunman could even be looking for her." They exchanged horrified looks.

A tremor of panic shook Jade's chest. She bent over Maria and patted her face. "Maria. Maria? You need to wake up."

Nothing.

She brushed a hand across the back of Maria's head, lifting it. Wetness registered. Her hand came away bloody.

54

You're going to die.

Chris's finger tightened on the trigger, the muzzle of the AR-15 dancing only inches from my face.

Find a way to buy time.

Gasps exploded out of me. "Your mother still loves you, Chris, but she thinks you're dead."

Emotionless eyes stared. "I *am* dead."

"Don't you want to see her again?"

His jaw muscles bunched. "Leave my mom out of this."

"Did they erase your memories of her so you'd be easier to control?"

"Shut up!" Still, he hesitated to pull the trigger. Why? Could a battle be raging in his mind?

Sweat stung my eyes. Ignoring my aching temple, I said, "Do you know what your mom used to say every year on your birthday?"

He blinked but remained silent.

In my peripheral vision, people flanked us. My tackling him had both turned his sights on me and allowed them to surround us. Regardless of what happened to me, Chris wasn't walking away from this one.

"Drop the weapon!" The unmistakable bark of a cop scraped my nerves raw.

I lifted a cautionary hand.

Just wait. Let me reason with him. Please.

If somebody shot Chris, he could pull the trigger in reflex. Surely the cop knew this, but disarming Chris before he hurt or killed others made sense. I just prayed some common sense factored into his decision.

I wet my dry lips with a tongue leached of moisture. "What do you think she said every year on your birthday, Chris? You want to know, don't you? Shoot me, and you'll never find out."

No response. Dead eyes fixed on mine. What could he be waiting for?

Still a stalemate. And no assurance I'd walk away from this. I tried to calm my panting and ignored my aching chest from his weight bearing down on me.

"Okay, Chris, I'll tell you. Every year on your birthday, your dad released the number of balloons for the age you would have been had you lived. Do you know what your mom always said as the balloons drifted away?"

His eyes moistened. Only inches from my face, the muzzle jittered. "Tell me."

The emotional Chris, the real Chris, had manifested if my theory proved to be correct …

"She said, 'I'm sure he's in a better place.'"

During our stare down, he swallowed.

"But is that true, Chris? Are you really in a better place?"

A bead of sweat trickled down his cheek. "I'm in hell."

"No, this is only a taste of it. You can go to heaven, Chris."

"No. It's too late for me. Look at what I've done."

"You mean, what *they've* made you do."

A sarcastic chuckle. "You think anybody's gonna buy that?"

"I do, Chris, for what it's worth. I know what it's like to wake up with blood on your hands and have no idea what they made you do. I know what it's like to feel trapped."

His eyes widened.

"They put something in your head, Chris, to control you. I know, I have an implant too. But I have a little surprise."

He swallowed. Waited.

"See that watch on my wrist? It's really a wireless jammer I turned on only moments ago. Because you're so close to me, it's not only blocking the controlling signals to my implant. *It's blocking yours, too.*"

"What?"

"It means you're free, Chris. You *can* choose to do what's right. You don't have to do what they want anymore. Put the gun down."

A war raged on his face, a grappling with truth. "I … I don't think I can."

"Of course you can. They're no longer in control. You don't have to play their sick games anymore. Please, Chris."

The moment taunted both of us. So close to freedom. But I could tell from his eyes that surrender was by no means on the table. He'd die first before surrendering.

A quick movement flared to Chris's right. The cop closing in?

Chris glanced to the side for an instant.

It was enough.

I grabbed the barrel with both hands, shoved it away from my face. Someone grabbed me, dragged me from Chris. Bystanders tackled Chris Van Lanen before he could even flirt with the idea of killing anyone else.

55

Maggie whirled toward Cynthia. "What happened to her?"

"Nothing as far as I know. Like I said, when shots were fired, we both ran here. Maybe she hit her head while we were fleeing. Beats me." Cynthia rose, thrusting her hands behind her. The glint of something shiny caught Jade's eye.

"Hey, what have you got there?" Jade reached for her hidden hand, but Cynthia evaded her grasp.

Maggie's fingers clamped around Cynthia's wrist and forced her hand into view. Cynthia clutched a small hand-held device composed of glass and steel. Similar to a syringe but larger.

Keeping Cynthia's hand and the device at a safe distance, Maggie said, "I know who you are. You played nurse and injected a man with a brain implant while he was unconscious in the hospital, didn't you? Is this the device you used?"

Cynthia pressed her lips tightly together, eyes defiant.

Jade stared at her, then glanced at Maria Lamont. The justice's head wound. What other explanation could there be?

No, no. This can't be happening.

Maggie began prying the device out of Cynthia's hand, but Cynthia relinquished it without any fuss. "Here, take it. You can have it, for what good it will do you now."

Pocketing the device, Maggie pulled out her Glock. Pointed it at Cynthia's face, voice shrill. "Face the wall! Hands in the air. Now."

Cynthia complied. "It doesn't matter. You're too late."

Jade stared at Maria. The shooting had been nothing but a diversion.

Maria had been the true target all along—not to kill her but to control her. She'd historically been the swing vote for crucial Supreme Court decisions. Give her a brain implant, and the Justice Club could control the more controversial judicial rulings as long as they wished.

The Justice Club now controlled the justice? No, this couldn't be. If Landon hadn't successfully found a way to have his implant removed, what hope did they have of helping Maria?

Spirit flagging, she shot a *What do we do now?* look at Maggie. But Maggie kept her gun and focus trained on Cynthia.

Jade crouched next to Maria and patted the justice's face. Why didn't she wake up? Had she been drugged?

Maggie whimpered.

Jade whirled toward her friend. Too late.

An older, gray-haired man had grabbed Maggie from behind and thrust a syringe into her neck. Maggie wilted, her eyes rolling into her skull. Her gun clattered to the floor.

Jade grabbed the Glock before Cynthia could. She pointed the gun at both of them, barrel dancing, and tried to recall the brief firearms lesson she'd had once upon a time.

The man pulled out a second syringe and stepped toward Jade. Robotlike. Face expressionless. Hallmarks of an operative.

Spiders crawled up the back of Jade's neck. She edged toward the stage door, which was still blocked by the chair. Face this man and Cynthia or flee to the stage and risk running into Chris with his rifle?

Jade maintained a two-handed grip around the gun. "Stay back! Or I'll shoot."

They kept coming.

She pulled the trigger.

ADAM BLUMER

Click.

Nothing happened. Jammed?

Stay or run? Did she have a choice?

56

Armed cops and other law enforcement ran toward the stage from all directions. Other folks, dressed like commandos, with "ATF" scrawled across their backs, surrounded Chris, cuffed him, and led him away through a side door. He didn't resist, face expressionless.

Numb.

No other word could describe my reality or the shock of what I'd seen. The numbness seeped through every fiber of my body. The sobering amazement that I'd somehow survived when others hadn't.

I cradled my throbbing temple. Stunned to find strength in my legs, I ambled away from where the shooting had begun and sat on a piano bench in a daze, thinking I'd found a moment for a breather. Until the carnage painted in broad strokes of red across the auditorium made my gorge rise.

Steering my gaze elsewhere, I put my head down and took deep breaths. Laced my fingers across the back of my neck. Somehow kept the light-headedness at bay.

A woman stooped in front of me, said she was a nurse. She checked my vitals and said I was one of the lucky ones. Deserting me, she headed to the next body, in search of life or another confirmation of death.

Guilt chafed me. Could I have done more to prevent this tragedy? I'd wrestle with that question later. But right now—

Where was everyone? Amee? Members of my band? Had some of them been killed?

Maria Lamont. Could her corpse number among so many?

She'd been watching the concert with Cynthia. Where had they gone? I got up and looked that direction.

Jade dashed toward me, fear tattooed on her face. Where had *she* come from? She'd been here for the concert? At least I didn't have to worry about an operative going after her at home because I had interfered in Justice Club plans.

She grabbed my arms as if to steady herself, her pupils rocketing from side to side. "Landon, you gotta come quick. Cynthia and some man—they're coming after me. And I think Justice Lamont is in trouble."

"What are you talking about?"

"This way. Quick."

"Wait."

I grabbed the nearest cop, and Jade described the threat. Hand on his holstered gun, the officer led us across the stage to the side door. The door swung open. No obvious sign of anyone pursuing Jade. The cop went first, gun drawn, only to reappear seconds later.

"Everything looks clear to me." He muttered a few words into his lapel mic and took off down the corridor, sidestepping bodies.

We tentatively stepped across the threshold. Justice Maria Lamont and Maggie Songbird lay side by side, as if passed out or dead. The sight pushed the air out of my lungs.

Jade watched the cop's retreating back. "But Cynthia and that man were right here. They were coming after me, and all I had was Maggie's gun." She pulled it out, and I drew back, surprised.

"How did you get that?"

She told me the story, and I accepted the Glock, jammed or not, wondering if I'd need it.

My gaze fixed on the two women. "What's wrong with them?"

"They've both been drugged." She crouched beside Justice Lamont. "And it's worse for Maria. Landon, I believe Cynthia injected a brain implant into the justice."

My blood ran cold. "Why do you say that?"

Jade explained what she and Maggie had witnessed. "Come see."

I crouched beside her, and she showed me the bloody mat of hair on the back of Maria's head. She fished the implant injector from Maggie's pocket, the steel glinting in the half-light. I chose not to touch it.

The ramifications of her words sucker-punched me. "They can really do that? *Inject* an implant?"

She described how Cynthia, posing as a nurse, had allegedly injected the implant into John Smith. Turning to Maggie, she nudged her to awaken her. No response. "She might be out for a while. The man stuck a needle in her neck, and she went out like a light. I'm assuming they did the same thing to Justice Lamont." She studied both women, brow furrowed. "What should we do?"

All this time I'd thought I was designated to be the trigger guy. They'd set me up as a decoy, a realization that drowned me in a strong sense of being used.

I fished through Maggie's pockets, found a magazine of ammo, and loaded it into the Glock, replacing the old. Rising, I appraised the situation. "Justice Lamont's protection needs to be our top priority now."

"There are cops everywhere. Shouldn't we just grab one, tell him who Maria is, and explain what happened?"

"Not all cops can be trusted," said a familiar voice behind us, "but you can trust this one."

I whirled. A police officer emerged from the shadows, or so I thought due to his garb until his face registered, complete with brown hair and a matching mustache.

"Monty!" I said. "Have you been hiding here all this time?"

"I told you I'd be here to help if I could." Wasting no time on greetings, the lean older man knelt beside Maria Lamont and checked her vitals like he possessed medical training. "She's unconscious but fine. There may still be time."

"Time for what?" I said.

"Time to get her out of here before Justice Club operatives come looking for her. I have friends who can remove the implant."

My eyes widened. "Is that possible?"

"I'm sorry, Landon. I would have found a way to remove your implant long ago if there had been an easy way. Yours came about by a deep insertion. Hers is more superficial and is simpler to extract for those with the right skills."

"Landon, who is this guy?" Jade said.

I made quick introductions; we were wasting precious time.

"They've wanted Justice Lamont for a long time," Monty said, "and they probably think they succeeded." He eyed my wireless jammer. "They were probably already monitoring her until you showed up. Now that you're here with your jammer, she's off the grid. They'll know something went wrong. We've got to get her and us out of here now. Which reminds me."

He pulled out a small pistol-like device and injected a jammer into Maria's arm. For good measure, he gave me another one, making my jamming watch redundant.

Maggie sat up, groggy and disoriented, her hand pressed to her neck. She asked about her gun, and I returned it. The agent rose unsteadily, assisted by Jade, and asked what was going on. Jade quickly summarized.

Maggie grimly glanced at Justice Lamont, then faced Monty. "I'm Special Agent Maggie Songbird with the FBI. I recognize you from the photo of a Catholic priest. Is that who you are?"

"No, I'm no priest, but there's no time to explain now. We've gotta get Justice Lamont away from here."

"In the absence of her US Marshal protection," Maggie said, "I'm assuming the role of her protector. You're not taking Justice Lamont anywhere until I know who you are and which side you're on."

"I'm Monty, and I work with the resistance. Landon has been assisting us by working inside the Justice Club."

"I'm well aware of that," Maggie said with a critical eye. "What are *you* doing here?"

"We both want to keep the justice safe. I have friends who can remove her implant if we hustle. Does that tell you which side I'm on?"

Maggie took a deep breath. "What do you propose?"

"We need to get the justice out of here."

"Obviously," Maggie said.

"The place is crawling with cops, EMTs, and wounded people. If everyone pitches in, we'll blend right in."

"And take her where?" Maggie said. "We don't want anyone to think we're kidnapping her."

"That's where you fit in," Monty said. "Call your superiors. Tell them that, in the absence of obvious US Marshal protection, the justice is in your protective custody. Say she's hurt and that you're taking her to a hospital."

"Is that where we're going?" Maggie said.

"Later, you can take her there, but I have another destination in mind first."

"Where?"

Monty hesitated. "Do you want the implant removed, or don't you?"

"Of course, but I don't even know for sure who you are or where you want to take her. I'm not going to stand by and just let you—"

"I mean no disrespect," Monty said, "but I don't think you've been listening. The Justice Club designed this whole mass shooting as a smoke screen simply to gain control of Justice Lamont. They succeeded in giving her an implant, but we may be able to undo their work. Thanks to wireless jammers, the justice is currently removed from their control, but that's only a Band-Aid."

Maggie shrugged. "So what's the problem?"

"She's off the grid. Justice Club operatives are on their way here right now to find out what went wrong. If they discover we're trying to rescue her, they'll kill all of us simply to keep her exactly where they want her."

He stepped closer, his face mere inches from hers. "So what do you want to do? Continue to debate this, get us all killed, *and* ensure the Justice Club maintains control of Justice Lamont? Or work with me so we can get the justice safely out of here and to someone who can remove the implant? It's your call."

57

People crowded the corridor, a chaotic scene. Some sat on the floor and wept, while emergency responders knelt over them to determine the extent of their injuries. In the background wailed the incessant hallmark of ambulances. An occasional cop or ATF sauntered by, talking into lapel mics or walkie-talkies. Voices drifted from speakers amid bursts of static.

Due to the chaos, nobody thought it strange to see the four of us carrying a woman toward one of the exit doors. Maggie led us to her rental sedan, and at her directive, we carefully lowered Maria onto the back seat. By now the sun had long set, and shadows lengthened across the chaotic parking lot.

"I'll call the assistant director," Maggie said, stepping toward the driver's side door. "I'll tell him exactly what you suggested, Monty."

Monty obstructed her path. "Sounds like a plan. But if anyone is driving the justice to safety, let it be me. I know exactly where to take her."

She locked eyes with him, jaw set. "Don't be silly. I'm not lying to the assistant director. I'll be driving and taking full responsibility for Maria's safety. Remember, you said we didn't have time to wrangle about this."

"Fine. But later, when you take her to the hospital, they'll discover the head injury. If they wonder what happened, there could be a thousand other explanations."

"Believe me, the FBI is well aware of the conspiracy involving these implants," Maggie said. "If the truth about Maria's implant comes out, what do you care? You can ride off into the sunset. I'll be the one left behind to provide explanations."

Monty nodded. "Fair enough. You drive the justice with Jade. Landon and I will lead the way in my Jeep."

Still Maggie hesitated, measuring Monty with her eyes.

"You can trust him," I said. "I would have been killed long ago if he hadn't helped me."

Maggie said, expression stony, "Okay, fine. It doesn't look like I really have a choice. If I take Justice Lamont to a hospital, they won't have a clue what to do about this implant, but you offer a solution."

"Exactly," Monty said.

Maggie and Jade got in the rental sedan, while I followed Monty across the parking lot to his Jeep. "Are you sure I should come with you?" I said after getting in. "Shouldn't I stay behind and do more inside work with the Justice Club?"

Before answering, he started the engine and pressed the accelerator, making a beeline for the parking lot exit. "Only if you intend to be a martyr, but I'll never let you do that. If you go back now, they'll kill you. The whole world, including the Justice Club, knows—or will soon know—you did everything you could to stop Chris tonight. Landon, I think you're one spy who should come out of the cold. You accomplished your mission."

"But people were killed. I failed."

"What are you talking about? There's no way you could have known what Chris would do. Think of how many more people would have been killed if you *hadn't* tackled Chris? What you did took guts."

"Wait. You were there?"

"Sure I was. Did you really think I'd leave you to the wolves? I came to extract you. Your role of working for us on the inside of the Justice Club is over."

THE DRIVE TOOK us a half hour out of town and deep into the California countryside, with dirt roads and forests and vineyards everywhere. Night encroached, the Jeep's headlights tracing a path down the road.

I peppered Monty with questions about his appearance at the concert and how he had known about the mass shooting tonight. He maintained a mostly tight-lipped response and gave a small smile.

"You are better off not knowing some things, Landon. I've told you that before. That way, if anything were to happen to you—"

"You mean, if the Justice Club ever got me back."

"They'd never be able to extract from you information you don't possess. Even if they sorted through your memories, they'd get nothing."

"They can do that? Search my memories, I mean."

"Of course. You'd be amazed by what these people know. How else could they have known so much about the school shooting when you were a kid? We hacked into their system and downloaded data about those memories. That's how we know so much about you, too."

Monty pulled into a small driveway blocked by a closed steel gate. He gave me a key and instructions to unlock the padlock and open the gate for us. I did as instructed.

We followed the driveway deeper into the woods. Just when I wondered if we'd ever reach our destination, we arrived at a clearing, illumined by floodlights. A concrete building, smaller than a garage, occupied the middle. We parked in front and got out.

I went to Maggie's vehicle to help them carry Justice Lamont out. To my surprise, the justice was awake and stepped out of the sedan, studying me with wide, fearful eyes.

"I explained what happened to her," Maggie told Monty in a hushed tone, "but she doesn't believe me. She thinks my creds are fake and that we've kidnapped her."

"Can you blame her? She'll thank you later, though. C'mon, we need to get her inside."

Though the justice clearly didn't like it, she allowed them to lead her into the structure without resistance. We crowded into a small elevator, which plunged deep into the heart of the earth.

"What is this place? Where are we going?" Jade said to Monty.

"Welcome to the homes of tomorrow." Beholding our puzzled looks, he said, "This is an old missile silo converted into luxury condos for the superrich. For *only* two million dollars, you can buy one of the condos down here and live safely if there's an apocalypse on the surface."

Maggie shot Monty a doubtful look. "Did you say two *million* dollars?"

"It's worth every penny considering the amenities. There's a pool, a movie theater, even a library. The resistance wisely purchased one of the condos at the bottom. Because the place is so deep below the surface, no wireless signals can penetrate, effectively freeing anyone with an implant from the Justice Club's control. It's a safe house of sorts and a medical hub. These surface implants have become quite common lately, and we have staff equipped to remove them without much time or difficulty."

He took Justice Lamont's hands in his and met her concerned look with a small smile. "Please be at ease. Believe me when I say we will take the utmost care of you, especially considering that you're our honored guest. We have experienced personnel who will make you comfortable and complete the procedure in no time."

The lines between Justice Lamont's brows deepened. "So this really isn't a joke, huh?"

"Like I said," Maggie said, "it's no joke."

"I don't like the idea of people using me for their sick agenda." Justice Lamont shook her head. "Fine. Let's get this show on the road."

When we reached the bottom, elevator doors whooshed open, revealing pristine, white halls and people in blue medical apparel coming and going. A pretty black woman in surgical garb met us, gave Monty a nod, and put an arm around Maria. "Not to worry, Justice Lamont. We'll take really good care of you. Soon we'll give you some-thing to make you sleepy, and later all this will be nothing more than a memory, okay?"

The justice glanced back at us, worry lines deepening in her forehead, but assented to being led down the hall and into a side room.

Monty led Jade, Maggie, and me to a white-walled room filled with multicolored couches, easy chairs, and a coffee station. A clock on the wall announced it was after nine p.m. The largest TV screen I'd ever seen occupied the far wall, where news feeds from four different cable TV networks filled the split screen, the sound muted. Headlines and video provided coverage of the massacre in Los Angeles. Having already seen enough, I averted my eyes.

Monty gestured to the seating area. "You might as well make yourself at home. Coffee anyone? I could order some light refreshments if anybody's hungry."

Jade, Maggie, and I took our seats, eyes meeting and a silent message passing between us. After the bloodbath we'd witnessed not long ago, we had no appetite to eat or drink anything. Still, Monty sauntered over to the coffee bar and came back with a steaming cup.

I took a deep breath and blew it out, fingers massaging my aching temple, no doubt the location of a nasty bruise. My tongue throbbed from where my teeth had clamped down on it. Fatigue I'd long suppressed slammed into me, signaling how tired I must be after everything that had happened today.

Yet I was relieved. The concert of concerts was over, people were dead, and somebody (if Monty could be believed) would hail me as a hero. But since my role with the Justice Club had been severed, I was probably on their Top Ten Most Wanted list.

What did Amee think about my being a turncoat? If she'd been able, she never would have allowed me to escape. Something told me I hadn't seen the last of her.

"On the way, I confirmed that Thad, a field agent who was working with me at the Amberson Theater, is okay. He vanished on me, but he's fine," Maggie said to Monty. "I also called the assistant director and told him I had the justice in my custody. He understood. According to early reports, he said, at least twenty people were killed and more than fifty were injured at the concert tonight."

Leaning forward, I raked my fingers through my hair, not wishing to hear more statistics. Visual snippets of the aftermath flashed in my left mind screen, images of bodies lying in bloody pools. A circular rub on my back prompted me to lift my head.

Jade's concerned eyes met mine. "Landon, don't blame yourself. There was nothing more you could have done. Chris obviously had been trained and prepped."

But so had I. Trained and prepped to do what? Apparently to be taken advantage of. Oh yes, they'd used me.

Part of me wanted to punch someone. And make them hurt bad.

I gave her a nod, though my heart failed to relent with its accusations. If only I'd been quicker, tackling Chris sooner and harder. Could more lives have been saved?

"Landon, before you get too cozy," Monty said, "I have a little surprise for you. There's someone here I'd like you to meet."

Movement to my right caught my attention. A familiar elderly woman with gray hair, also dressed in blue surgical scrubs, gave me a knowing smile and sank into a chair across from me. "Do you remember me, Landon?"

In my mind screen, a video clip played.

A woman with brown eyes, twice their normal size, ogled me through thick, silver-framed glasses, which went well with her salt-and-pepper hair. "I must be one of your biggest fans," she said with the cutest Texas drawl.

Leslie Neumann minus the glasses.

I sprang to my feet. "But—but I saw you jump off the balcony. I thought you were dead."

Leslie opened her mouth to reply, but Monty interrupted her. "Sorry, Landon, it was all part of a show intended to make the Justice Club *think* you'd pushed her."

Still staring at Leslie, I said, "I don't understand. There had to be a body on the sidewalk by midnight. That's what the instructions said."

"A street vagrant," Leslie said. "She'd been hit by a car and was already dead. The resistance used her corpse and planted her on the sidewalk to make her look like me. They even made sure she had injuries matching a great fall."

I turned on Monty, choking on the whiff of betrayal. "You tricked me. You—you made me think—"

"Now Landon, hold on," Monty said, holding up a hand. "Just listen, okay?"

I sat down and bit my lip, fuming because of what they'd put me through. If this explanation didn't satisfy me—

"Leslie was the intended mark, all right," Monty said. "A brain surgeon with her skills doesn't show up every day, wanting to fight the Justice Club. We'd recently signed her on to help us, and that's why the Justice Club wanted her dead. Because of inside sources I've told you about, we learned about their plans to terminate her. We also knew about your assigned kill order."

Leslie nodded. "Landon, I know you feel used at the moment, but hear us out. You were chosen to take me out as your rite of passage, so to speak. For you to continue helping the resistance on the inside, the Justice Club needed to believe you had carried out your first kill order."

"The plan was simple really," Monty said, folding his hands. "We knew you wouldn't be able to go through with pushing Leslie off the balcony, so we planned everything to make it *look like* you had. We orchestrated a glitch in the Justice Club's video surveillance system at the moment Leslie jumped, so they never actually saw you push her. But since they had a body matching Leslie on the sidewalk, they assumed you had. But we needed *you* to believe Leslie had jumped, too."

"I can see tricking the Justice Club," I said. "But why deceive me? Now that I recall, I never looked over the balcony railing to be sure Leslie had jumped."

"Because of your fear of heights, we gambled that you wouldn't," Monty said. "We rigged a special net to catch Leslie as she fell."

Leslie's eyes widened with delight. She clasped her hands. "Oh, it was so exciting. I haven't had as much fun since I went parachuting years ago. Over the railing I went. And sure enough, Monty was right there on the fiftieth floor to whisk me away before anybody was the wiser."

I massaged my aching temple. "But the DNA. Certainly—"

"All staged for the Justice Club and the police, right down to the smallest detail," Monty said.

"And staged for me too. I still don't understand. Why trick *me*?"

"You needed to be genuinely remorseful after Leslie jumped," Monty said. "What sort of acting would you have pulled off later in the bar with Amee if you had known the truth? She needed to see how upset you were, because you really were, and you scored."

"There's a reason I'm a pianist and not an actor," I said. "It makes sense now that you've explained it to me."

"So you'll forgive us for our little deception?" Leslie said, eyes twinkling.

"Forgiven." I hesitated. "But what about your son, Donny?"

A shadow seemed to pass across her face. "All true. He loved your music but could never be the composer you are. I miss him terribly, but explaining what really happened that night isn't the only reason why I'm here. You want that implant removed, don't you? How about we get rid of it once and for all?"

I stared at her. "What?"

"Our meeting at the Waldorf Astoria was really twofold. We just talked about the first reason, my pretend suicide. But there was another reason. I wanted to evaluate your motor reflexes and especially peer into your eyes."

"My eyes?"

"Absolutely. Anyone who has an implant like yours cannot hide the evidence in your eyes from someone trained who knows what to look for. I won't bore you with the details, but I could tell by looking into your irises then and right now that no residual damage would occur by removing your implant."

"So what do you say, Landon?" Monty said, slapping my back. "Want to get that nasty thing removed? Leslie can do the procedure right now."

"Landon, what are you waiting for?" Jade said.

"You really mean it?" I said.

Monty nodded. "I wouldn't have brought Leslie if we didn't mean it."

Leslie clapped her hands together, smiling. "Shall we get you prepped for surgery?"

A blaring alarm, as jolting as a siren, forced our hands over our ears. I jumped up. Monty dashed from the room, with Leslie following close behind.

58

econds later, the alarm ceased. Jade, Maggie, and I exchanged bewildered glances.

"What was that?" Jade said.

"I don't know," I said, "but it didn't sound good."

Monty rushed back, his usually immaculate hairdo slightly disheveled. "I'm afraid we have a slight change in plans."

"What's happened?" Maggie said.

"Someone lacking proper clearance breached the surface entrance. Somehow the Justice Club has found our location."

Amee is coming. She still wants Justice Lamont. Ironic that the Justice Club wants the justice.

"How?" I said. "We've had wireless jammers the whole way here."

Monty shrugged, nothing less than weariness reflected in his eyes. "I have no idea how they found us, but that's the least of our worries."

"What about Justice Lamont?" Maggie said.

"She's in the middle of surgery as we speak, and Leslie is assisting to speed things up. In case of this type of scenario, we have measures in place to stall the Justice Club from reaching us, but that will buy us maybe fifteen to twenty minutes. That's just enough time to finish the justice's surgery, but it won't allow enough time for your surgery, Landon. I'm sorry."

I shrugged. "It's okay. The justice is more important anyhow. But if they're coming, does that mean we're all trapped down here?"

"No," Monty said. "We have an escape plan, a tunnel to a second silo. As soon as her surgery is over, you should go."

WHEN HAD twenty minutes ever passed so quickly?

Monty led us to the tunnel entrance while Maggie pushed Justice Lamont on a gurney, Maria's face serene like she was amid happy dreams. She wouldn't be conscious, Monty told us, for quite some time. Better she be ignorant of the potential danger.

Beside Monty stood an open door, which had been hidden behind a filing cabinet. Beyond that stretched a cement-block corridor disappearing into blackness.

Once flashlights were passed out, Monty said, "There are no electric lights, so you'll have to make do with the flashlights. Beyond a few rats, you should be alone."

"We'll be fine," I said, though Maggie had made a face at the mention of rats. "You're not coming with us?"

A bittersweet smile. "Sorry, Landon. We have more than adequate personnel to deal with the Justice Club, but they'll be counting on me to join them. We have quite a fraternity here. A family really."

"Will we ever see you again?" I said.

A shrug. "Oh, you never know, Landon. I have a way of popping up."

I motioned toward the door. "So we just follow the tunnel?"

"Maybe a half mile before you reach the other silo."

"That far?" Jade said.

"There are some side tunnels, but don't worry about them. When you reach the other side, you'll come to a door like this one. Here's the key to unlock it." He handed it to me.

"Once you're inside, just flip a switch for the lights and take the justice to the surface in the elevator. You shouldn't meet any resistance. The silo has power but is currently unoccupied."

He turned to Maggie. "Outside there will be what looks like an ambulance waiting for Justice Lamont. Our driver should be waiting for you. He'll take you and the justice to the hospital and offer protection along the way."

"Protection from what?" Maggie said.

"In case, for whatever reason, the Justice Club intercepts you. Let's hope that doesn't happen. If you believe in God, it would be a good time for a prayer or two."

Maggie said nothing but fingered her holstered gun.

"What about Jade and me?" I said.

"A second vehicle, a sedan with plenty of fuel, will be waiting for you. The keys will be in the ignition."

I glanced at Jade. Both apprehension and hopefulness coalesced on her face. Turning back to Monty, I said, "But—but where should we go?"

He shrugged. "That's up to you. You're a free man, Landon."

Free? Won't the Justice Club be looking for me?

"If you're wise, you'll get as far away from here as possible," he said. "There will be a GPS in the car to help you find your way. In the glove compartment, you'll find a loaded gun, a disposable cell phone, and two phony passports. Use them wisely."

Freedom. This was my first taste of it, but it didn't register beyond basic facts. The Justice Club had no way of monitoring me, and I had Jade at my side. What more could I want? I ached to wrap my fingers around that steering wheel, press that accelerator, and literally leave my worries behind.

Jade would probably have a suggestion or two as to our destination. Another clueless road trip. But weren't they the best kind?

A second alarm blared from the hallway from which we'd come, though this time not as deafening as the one earlier. Monty rushed away from us, then turned suddenly for one last farewell. "Be safe. Maybe I'll see you again. Goodbye." His eyes met mine. "Oh, Landon, forgive me. The news slipped my mind until now, but it's important.

It's about your father. As of yesterday, he had vanished from the psychiatric ward."

"Vanished?" What connection did Monty have with my father? I'd forgotten to quiz him about his role as the visiting priest.

"Nobody has any idea how he got out or where he went," Monty said. "Your mom, of course, is probably worried sick, so you might want to get ahold of her."

The last time Monty had given me instructions about my mom, somebody had been about to harm her. "Thanks for letting me know," I said.

What could all this mean?

Monty rushed off, leaving us to face the dark corridor with nothing but the justice out cold on a gurney, our flashlights, a key to the door on the other side, and a rush of renewed hope.

Escape had never been so close. Or freedom tasted so sweet.

Could our exit be so easy?

59

Thursday, March 31

We followed Monty's instructions without any issues. When we reached the elevator and got in, Maggie said to me, "I have a confession to make, Landon. A personal reason prompted me to request being assigned to your case."

"I'm not sure I understand," I said.

"I wanted to ask you something a while back, but … well, there never seemed to be the right time. It has to do with my husband, who has been existing in a persistent vegetative state for the last eight years."

I punched the button for the surface. "I'm sorry to hear that."

"I noticed your wedding ring," Jade said, "but I didn't think it was my place to pry."

"Bill took me to one of your concerts in Atlanta as an anniversary present," Maggie said. "He and I had been on shaky ground for months because I thought he was having an affair. I didn't know at the time that I was completely mistaken."

She grimaced and shook her head, still pained by the memories. "We had a terrible argument just before the concert, and the only reason I still went was because Bill had paid so much for the tickets." A sad chuckle. "After the concert, on the way out of the parking lot, a drunk driver drove into the driver's side of our car. Bill was struck."

A clue of recall tickled my memory. "I'm so sorry. I do seem to recall hearing something about that."

Maggie raised her eyebrows. "Then it's possible you may remember."

"Remember what?"

"Near the end of your concert that night, when you were playing requests, you said a man had requested that you play 'People Will Say We're in Love.' Could that have been my husband? See, Bill was a trained vocalist and sang that song to me when he proposed. I've wondered for years if the request was his way of trying to patch things up with me, but I never knew the answer due to the accident."

Despite my occasional memory gaps, some things I'd never been able to forget. "So he really sang that song to you atop the Empire State Building?"

Nodding, she pressed steepled hands together against her lips as if in prayer, tears glossing her eyes.

"Then it was your husband all right. He said the two of you had a terrible fight, and he wanted to make it up to you. He said you'd understand."

Wiping her eyes, she said, "Wow. I never dreamed you'd remember all that. Thank you, Landon. You have no idea what it means to me to know his last intent before the accident."

AT THE SURFACE, a long-grassed meadow stretched before us beneath a starlit sky. There was no sign of anyone except the ambulance and its driver. He waved at us from his open window and tapped his watch. The ambulance driver and I placed Justice Lamont in the back, still out cold.

"Well, Landon," Maggie said, squeezing my hand, "I guess this is goodbye. If it hadn't been for you, Jade, and Monty, the justice would have been in serious trouble."

"Thanks to you," I said, "we got her here in time to make a difference. Thanks for extending your trust."

"I didn't really have a choice, but I'm glad I took it. The country will probably never know the full story of what you did today."

"I wouldn't frankly *want* them to know everything."

"So where will you go now?"

"I'm not sure. Jade and I haven't exactly talking about it yet." Jade, unusually silent, just smiled at me uncertainly. We had so much to discuss, so many plans to make. And now wasn't the best time to chitchat about them.

"You better go," I said, "before the Justice Club realizes you're escaping through the back door."

Jade gave her a quick hug. "Goodbye. I'll give you a call sometime, okay? It was nice working with you. Stay safe."

"Likewise. You two take care." Maggie gave us a knowing smile, then hopped into the ambulance. Seconds later, they were gone.

"THINK Maggie and Justice Lamont will be okay?" Jade said.

"I certainly hope so. Otherwise, this has all been a major waste of time." Could we really just drive away? Until we were dozens of hours from the silo, it wouldn't take much to spook me.

I gripped the steering wheel and scanned the highway stretching before us, unnerved but trying not to show it.

"Wow," she said. "I never thought we'd finally find some time to spend together."

"Yep, plenty of time, wherever we choose to go."

"No way we could fly?"

"Afraid not. They'll be looking for me."

And they could be looking for you too.

Dare I tell her about the disturbing photos from the attack at her house? Deciding to remain mum, I determined not to let her out of my sight.

"Monty said you're a free man," she said, "but you're not free at all, are you?"

"I suspect he was joking."

"That's why you've been checking the mirrors nonstop."

"You've noticed?"

"It's pretty obvious."

"If I really cared about you, Jade, I'd drop you off at the nearest airport with a plane ticket home. I'm just putting you in danger again, and I'm bad company for a woman who likes to be safe."

She glanced at me, and our eyes met. "If you're a hunted man, then I'm a hunted woman. You're not leaving me behind, Landon. Not this time. Whatever happens, we face it together."

I looked back at the road, jaw clenched.

"Landon, I mean it."

I glanced at her. Blue eyes met mine, determined and unflinching. "I can see that."

She encircled my arm with her hand. "We haven't really talked about it yet, but where should we go?"

"I just headed northeast for no real reason except to get as many miles between us and that silo as possible. I haven't even thought about where we're going, but I suppose Michigan would make sense. Of course you want to see Henry and your dad."

Jade said, "You must be thinking about your dad and how worried your mom must be."

"You could say that. I can't imagine where my dad could be right now. It doesn't really make sense."

"What doesn't?"

"When I saw him at the psych ward, he was in little more than a vegetative state. He couldn't even feed himself, never mind use simple forms of communication like talking. How does a man like that suddenly escape? And even if he did, where could he have gone?"

"I believe your mom said he essentially woke up after your visit. She couldn't get him to stop babbling."

"But babbling about what?"

"No idea. I don't think it made any sense."

A priest had visited my father, and Monty had fit the photo, though he'd said he wasn't a priest. A clever way to see my dad every week, but visits for what purpose?

Monty had given me a single name to whisper in my father's ear. But why?

Ahead, our headlights washed a road-closed sign and a detour sign directing us to a side road. I took it, assuming construction.

The phone in the glove compartment rang. Jade found it. "I forgot all about the phone. Should I answer it?"

"Sure. Monty knows the number. Maybe it's him."

"Hello?" Jade said into the phone. "Oh, hi, Maggie."

How did Maggie know the number? Maybe the ambulance driver had shared it.

Another detour. Another side road. But no sign of road construction.

"I'm so glad, Maggie." Jade nodded and smiled as if chatting with her best friend. "That's wonderful news. I'm so glad."

Jade met my eyes, nodding. A picture of relief. "You made it to the hospital, and Justice Lamont is doing fine. And the FBI is providing around-the-clock surveillance. That's wonderful … uh-huh … What's that?"

Far ahead, something glimmered. Maybe somebody with a broken-down car. But why leave it in the middle of the road?

Trees hemmed us in on both sides. No exits. No side roads. And a sudden absence of traffic.

An uneasy vibe stole over me. I touched the brakes. "Uh, Jade. There's something ahead. I'm not sure …"

Pulling the phone away from her ear, Jade said, "Maggie wants to talk to you. Said it's important. Something about a discovery in Amee's past you need to know about."

I accepted the phone and greeted Maggie. While she filled me in, my focus narrowed on what stood before us. I slowed, my mouth turning dry. Jade clutched my arm.

Ahead lay a police barricade. Doors ajar with cops using them as shields. Pointing guns at us.

In the glow of our headlights, a familiar figure paced in front of the barricade, arms folded across her chest, apparently waiting for us.

"Landon, do you see why these details are important?" Maggie said.

"Yes, I do, but Maggie, we're in trouble."

"What do you mean? What's happened?"

I filled her in. "I didn't expect to see her again."

"See who?"

"Amee Presley. She's here, waiting for us. And apparently with a bunch of policemen doing her bidding."

60

Turning around and fleeing the way we'd come didn't seem wise. The police would just chase us down. I braked to a stop.

Remembering the gun in the dashboard, I ignored it and got out of the car, directing Jade to stay put, her eyes rounded. I turned the phone's speaker on. Maggie insisted on staying on the line. Maybe she had a plan.

Seeing so many guns trained on me and Jade made sweat pop out on my forehead and flood my armpits. I remained beside the car and kept the driver's door open in case I needed to jump inside. "Hello, Amee. Fancy seeing you here."

Smug satisfaction rang in her voice. "Hello, maestro. On another road trip, I see. And such a cozy ride with your old flame at your side."

"What do you want?"

"What do you think?"

She sauntered toward me, three cops covering her from behind, guns aimed. She stopped, the breeze tousling her shoulder-length black hair. "You seem to have forgotten a conversation we had once. I told you there was no walking away from the Justice Club. Either you're all in, or you're dead."

"Except I'm free, Amee. You and your puppet master can't control me anymore. And you know it."

She pulled out a sleek, silver smartphone. "No?"

"Be my guest. You know it won't work. But you've known that for some time, haven't you? Once you and your buddies realized you couldn't control me, you decided to use me instead."

She shrugged. "One can always try. Part of you still wants to do evil, Landon. I can still tempt you."

"But like I said, Amee, I'm free. I *can* say no."

"Free? You must be blind because several cops with guns aimed at you would say otherwise." She slid the smartphone into her pocket and pulled out her hand, this time clutching a gun, which she pointed at my face. "Step away from the car, Landon, and put your hands up where I can see them."

When had she learned to use a gun?

My scalp tightened. "So, what—you and these policemen want to arrest me? Why?"

"I said, step away from the car and put your hands up."

I complied. "Usually somebody has to commit a crime to get arrested."

"You did worse than that, Landon. You interfered."

"If sparing innocent people from being killed by a madman is interfering, then I'm guilty as charged. Most people would say I was acting like a hero. Strange definitions in your world, Amee. Right is suddenly wrong. Wrong is right."

She advanced a step; cold, wrathful eyes bore into mine. "I'm not finished with you, Landon Jeffers. You come quietly with me now, or she dies. Those guns aren't aimed at you anymore, maestro. Remember, I told you that if you messed with our plans, she'd be six feet under. Did you think I was joking?"

A glance at the cops confirmed her threat.

"So the question is," she said, "how much does Jade mean to you?"

What a question!

Could Monty's getaway car offer special features? Maybe bulletproof glass?

Doubtful.

And while the sedan might conceal Jade, it wouldn't keep her safe from bullets. Definitely a theory I didn't want to test.

I kept my gaze fixed on Amee, hoping Jade had overheard. From the corner of my eye, I discerned her slither below the windshield. Smart girl. If even smarter, she'd remember the gun in the glove compartment. But then again, if she took on Amee with a weapon, the cops would probably open fire.

But would the cops really kill her in cold blood? The threat rang hollow.

Unless …

Amee eyed the phone in my hand at the same moment a tinny-sounding voice called my name. I pressed the phone to my ear. "Maggie, did you hear all that?"

"I sure did. Put her on the line."

I held the phone toward Amee. "Someone wants to talk to you."

A question in her eyes. "Who is it?"

I remained silent.

Amee stepped toward me and accepted the phone, backing away, the gun still trained on my face.

"Am I speaking to a Miss Amee Presley?" Maggie said from the speaker.

"Yes, you are." Annoyance and impatience rang in her voice. "May I ask who this is?"

"This is Special Agent Maggie Songbird from the Federal Bureau of Investigation. I don't believe we have met, Amee, but I just overheard you make a criminal threat on Jade Hamilton's life."

Amee laughed. "So sue me."

"You think this is funny? I've got some news to sober you up. According to my colleagues, your real name is Annie Strobel. One of my agents lifted your DNA from a coffee cup after the concert in New Orleans. Quite careless of you. It just so happens, Miss Strobel, that there's a warrant out for your arrest in New England."

She shrugged, eyes on the phone. "Why would someone want to arrest *me*?"

"I understand you like needles. Apparently, you like them so much that you injected an entire family with a lethal substance back in Connecticut. I guess you had one foster family too many."

Amee remained silent, her expression stony.

"The FBI is involved because you crossed state lines and tried the same lethal injection on a few more people. I say 'tried' because two of them died, but one survived. About an hour ago, she picked out your mugshot from a police lineup. In short, we have a DNA match connecting you to these murders and an eyewitness for attempted murder. In other words, it's a slam dunk."

A smile tugged on Amee's lips, her gaze flicking to me. "So why don't you come arrest me then?"

"I'm on my way there as I speak. So don't go anywhere."

Amee laughed again.

"Something has tickled your funny bone, I see. You leave, and you're in even bigger trouble, Annie Strobel. And if anything should happen to Landon Jeffers and Jade, you'll be the target of a massive manhunt. Got it?"

Face slathered with disdain, Amee thrust the phone toward me, but Maggie wasn't finished. "And what's this business with a police barricade? How did you arrange that, I'd like to know. I'm not sure who you're working with, honey, but weaponizing the local police to make a phony arrest ... well, I can't even count how many felonies I could get out of that one."

"You think you scare me?" Amee said. "Think again."

"I have a colleague on the phone with the local sheriff there as I speak. The sheriff is trying to figure out how you bypassed his authority and got his officers to set up a barricade to stop Landon."

"You're bluffing," Amee said.

I eyed the cops. No change in the status quo. Guns still pointed at the car. At Jade.

"You think so, huh?" Maggie said. "What if I'm not? Those officers you've got lined up behind the barricade will soon have their guns pointed at you."

Amee bit the inside of her cheek, the first sign of uncertainty. Then: "What do you want?"

"Turn yourself in."

Amee scoffed.

"I guess I'm quite the comedian today, but here's something you should seriously consider. Let Landon and Jade go, and I promise you'll get a fair trial."

"Listen up, Miss FBI. This is what I think of your silly proposal." Amee cursed and flung the phone down hard on the cement, smashing it. With her heels, she stomped on whatever remained, then lifted her gaze to mine, both hands on the gun grip, arms extended.

"Now where was I before this incredible waste of time? Landon, you're coming with me. *Now*."

"Or what? You're going to have these fine officers shoot Jade down in cold blood just because you said so?"

"They will if I tell them to. But that's only the beginning, or did you forget? Now that the Justice Club is finished with Landon Jeffers, I've been given the pleasure of terminating you."

"And just like that, you can make the local police do whatever you want?"

"You forget that the Justice Club has had its fingers in local law enforcement for years. This is child's play. By now you've realized that certain people with something in common can't resist orders from the Justice Club, even if they wanted to."

She controlled this many cops through brain implants? Could she be the one bluffing now? But what if what she suggested was true?

The possibility chilled me.

Somebody had to stop the Justice Club once and for all. Before long, they'd infiltrate the military. Make fine young men turn their guns on brave Americans. Instigate a government coup.

The implications numbed me. And simultaneously ticked me off.

This had to stop. Right now.

But how?

The fingers of my right hand moved to the clasp of the wireless jammer's wrist band. If the cops were being controlled through implants …

"Landon, come with me. Now. Nobody has to die. I'll let Jade drive away."

No way. You'll kill me in cold blood. And then you'll kill Jade just for the fun of it.

Would my sudden movement make her fire?

Time to find out.

61

I flung the jammer toward the police barricade.

My movement confused Amee, who whirled toward the cops. The policemen rose and lowered their weapons. They eyed each other in confusion, the controlling signal disrupted. Daydream state shattered.

The distraction worked. Grabbing Amee from behind, I reached for her gun. But grunting and cursing, she didn't give it up so easily. We fought for it, and the gun went off in the air.

The cops streamed as one toward Amee, guns aimed at her. "Drop it!" one yelled.

"What are you doing?" she screamed at him. "You're supposed to do what *I* say."

"Ma'am, we don't know what you're talking about," the nearest cop said. "But you're going to get somebody hurt if you don't stop firing that gun. Please, put it down on the ground. Now."

With a curse, Amee complied. Another cop came up behind her and grabbed her from me while another pulled out handcuffs.

"What are you doing?" she screamed.

"Doesn't feel good to have those hands restrained behind you, does it?" I couldn't help saying.

"Ma'am, we just got a call from the sheriff," said another cop, cell phone in hand. "Seems you're in deep trouble. You have the right to remain silent ..."

They led Amee away, her hate-filled glances cast our way, the air rent with her curses.

I just watched and whispered a grateful prayer to the Almighty. Seconds later, Jade put an arm around me and leaned her head against my shoulder. Such a heavenly sensation. Dare I entertain the notion of a future filled with more of this? Could it be possible, a man on the run from the Justice Club and smitten at the same time?

What had Jade said earlier in the car?

If you're a hunted man, then I'm a hunted woman. Whatever happens, we face it together.

On the run once again.

But this time together.

In the middle of the road, I spied the wireless jammer, awaiting the next car to come along and destroy it completely.

I grabbed it and held it reverently. Twice it had saved my bacon.

One of the cops sauntered toward us, apology heavy in his eyes. "I'm sorry about all this, folks. Nobody can figure out where this barricade came from. And we have no clue what this woman had against the two of you, but you know what? Sometimes people are a few fries short of a Happy Meal, if you get my meaning."

He smiled a gap-toothed grin. "That situation was pretty confusing, but since that last part involved you and her gun, we need you to come to headquarters and make a formal statement."

"Seriously?"

He nodded. "Seriously. Sorry about that."

I glanced at Jade. "I guess we have no choice."

They had plenty to hold her for a long while, but perhaps my statement would help even more.

AN HOUR LATER, we were ready to leave police headquarters. Before we left, I handed the wireless jammer to Turner, the gap-toothed officer.

He accepted the jammer with raised eyebrows. "What's this for?"

"Just keep it. Believe me, you need it more than I do."

Puzzled but grateful, the officer nodded and sauntered away. Later, someone ought to take a closer look at this police department.

Crossing the parking lot to our car, I glanced at Jade. We looked into each other's eyes and smiled. We'd done our duty, but now it was time to make tracks. I'd sensed a measure of safety being surrounded by cops, even those with brain implants, but now we were on our own. I pulled the keys out of my pocket.

Night had descended, cricket song loud and mesmerizing. Only a campfire with s'mores could have made the moment cozier.

"So, can we go now?" Jade said, hands on her hips.

"And go where?"

"I miss Henry and my dad, and your mom will be worried sick."

"We can call them on the way and let them know what's up."

Jade nodded.

Someday I wanted to take her to Disneyland, since she'd already been to Disney World; I knew how much she loved those Disney dwarves. But now was hardly the right time for such a trip, and I kept my thoughts to myself.

Jade said, "Think we'll have any more trouble? Amee could have called in our vehicle. Folks could be looking for us."

"Folks are already looking for us. You can bet on it. But at least Amee won't be there." My gaze swept the trees, cloying darkness splashing the spaces between them.

But there are a thousand Amees out there, driven by the same agenda. Where can we go to be free?

"God's in control," Jade said as if she were my mind reader. "He's watching over us. And if we do have any more trouble, we'll face it together, right?" She reached for my hand. Laced her fingers in mine. "We're a team now, Landon."

I nodded. "That's exactly what we are."

And maybe we could be a whole lot more.

"Are you hungry?" she said.

"Starved. You?"

"A burger would sound pretty good right about now, wouldn't it?"

"With lots of cheese."

"And don't forget the pickles."

I grinned. Still a pickle freak, even after all these years. "Then on our way we find a burger place, enjoy ourselves, and choose not to worry."

"Right. We need to think positive."

"Agreed," I said, her role as positive thinker secured.

And when it got dark and we needed somewhere to sleep? We'd figure that part out when the time came. We'd slept in cars before but never just the two of us.

Back in the car, I inserted the key in the ignition. Hot breath gusted on the back of my neck. I whirled.

Somebody. In the back seat.

Flicking on the dome light, I gasped.

My father cowered, arms raised like he feared I might strike him.

My *father*?

"Dad? What—what are you doing here?"

He lowered his arms. Brown eyes widened in recognition, bushy black eyebrows raised in surprise. The alarm in his expression faded, replaced by a smile. "Lan-lan. Don-don."

The last time I'd seen my father, he'd been mainly unresponsive in a psych ward. And now he'd just said my name for the first time in years.

How many years had passed since we last connected—I mean, *really* connected? I could only eyeball him.

"Isn't that something?" Jade said. "I guess he must have sneaked into the car during the confusion."

Sneaked in?

My head swam with questions. "But—but how did he know where we were? How did he even get here?"

Jade shrugged. "Does it matter? Maybe he hitched a ride on that semi that passed us a while back."

I shook my head. "But then he backtracked on foot until he found us?"

Doubtful.

"Or maybe he hitched a ride with one of the cops at the barricade. They could have picked him up somewhere."

That option seemed more plausible. An odd hitchhiker would have fit the bill.

But why would Dad come here now?

He leaned forward and rapped my skull. "Dad-dad follow. Follow Lan-lan Don-don head." Another silly grin. So obviously glad to see me. Just as I was to see him, and yet …

What could he be talking about?

Follow Landon's head?

"Maybe your dad can track your implant somehow," Jade said. "Maybe that's what he means."

What other explanation could there be? Maybe he'd somehow known I was in danger and thought he could help. But breaking out of the psych ward and seeking me out, all the way from Michigan? Could the scenario be possible?

How could *he* help *me*, a wanted fugitive of the Justice Club?

My gaze scanned the empty road around us, suspecting Monty had played a hand in this implausible reunion. Had Monty followed us and dropped Dad off? But surely I would have seen Monty if he had.

"Hold on," I said. "Let's think this through. If Dad can track me, he must have some sort of gadget for doing so."

"Good point. I guess he must." Jade looked him over.

Gray sweatshirt, blue jeans, sneakers. Nothing obvious unless he had a smartphone in his pocket. A smartphone with the right app could explain it.

Wait.

Where had that backpack come from?

Jade must have read my mind because she dug into it while my dad gazed at her, transfixed as if finding her too pretty to look anywhere else.

"Just clothes, some cash, water, and energy bars," she said. "Not a phone. Nothing."

Why complicate matters? Evidence suggested he comprehended us just fine. "Dad, can you understand me?"

He nodded vigorously with an endearing gaze, the love of a father for his son. If I hadn't been so bewildered by his presence, I might have gotten misty eyed.

"Okay, Dad, we don't see any tracking gadget. So how on earth did you find me, huh?"

But even while I asked the question, I recalled Monty's injection in my shoulder, effectively blocking transmissions. So if signals were blocked, how on earth could—?

Dad leaned forward and rapped my skull again. "Dad-dad head follow Lan-lan Don-don head."

Monty had asked me to whisper a single word in my dad's ear. Could it be that the power of a single word uttered in my voice, as individual as a fingerprint, had unlocked something in his brain-damaged head? Like a password?

"I know this sounds crazy, but I'm wondering if he has an implant too," I said. "And maybe somehow his implant can communicate with mine. Is that how you knew where to find me, Dad?" Despite Monty's jammer? Perhaps operating on another frequency?

Dad's head bobbed, his smile widening.

But if he had an implant, when had he gotten it? Had he once been a malfunctioning operative too? New questions clogged my brain.

"How fun!" Jade said, gripping one of Dad's hands. "Now it's the three of us all together."

I stared at her, not lost on the positive spin she was putting on our situation. For all we knew, we were still in danger and far from home. Maybe Mom, Henry, and Gordon were too. Until we were all together again in a safe place and devised a new plan to ensure future safety, this was hardly a vacation trip.

"Mr. Jeffers, are you hungry?" Jade said.

Dad nodded vigorously. Licked his lips.

Jade looked at me. "Um, Landon, are we going to just sit here all night?"

"Oh, sorry. Yeah, I guess we should get going. Maybe we'll learn more on the way."

Jade must have sensed my frustration. "Look, we don't need to know all the answers to drive away, right?" She flicked on the dash-board GPS. "Look, I can navigate."

"Good. Let's head northeast and start making our way toward Michigan. Then call my mom and let her know Dad is okay. But first, we eat."

Jade figured out where we were, and the plan made sense. We grabbed burgers at a drive-through on the way and ate like ravenous beasts, Dad included.

Figuring Dad was at last pacified, I merged onto the busy highway, heading northeast. But Dad bellowed from the back seat. "No! No! NO! Wrong, wrong, wrong way!"

EPILOGUE

Jade tried to calm him down.

"Dad," I said, glancing at him through shadowy light in the rearview mirror. "What is it? What's wrong?"

Dad shook his head, scrunched up his eyes, and pounded his fists against his head. "North-north. Bad-bad!" he shouted.

"I guess he doesn't want us to go this direction," Jade said.

I raised my voice, trying to talk above my dad's loud babbling. "But why should he care? Dad, don't you want to go home?"

Then again, if I took him home, wouldn't officials just put him back in the psych ward? A new wrinkle.

Dad groaned. "Lan-lan. Don-don!" He writhed, jerking his head from side to side with a grimace. Fists pounded against his head again. "So! Nor! Ah!"

"What did he just say?" I said.

"I don't know. I'm afraid he's going to hurt himself," Jade said. "Take the next exit." She grabbed his wrists in a vain attempt to prevent self-harm, but he jerked away. Began striking himself again.

"Landon, he won't stop. I don't know what to do."

"Okay. I know this may sound crazy," I said, looking ahead, hoping for a close exit, "but maybe Dad's here for a reason. Maybe he's sort of a navigator to steer us to the next place on our journey."

"Well, wherever it is, it must not be Michigan."

"If we find out where we're supposed to go, maybe he'll be happy."

As soon as I pulled into a gas station parking lot and slowed, Dad stopped striking himself. Panting, he stopped pushing his head back against the seat and closed his eyes, corded neck muscles relaxing.

Could someone inflict pain through his implant if we headed in the wrong direction? What other explanation could there be? But who didn't want us heading northeast? And why?

I parked the car and faced him. "Where, Dad, are we supposed to go? Tell me!"

His gaze locked onto mine, desperate and pleading. "So. So. So."

There was something magical about our connection, something I'd missed out on for years. "Do you want to go west, Dad? Is that what you want?"

He shook his head, face reddening. "No. No. No!"

"Then where, Dad? Help me out here. Tell me where we're supposed to go."

His face scrunched up, lips puckering as if exerting great effort. He labored to pronounce each syllable. "So. Nor. Ah. So. Nor. Ah."

"What's he saying?" Jade said. "It sounds like—"

"Do you mean Sonora, Dad? Is that what you're saying?"

A relieved smile. He nodded excitedly, clapping his hands. "So. Nor. Ah."

"I was wrong," I said. "Sonora isn't the name of a person. It's a location."

Jade's eyebrows hiked. "Are you sure?"

"Not positive, but I don't know what else he could mean."

"I've heard of Sonora, California. Is that what you mean, Mr. Jeffers?"

Dad groaned and shook his head, readying those fists to start striking himself again.

Jade studied the map. "Wait. Hold on. I see a Sonora, Texas, unless he means a state in Mexico." She turned to Dad. "Is that what you mean? Do you mean Sonora, Texas?"

Dad nodded and grinned. He clapped his hands.

"I guess that must be the place," I said. "Ever heard of it?"

"Nope. I'll look it up on my phone—glad we still have that—and see what I can find out." A pause. "Wow. That's quite a trip."

"I'm sorry, Jade. I know you want to get home to your dad and Henry."

She bit her lip. "Yeah, I do, but whatever is going on with your dad must be important. Let's see where the path leads us. I'm okay with extending the trip another day or two if we need to."

"It's after midnight. Should we find a hotel? I could use cash, and we could sleep a few hours at least."

She shook her head. "No, let's just keep going. I'm too revved up now to sleep."

"I feel the same way."

"What do you think we'll find in Sonora?"

"No clue."

After grabbing coffee, we merged back onto the highway, this time heading southeast. Expecting another tantrum, I eyed Dad in the rearview mirror, but he only peered out the window, calm and contented. Hours later, he'd curled into a ball and fallen asleep.

Adjusting my hand on the steering wheel, I glanced out the windows. Little more than shadowy glimpses of barren, rain-starved fields. Scraggly, choked brush.

Jade shook her head. "Where'd the grass go?"

"We're definitely not in Michigan anymore. Did you find anything interesting about Sonora?"

Jade studied her phone, its glow illuminating her face. "Yeah, we're talking a town of only about three thousand people. Not much there beyond a few ranches, hotels, and underground caverns, if that's what drives you wild."

"Maybe this is a mistake."

If Sonora held significance beyond the importance of whispering the name in my dad's ear, why hadn't Monty mentioned it? He often provided more smoke than light.

But perhaps he hadn't mentioned Sonora on purpose. Maybe if I knew too much about what lay ahead, I would turn around and head in the opposite direction.

Remembering that Sandra didn't have a cell phone, Jade sent her dad a text, telling him they were okay and where they were headed. He was probably in bed and wouldn't see the message until morning.

Jade grabbed my right hand, her touch electric. "Hey, you okay? You seem miles away."

"Just thinking."

"About?"

"About being hunted by the Justice Club and what that means not only for me but for all of us. About seeing my dad again in such a strange turn of events. About the mysteries of life over the last year and what God intends to do through them. Things have been crazy, as you know."

"Well, at least now you don't have to puzzle through those mysteries alone."

"Jade, I really think—"

"Nope," she said, shaking her head, arms folded. "You aren't going to leave me somewhere so you can drive off and face the danger alone. In case you haven't noticed, I'm a big girl. I don't need you to protect me all the time. Nor do you need to carry this burden by yourself. Let me share some of it, okay? I can handle it."

"Okay, fine. I'm not going to leave you behind."

"Glad to hear it."

"Besides, I like having you here with me."

"You do?"

I met her eyes and dived deep. "Yeah. Over the last few weeks, I haven't been able to stop thinking about you. Going back home last fall may have been one of the best things that ever happened to me, even though it was because of my supposed cancer."

"Because of me?"

"Mostly because of you, Jade. Can you guess when it started?"

"No. Tell me."

"It was back in Iron Valley when that cop, Galotta, pointed his gun at your head. I realized what I'd have left if I ever lost you—besides God and my family, of course."

"And what would that be?"

I looked at the road, avoiding her searching gaze. "Nothing. Life would be one big, fat zero without you."

"I feel the same way about you, Landon. I can't believe we walked away from the wonderful connection we had in high school. I look back at those lost years with a lot of regrets."

"But you don't have any regrets about being here with me now, do you? Because if you do, I can exit this highway right now and—"

Her finger met my lips, held me in a trance. "What did I just say? You're not leaving me behind. Whatever we face, we face together. Just admit it."

"Admit what?"

"You need me."

Her face inched closer to mine, her blue eyes melting my soul. The scent of strawberries tickled my nose. I had to force myself to look at the road. Struggled to stay in my lane.

"Jade, I—"

"Shh. I'm not leaving you. You try sneaking off without me, and I'll hunt you down."

During all the years we'd known each other, we'd never so much as shared a kiss beyond her peck on a school playground when I was a kid. Now her lips brushed my cheek in a sweet, chaste kiss overflowing with hope and promise.

With it came an understanding I couldn't ignore. She loved me as much as I loved her. This truth, warming my chest, was a combination of joy and the scary reality of two people on the run, all mixed.

While I gazed at her, mesmerized, the car must have drifted from its lane.

From the backseat, Dad lunged toward us, knocking us apart. His hand shot forward at lightning speed and grabbed the steering wheel. The car lurched back into its lane.

I stared at my dad in the rearview mirror, gasping.

He grinned. "Dad-dad keep Lan-lan Don-don safe."

Jade smiled at me, a pinkish hue in her cheeks. "So I guess now he's not only your compass but also your protector."

And my chaperone.

"But a protector from what?" I said. "Or whom?"

"Sounds like we might be heading into danger. You sure about Sonora?"

"Nope. But I'm sure about us." We laced our fingers together, and I decided that, come what may, nothing would detract from the promise, the beauty, of this moment.

Of right now.

Of the two of us facing tomorrow's unsolved mysteries together.

WANT TO READ MORE?

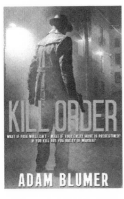

I hope you enjoyed *Termination Zone*. If you missed *Kill Order*, the novel that comes before *Termination Zone* in the Landon Jeffers Thriller Series, I highly recommend it.

Kill Order has very much the same flavor and pacing as *Termination Zone*, but it provides more backstory on what led the characters up to this point. You can download a copy here:

AdamBlumerBooks.com/kill

Or, if you prefer, you could wait for when *Kill Order* is on sale or being offered in a special giveaway. To stay informed about these special sales or giveaways, be sure to **subscribe to my newsletter** by going to my website at the link below and signing up. I love to share special deals with my readers. Just for signing up, you can receive a **FREE** copy of my first novel, *Fatal Illusions*.

AdamBlumerBooks.com/newsletter

What Is Kill Order About?

What if free will isn't? What if your every move is predestined? If you kill, are you guilty of murder?

Grammy-winning pianist Landon Jeffers's brain cancer has given him only a few years to live. But when he sleeps, the forgotten terrors of his past torment him. When he wakes, shameful memories come rushing back. Desperate for answers, Jeffers discovers that a brain implant intended to treat his cancer is really a device to control him, forcing him to commit terrible crimes. Now he's being manipulated by an evil crime syndicate and a crooked cop.

When he sleeps, the forgotten terrors of the past come alive ... and his future is a dead ending.

"With *Kill Order*, Blumer delivers another high-concept, high-stakes thriller. With an expansive cast and an intricate plot, readers will find themselves on a relentless ride that races forward to the final page. Fans of Dean Koontz's thrillers will like this novel. But *Kill Order* offers even more: a look into responsibility and guilt, culpability and fear."
—Aaron Gansky, author of *The Bargain* and *Who Is Harrison Sawyer?*

"Adam Blumer has created a story that parallels Stephen King and Ted Dekker's offerings with his own unique voice. *Kill Order's* inspiration thread is the added spice that makes this thriller unique and satisfying. Blumer's what-if idea is well-researched, and the intrigue and raced for your life moments are well-executed."
—Multi-award-winning author Cindy Ervin Huff

"*Kill Order* is a fast-paced, masterfully written psychological thriller with surprising twists and turns that will keep readers engaged until the very last page. I highly recommend it!"
—Nancy Mehl, best-selling author of *Dead End*

WILLING TO HELP ME OUT?

If you enjoyed this novel, you can do me a big favor by taking a few simple steps. First, tell your friends. Word of mouth is still the number-one seller of books.

Second, please consider rating the novel and leaving a review. Each novel I write is several years in the making (mostly evenings and Saturdays after my day job of editing books for others). It means so much to me when readers let me know they enjoyed my novels. As for the review, a simple "I enjoyed it" is sufficient, though you can say whatever you wish. You can write a review for *Termination Zone* by following this link:

AdamBlumerBooks.com/TZreview

CHECK OUT MY OTHER NOVELS

Fatal Illusions, Book 1 of the North Woods Chronicles

An Amateur Magician, an Unassuming Family ... a Fatal Illusion.

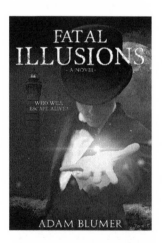

AdamBlumerBooks.com/fatal

Haydon Owens wants to be the next Houdini. He has been practicing his craft and has already made four women disappear. All it took was a bit of rope and his two bare hands.

The Thayer family has come to the north woods of Newberry, Michigan, looking for refuge, a peaceful sanctuary from a shattered past. But they are not alone. Little do they know that they are about to become part of Haydon's next act.

Time is running out and already the killer has spotted his next victim. Who will escape alive?

The Tenth Plague, Book 2 of the North Woods Chronicles

Water turns to blood. Flies and gnats attack the innocent.

AdamBlumerBooks.com/tenth

Marc and Gillian Thayer's vacation resort becomes a grisly murder scene, with a killer using the ten plagues of Egypt as his playbook for revenge.

When their friend turns up dead, Marc and Gillian put their vacation on hold, enlist the help of a retired homicide detective, and take a closer look at the bizarre plagues as they escalate in intensity. Meanwhile, a stranger is after the Thayers' newly adopted baby. Will they uncover the truth behind the bitter agenda before the tenth plague, the death of the firstborn son?

Mistletoe and Murder: A Christmas Suspense Novella Collection

Silent Night, Deadly Night. Welcome to a Killer Christmas.

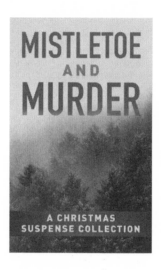

AdamBlumerBooks.com/mistletoe

Danger and suspense await you this Christmas season in *Mistletoe and Murder: A Christmas Suspense Collection* featuring ten individual novellas of suspense from some of today's most talented Christian suspense authors.

Come with us on a heart-racing journey through the holidays as USA Today, Christian Booksellers Association, and ECPA Bestselling authors Mary Alford, Adam Blumer, Liz Bradford, Vicki Hinze, Shaen Layle, Loree Lough, Nancy Mehl, Cara Putman, Lynn Shannon, and Virginia Vaughan, weave tales of suspense that will have you flipping pages well into the new year.

SIGN UP FOR MY NEWSLETTER

To stay informed of Adam's new releases and special sales, be sure to **subscribe to his newsletter** by going to his website at the link below and signing up. He loves to share special deals with his readers. Just for signing up, you can get a **FREE** copy of Adam's first novel, *Fatal Illusions*.

AdamBlumerBooks.com/newsletter

ACKNOWLEDGMENTS

So many people. So many words. And getting them right always takes a team effort.

So many folks over the years have lovingly encouraged me along my path to publication; I'd never have sufficient space to thank them all. For this novel, in particular, I am indebted to the following people, who played a significant role in getting this project from idea to published word.

Street Team members, thank you for your diligence in promoting my books and in encouraging me when I was nearly ready to throw in the towel.

Kari Fischer, Heather Mitchell, and Philip Crossman, thank you for the excellent critiques as beta readers.

Elaina Lee, thank you for the beautiful cover.

Lesley Ann McDaniel, thank you for the excellent proofread.

Members of the Christian Indie Authors Facebook group, thank you for the tips and advice. This is a great place to hobnob with those who have walked a few miles in self-publishing shoes.

Retired policeman Jason Curtman, thank you for the procedural advice and encouragement, especially about the AR-15 and bump stocks. My father-in-law, Richard Melzer, also offered helpful advice.

Luana Ehrlich, Dan Walsh, Heather Gilbert, Jan Thompson, and other self-publishing authors, thank you for describing the joys of "going indie." I also appreciate your patience in fielding my many questions. I am enjoying the journey so far.

Mom, thank you for always being there and cheering me on.

My wife, Kim, thank you for being my first reader and supporter.

God, thank You for giving me the desire and ability to write, and for opening doors and sometimes closing them. Your way is always best.

ABOUT THE AUTHOR

Adam Blumer fixes other people's books to pay the bills. He writes his own to explore creepy lighthouses and crime scenes. Winner of writing awards in high school and college, he is the author of four clean Christian thrillers: *Fatal Illusions*, *The Tenth Plague*, *Kill Order*, and *Termination Zone*. He also contributed the novella *Death the Halls* to *Mistletoe and Murder: A Christmas Suspense Collection*.

A print journalism major in college, he works full-time from home as a book editor after serving in editorial roles for more than twenty years. He lives in Michigan's Upper Peninsula with his wife, Kim, and his daughters, Laura and Julia. When he's not working on his next thriller, he's reading, hiking in the woods, playing Minecraft, or learning new chords on his guitar.

Committed to writing novels that are free of profanity, vulgarity, and sexual content, he is a member of American Christian Fiction Writers (ACFW) and The Christian PEN. He works with literary agent Cyle Young of Hartline Literary Agency. You can learn more about Adam by visiting his website: AdamBlumerBooks.com.

To get an e-mail alert when Adam releases a new book or has a book sale, be sure to **subscribe to his newsletter.** Simply go to his website, AdamBlumerBooks.com, and click on "Sign Up."

Other ways to connect with Adam:

facebook.com/AdamBlumerNovelist

twitter.com/adamblumer

instagram.com/adamblumer

amazon.com/author/adamblumer

bookbub.com/profile/adam-blumer

goodreads.com/adamblumer

pinterest.com/adamblumer

youtube.com/adamdblumer

Made in the USA
Monee, IL
03 November 2020

46647576R00189